BONE BIRD

BONE BIRD

DARLENE BARRY QUAIFE

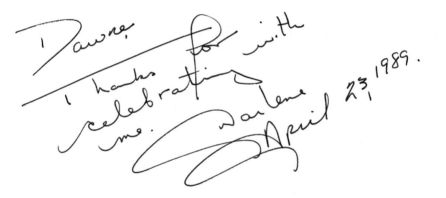

Dawne,
Thanks for ... with
celebration
me.
Darlene
April 23, 1989.

TURNSTONE PRESS

Turnstone Press
607-100 Arthur Street
Winnipeg, Manitoba
Canada R3B 1H3

Turnstone Press gratefully acknowledges the
assistance of the Canada Council and the
Manitoba Arts Council.

Cover illustration: *Wave Length* by Dianne Bersea,
coloured pencil on rag paper, 11"x15".

Illustration, page 1: Dianne Bersea

This book was printed and bound in Canada
by Hignell Printing Limited.

Canadian Cataloguing in Publication Data

Quaife, Darlene A. (Darlene Alice), 1948-
  Bone bird

  ISBN 0-88801-133-4

I. Title.
PS8583.U33B6 1989   C813'.54   C89-098030-6
PR9199.3.Q33B6 1989

A wake song for my mother and father who taught me to care.

A joy song for Ron who taught me to climb mountains.

ACKNOWLEDGEMENTS

These pages are testimony to the encouragement and support
of Rudy Wiebe, Dr. Juliet McMaster and Dr. Rod Wilson.

To Dennis Cooley who met me on the page—
a meeting of minds.

Recognition must be given to friends and colleagues who
helped foster a sense of achievement during this long project,
in particular, Catherine Ford for her unwavering confidence,
and Dianne Bersea for giving my vision wings.

Long hours were contributed by Pat Parke,
Karen Falk and Chris McLachlan.

Thank you for being there Ron, Flora and the family.

Also, thanks to Alberta Culture and Canada Council for
financial assistance and thus the luxury to work.

The map is not the territory.

—Alfred Korzybski

Having the word, you don't have to count stars
or grains of sand. We've traded knowledge for
feeling, which is also a way of getting inside the
truth of things.

—Ermilo Abreu Gomez

Empathy is the child of imagination.

—D.B.Q.

BONE BIRD

Night rain in the winter drones everyone deeper into sleep. Spring rain drives nails through dreams. On this serrated coast at the edge of the world, the first spring rain had everyone in Tanis Bay restless in their beds. Their houses drifted into fog and were lost. But the rain was a clear, hard rattle against roofs and earth. Clean penetration in the dark, rain spiking holes in half-dreams freeing them to seep out and mix with night inside heads meant to rest on pillows. These skulls grew giant cedar, limbs tangled with witch's beard, the fog hugging a raven to a branch. And a rising creek, its sound lost even as it drove out to broken-down stone fish traps, looped on the tidal flat.

The spiky wet had punctured the bubble of air that made Shea Cleary snore and his wife, Teodora, rolled over to check his breathing. The noise of the rain on the cedar shake roof had forced him off his back; he lay on his side, one ear silent against the pillow. His breath was sharp and shallow in a chest caved in over his heart.

Sixty-one years of the dense green smell of Vancouver Island's forest had not erased the red lands. The hard rain still raised the tang of wet creosote bushes in Teodora's nostrils. The drumming on the roof was the same drumming she had heard in another lifetime on the sunpacked desert floor. This first rain of the spring made Teodora think of another spring, the Sonoran Desert and her real wedding. She would ask Shea in the morning if the rain reminded him of the Papago village in Arizona. It was there she learned to grow a single fingernail, not cutting it for nine months so it was long and curved, made sharp on the edges by rubbing with a sandy stone. A knife without iron or steel to cut away the mother cord from the newborn. She had gone with her friend, both new brides, ready by village tradition to be inside the small house during a birthing. Her Papago hosts did not know that she had been the medicine woman at many births. To them she had become a woman with marriage, a child before.

Across Johnstone Strait from Tanis Bay in an overgrown house on Klaskish Island, Wil Charlie shifted to his back to listen to the fist of rain beating at the canvas patch on the roof. Augusta Charlie turned over too, but she heard the rain as it shattered against the waves like spit against teeth. In her half-sleep she is fifteen again and feels her Clan grandmother spreading bear fat all over her body. It is cold on the beach. Her nipples so hard that the old one rubs in pain with the grease. But she remains silent, the fat filling her pores so her skin can't breathe, her grandmother putting more and more on, until her legs can't stand still any longer and she runs down the beach and into the wet mouth of the ocean. The rain thins the grease in her hair and it runs down her forehead, burning her eyes more than the salt water does. The rain is icy needles stitching the waves together in front of her so that she can't see the island she must swim to. Up and down, the ocean breathing with her on its chest, up and down,

her arms flailing to be free of it, to reach the island . . . the warmth
of the little house her sisters of the Women's Clan have prepared
for her. How many nights are there in sixty-odd years? How
many nights since she sought First Woman on the floor of the
little house? Never enough to fix things. Never enough to keep
alive the faces of her lost children, the sound of kin voices, the
touch of her great grandmother's scaly lips. Never enough, yes.

In another house in Tanis Bay, Aislinn Cleary had been listening
to the rain ricochet off the tin roof. It made her think of Billy
Stone and the guys plinking at road signs with a battered Cooey
.22 when she was sixteen and cruising in old man Stone's pickup.
The whole gang getting wet and drunk in the box of the half-ton.
The guys taking turns sighting the gun off the cab roof when
Billy slowed the truck as they came up on a fluorescent black
and white target.

Billy was older than the rest of them and he had the waitress
from the Island Highway Service Station snugged up in the
crook of his right arm. Aislinn watched, studying the waitress'
upturned face, the Brandy Wine lipstick. The rearview mirror
held Billy's smile. He looked like a rock star out of *Rolling Stone*
. . . arrogant, powerful . . . and she longed to feel his touch as his
fingers explored inside the curve of Miss Brandy Wine's sleeve-
less blouse. If she closed her eyes, she could see his fingers, the
nails blunted and wrecked from working on his truck. They were
perfectly formed in her mind because she had used them often.
The first time was when her best girlfriend caressed the skin
stretched over her new breasts. They lay together naked on
Aislinn's pink bedspread, eyes shut, imagining each other's
hands were many times larger, harder, stronger. Now, she was
her own source: imagination a window. To stay in Tanis Bay
meant opening the window frequently and crawling out on the
ledge.

Aislinn heard her mother moan in the next room. She suspended her breathing and listened. The house was quiet and she was grateful the rain hadn't turned to tears in Fern's room. Tears on her mother's blank, expressionless face were grotesque, the sight filled her with horror. Her mother who so hated human weakness, who had mocked her husband's drunken, frustrated tears, her children's skinned knees and crybaby sobs, was locked inside a trembling body. Time was dissolving her like salt in the rain. Time and disease.

She wasn't crying, but Fern was awake under the tin roof. She whispered a slow litany: "It's rained from the day I was born. My life's been filled with rain. . . . My life is rain with no rainbows. What was the rain song we used to skip to in the school yard? My mother calling me, 'Fern, Fern, come in out of the rain, silly girl, no coat on . . . what do you think you were doing out there, young lady?' Did I really say, 'Tasting the rain'? Yes, I said it and she slapped my face for answering back. She could slap me all she wanted now; I wouldn't feel a thing. Too late, too late for not feeling . . . mother long since dead, father dead, husband dead . . . my body dead but the rain wakes my head and makes me think . . . I hate the rain."

— 1 —

THE MORNING SUN enticed a breeze up Tanis Bay that shook the water from the fingertips of trees onto the tin roof.

"Aislinn, where are you?" Fern's slow, measured words beat out a march on the wall between the bedrooms. "Aislinn, come get me up . . . I won't listen to the rain on the roof one more minute."

Aislinn let the shades up in her mother's room before she went to the dresser for a clean pair of woollen underwear her mother wore winter and summer.

Fern turned her head to the window. "Spring rain in England is pleasant, not like this. It's enough to suffocate a person, all those trees and clouds."

Aislinn glanced at the sun coming through the window, then peeled back the barely rumpled blankets and sheet covering her mother. Except for the tremors, her mother hardly moved now, her nightgown smooth over legs that looked like sticks. Aislinn slid what her mother still called "knickers" over bird's feet and up Fern's legs, pushing the nightgown ahead as she went.

"I hate the rain." The words came out flat, because Fern could no longer draw down her thin lips in her famous look of disdain.

"You've told me ten million times, mom." Aislinn pulled the nightgown over her mother's head.

"I should have married that Yankee soldier after the war and gone to California." The tight neck muscles made Fern's head stick out aggressively over her chest.

Aislinn stood by the bed, the nightgown crumpled in her hands. "I don't want to hear about it . . . you and your soldiers. . . ." She stared at the woollen vest that outlined ribs where breasts should have been.

"I have a right to my memories," her mother said. "I haven't got anything else left. I can see that just by the way you're looking at me."

Aislinn dropped the nightgown on the floor and quickly picked up a housedress from the bedside chair. Avoiding her mother's eyes with their bright, accusing light, she sat her up and swung her frail legs over the edge of the bed. She buttoned the dress on down the front and pulled knitted slippers over the tiny feet, then lifted her off the bed and carried her to a chintz-covered sofa chair in the kitchen. Carrying her mother about as if she were a child made Aislinn feel strangely old and patient. For a moment, she was protector more than nursemaid.

Fern read her daughter and, once in the chair, she always said something to re-establish her position. She was the mother, Aislinn was her child. No matter how helpless she became, that would never change. "Don't forget to phone in the grocery orders . . . you know how everyone gets when the store runs out of stock."

"Today is Tuesday, not Monday." Aislinn slid some lard into the frying pan.

"In that case I hope you did it yesterday."

There was very little tone to Fern's voice. She could no longer make her words spit like the fat in the pan, but Aislinn's ears still seared just as they had when she was a kid.

"Of course I did . . . now let's get this egg into you . . . gran will be waiting for me." Aislinn spooned the white and yellow fragments between Fern's lips, alternating with bits of soft toast. Fern muttered, "Did you bring home my magazines?" and got some of the egg on her chin.

"Damn it, mom, either eat or talk." Aislinn wiped Fern's chin with the dishrag. "Your magazines are right there on the table. Didn't you see them?"

Fern raised her hand to push the spoon away; instead she grazed the egg bowl with a slow, awkward movement causing it to rock. "You wouldn't talk to your precious grandmother the way you talk to me."

"Here, drink your milk." Aislinn put the glass to her mother's thin lips. "Mrs. Chambers is coming by this morning."

"Where's Clara Stone?" Milk bubbled into a white froth between Fern's words.

"Clara's going fishing with Sam this morning." Aislinn put the dishes in the sink and grabbed her raincoat off the hook. "And I'm gone . . . gran will be lifting grandad by herself if I don't get a move on."

"Why don't you just move in with them . . ." Fern looked blankly at the latest fashions on the tall, young women in the magazine Aislinn had laid open in her lap. "You should do something with that hair of yours."

"See you at noon." Aislinn was gone and the screen door banged shut on Fern's last piece of advice.

Teodora had Shea up and was shuffling him into his slippers when Aislinn opened the bedroom door. "Gran, you should have waited until I got here."

"The rain woke us up early." Teodora helped Shea out to the kitchen table. "It rained like that the night before we got married . . . don't you think so, old man?"

"Rain, I guess so, I sure wasn't thinking about rain that

night." Shea turned his head in the direction of Teodora's voice while he patted the table, checking with his fingers instead of his milkwhite eyes for the position of the breakfast dishes.

Aislinn placed her grandfather's hand on the handle of the mug she had just filled with tea. "What were you thinking, grandad? Were you scared . . . that's what gran says?"

"Well, look what I got myself into . . . your grandmother's scared the pants off of I don't know how many men with her talk of spirits. And what about the mumbo-jumbo she chants when she's doctoring someone?"

Teodora turned from the stove, the frying pan in her hand. "Old man, if it wasn't for my curing, you'd have been in your grave a long time ago."

"Hah." Shea blew on his tea, inhaling the steam with his second breath. "We Clearys are long in the tooth. It's the northern blood."

Aislinn sat down at the table to butter the toast.

Feeling his granddaughter at his side, Shea grinned. "Anyway, that heathen wedding wasn't legal . . ."

Teodora poured coffee for herself and Aislinn. "It may not have been white legal, but the gods saw our marriage, that's all that matters."

"Your hairpins are too tight if you think any kind of god would be interested in what that Papago chief had to say." Shea turned his head toward the sound of Aislinn stirring her coffee. "Two Bits was marrying off his nephew not long after we arrived in Burnt Seed. He had some strange notion we belonged together and offered to marry us at the same time. Your grandmother had me under one of her witch spells so I agreed. Can you imagine us sitting on the ground in the middle of Burnt Seed being harangued by the parents of the bride and groom? This was the marriage ceremony . . . damn practical when you think about it. The parents of the bride also spoke for your grandmother and they gave the two girls a real talking to in front of the whole village . . . put them in their place . . . made no bones about who was to be boss in the new families."

Teodora brought over a platter of eggs and fried tomatoes, and sat down at the table. "You've forgotten to tell our granddaughter one thing, old man . . . that Papago girl and me didn't have to accept you fellows, especially me since the Papago are not my people. Yaqui women are not married this way. You just remember that Yaqui wives can leave their husbands for good at any time, especially when they're old and cranky."

Aislinn took her plate and cup to the sink. "I'm glad you two love each other so much."

"What gave you that crazy idea?" Shea felt across the table for Teodora's hand.

"You're together, aren't you?" Aislinn put on her coat. "I'll see you after supper." She disappeared out the door.

"A heathen ceremony, is that what you think, old man?" Teodora helped Shea from the table to a nearby rocking-chair. She stroked the arm of the rocker. It always pleased her to remember that her son had made this thing of beauty in the good days before his accident when he had two hands to collect the driftwood he used for its graceful curves. "A heathen wedding . . . well it was a whole jar of beans better than what happened in San Francisco. Civil ceremony, hah. Believe me, there were no gods in that city hall building, just dead souls pretending to be people."

"Those government clerks were a cold bunch of buggers, that's for sure." Shea leaned his head back against the chair. His coarse white hair stuck out on either side where Aislinn had cut it too short to lie flat.

Teodora knew when he agreed with her he had had enough and was ready to sit and doze, drifting in and out of time while she washed the dishes and tidied the kitchen.

As she chased the cutlery around under white suds, she was reminded of the clouds that appeared above the blue Baboquivari Mountains at the edge of the desert. The clouds looked down on the village like godheads while the Papago parents married their children, and her and Shea. Their words had come to her through the changeling clouds where she saw the faces of her family.

The clouds had drifted up from the south, from Mexico. Had they floated unconcerned over the broken back of the Sierra Madre, casting shadows on the rockpiled graves of her village? Shea had helped her bury what the coyotes and birds had left of the bodies of her People. Collecting the scattered bones that lay about the plaza, under the torched cane-thatch of the ramada church and in the ransacked stone houses, she was glad her family had died those lonely years before. To die at the hands of the mountain, buried under the shriven rock of a fallen mesa cliff, was a gift compared to the village's death at the hands of Mexican soldiers. The federales had made it easy for her to leave Sonora for good, her People were either dead or scattered to the wind. She had only Shea to love her.

The clouds didn't cry at her wedding. No tears dropped from the fat cheeks of the clouds onto the desert floor. She was sure they saw no need since she had been freely watering the spot where she sat. The Papago acknowledged her tears. They understood that the sight of their village, the sound of the ceremony must make her grieve and they mourned at the thought of a lost village: the threads between human beings broken and buried.

All she had left when she arrived in Burnt Seed was the knotted cord around her neck. It was her rosary, self-made, to tell the beads was to tell her life—knots to remember by. When she left her home and crossed the Sierra Madre with the Yaqui guerrillas, she had started a map song to go with the knots. After two years of following the army, her map song had more words than all the prayers she knew, Yaqui and White. Under her fingers those early knots told of war.

Women and children packed onto the roofs of the boxcars and coaches of the hospital train that followed General Villa back and forth across the state of Chihuahua. Children blinded by

cinders from the locomotive's stack. All of them starving. The
thin tail of the revolutionary war-horse.

Slow starvation: the women followed their men and the food.
If the women had stayed on the ranchos like General Villa
wanted when he took their husbands, they would have starved
to death quickly. Villa gave them only enough food to keep their
deaths off his conscience. Food was for those who carried guns.
For women soldiers, but not for the viejitas who washed clothes,
cooked meals and lay down on their backs to be covered by men
with death in their eyes. The women came to her for immortal
root to return their moon blood; not enough food to feed the new
seed clinging inside and themselves too. She had done what she
could to cure their ills, but her herbs could not deaden the pain
of hunger.

And the peon soldiers with their terrible wounds. Torn apart
by guns as big as oxen. They had called to her, afraid of the white
medicine in the hospital train. They begged for her medicine as
a hedge against the Rolling Graveyard and its Mexican doctors.
What could she do? She couldn't fill holes the size of tortillas
with chewed tobacco leaves, or mend arms and legs hanging by
shredded flesh with a poultice of Brazil wood shavings. Her
medicine bundle was not made for the ravening spirit of war.

And had her friends among the viejitas lived beyond the day
she left them in Chihuahua City to cross back over the mountains
to Sonora with Shea? The war had gone on. The revolutionaries
were fighting each other when she married Shea in Burnt Seed,
Arizona, and married him again in San Francisco, California. By
the time she reached the treedark north, the peon general,
Pancho Villa, was an outlaw again. She heard these things, Shea
read to her from the newspapers, but she was never to know
about Mamacita, Leya, Anita, Dominga, Rosa. . . .

Teodora spoke to the dishwater as if it were a magic pool,
"What became of them?"

Shea opened his eyes at the sound of her voice. "What's that?

You talking to me, Teo?"

"Just talking to myself." Teodora pulled the plug, swirling the suds and the clouds down the drain. Now was a time for remembering, for closing the gaps and pulling all the knots together: the voices of her life making a single message.

Shea picked up the conversation where he had left it with his knife and fork at the breakfast table. "I remember the look on your face when Two Bits told you girls to always obey your husbands. He had a good way of putting it." Shea folded his hands on his chest and leaned back. "How did it go . . . something like, 'Your husband is like a chief to you. Don't talk when he's talking.' That was the gist of it anyway." He rocked forward. "I could tell he was wasting his breath. You know, you've always been too independent for a woman. I blame your uncle for teaching you his medicine." He relaxed in the chair. "That's not for women."

"Well, since you're awake and rambling, old man, then just you recall that Two Bits told you fellows not to beat your wives, but he didn't say anything about wives beating their husbands." Teodora flicked Shea's knee with the wet dish towel.

He jumped, then tried to hide his response by rocking back. "You should give your husband more respect," he said.

Teodora laughed. "Why should I start now? How about if I give you tea instead?"

"Go ahead, try and placate me with a cup of tea. You always played on my weaknesses. Not that I have many."

"No," Teodora punctuated her words with three more flicks from the wet tongue of the dish towel, "just tea morning . . . noon . . . and night. When I'm not filling the teapot, I'm fetching the chamber pot."

"Just as long as you don't get the two mixed up."

Dollars and cents and more cents. Aislinn chased the figures down the columns of the accounts book. Chasing pennies, her life was chasing pennies in a brokendown store in a dying town. 'Why' never figured into it. Without a doubt she knew why; what she didn't know was how long. How long could she stand it?

The summer she turned seventeen she'd almost made it out, almost escaped. But the rain betrayed her, always the rain. The Pacific Coach was late coming into the bus stop at the Island Highway Service Station, the rain so bad that the restaurant was full of truckers. She had no choice, there was no place else to wait and of course Billy's girlfriend was on duty.

Aislinn sat at the little table in the far corner near the washrooms, her back to the counter. She might not be noticed between the blocks of heavyset men hunched over their coffee the way they hunched over their steeringwheels, as if to make the circle part of themselves.

Miss Brandy Wine hadn't missed her, though. "Fancy seeing you here. You going somewhere?" Billy's waitress asked.

"Downisland to visit my aunt." Aislinn put her hands in her jacket pockets to keep them from ripping the edge of the paper place-mat. With her telltale hands out of sight, she knew Miss Brandy Wine wouldn't catch the lie; she wasn't a local.

"Yeah . . . bus is going to be real late tonight . . . part of the highway's flooded, had to do a detour. So, what'll you have?" The waitress did a quick check of the room, tracking empty coffee cups.

"A Coke . . . just a small." Aislinn didn't look up to meet the face above her. The waitress moved off and, released, Aislinn turned her head to follow the line of black arrows painted on the wall in front of her. They pointed to silhouettes on either side of a door. There was the outline of a woman in a long dress and powdered wig and one of a man in top hat and tuxedo. Ladies and Gents. She hadn't really noticed the figures before. Her gran and grandad would get a laugh out of Lady and Gent, their job and the company they kept.

The waitress set down her Coke. "What's so funny?" she asked.

"Nothing . . . a private joke." Tears there, again. What if something happened to her old folks while she was away? She better not start with all these men around. Reaching up, she took out the clip that pulled her hair back from her face, letting it fall like a curtain. She'd finished high school and that was enough. Her mother wouldn't miss her. The metal end of the clip was sharp where the plastic tip had broken off. She made the tears stop by focusing on the table top and lightly scratching her initials into the surface. Underneath, she added W.S., then boldly scratched a line through the W and cut in a B. Spider tracks. She would leave behind more than spider tracks to be remembered by. Pressing hard on the clip, over and over, she carved the letters, connected by a cross. There was a hand on her shoulder. Aislinn froze.

Billy dropped into the chair across from her. "So, what are you doing here?" he asked.

"Nothing . . . hanging out." Aislinn sipped her Coke, then set the glass down on top of her message. She kept her eyes on the Coke, stirring the ice with the straw. Miss Brandy Wine had given her one of the bent straws they put in little kids' drinks. She took it out and crumpled it into the ashtray.

"How did you get out here?" He was watching her face, not her hands.

For the first time since Billy sat down, Aislinn looked at him. She noticed his eyes hadn't changed since they were kids, even if everything else had; the irises were still dark, serious circles. "Walked out," she finally said.

"Shit, you must like it here a lot?" He looked around. "I can see why."

"Yeah, you seem to spend a lot of time here." She watched the ice cubes grow smaller, diluting her Coke.

"Sure, the old truck's a bummer, always breaking down.

Remember when I just got my driver's licence and I was playing big shot taking everybody to Goldeye?"

"I remember being stranded on that mudhole of a road in the pouring rain for hours. And you swearing at the carburetor until someone noticed the truck was out of gas."

"I bet you didn't know I wasn't supposed to have the truck that night. The folks were at a dance and I helped myself to the keys." He lowered his head and smiled to himself.

"Yeah, I heard later."

He raised his head to look at her. "Did you hear what dad did when I got home?"

Aislinn shook her head, no, although she had. She wanted to hear his version.

"The first thing dad says is 'Give me a dollar.' I had to give it to him in change, I was that broke. In one hand he's got my quarters and dimes, some pennies too, and in the other he's holding a bill of sale and the truck's insurance with 'cancelled' written across it. He says to me, 'You got wheels now.' Yeah, right, a truck with a teaspoon of gas in the tank and no insurance. The only high school kid in town with wheels but no social life. I spent all my spare time working to keep it running. Hell, nothing's changed."

Aislinn looked over her shoulder at Miss Brandy Wine. "Oh, I don't know about that."

Billy smiled and winked at the waitress pouring coffee. "So, can I give you a ride back home?"

Aislinn tried to hide her surprise. "Aren't you here to pick up your girlfriend?"

"No, she still has half her shift to work."

Aislinn examined the grey eyes across from her. "Is the truck in the garage here?"

"Nope, it's running fine."

She sat contemplating the flat, watery Coke that had reached the rim and sent sticky runners down the sides of the glass.

"Come on," Billy said. "I hear the bus is going to be hours late."

Aislinn shot a glance at Miss Brandy Wine. "Yeah, alright." She caught his little wave to the waitress.

Come to think of it, that was her last ride in the old pickup. Billy went downisland to work and her mother got sick.

Tired of marching her pencil down the columns, Aislinn closed the ledger. The front door of the store opened, the unoiled hinges reminding her that there were a lot of things left undone. From the little room at the back, she stepped out behind the counter.

They both stood just inside the door, quietly expectant, watching from behind their wrinkles for her face to appear between the curtains. Wil and Augusta Charlie always surprised Aislinn. She was sure they were surrounded by a soft yellow light, even though she couldn't see it. They always seemed warm to her. "What, it's you two," Aislinn said.

They smiled. Their quick, dark eyes absorbed all her edges: soft and hard. Behind the smiles they knew her.

Aislinn teased, "You always appear out of nowhere."

"Klaskish Island isn't nowhere, it somewhere, yes. You've been to somewhere," Augusta said, as she moved across the store.

Aislinn stepped from behind the proprietorial wedge of counter and hugged the humped shoulders of the old woman. In turn, she embraced the bone and sinew of Wil's frame, a fisherman's frame.

Augusta took down two large boxes of tea from a nearby shelf.

Aislinn got down a couple of boxes of digestive biscuits. Then another, as Augusta held up three fingers. "I see you two are staying for awhile. I'm glad. The Clearys need some fresh talk."

Wil cocked his head. "What . . . you want fresh talk from us old Indians? No can do . . . too old." He shook his head. The lines in his forehead were tight and grave.

Augusta poked him with a strong, bent finger. "Who you saying's too old? I still got plenty to say, yes, and some you haven't heard."

"Hah, I've heard everything you got . . . you haven't stopped talking since we been married," Wil said.

"If that's the truth, how is it we had ten children, yes?"

"It made no difference, you talked while we made babies too . . . telling me how to do it." Wil had to shake his head again, as if perplexed by the memory.

"Well, it must've worked, yes?" Augusta smiled, pleased with her wit.

It was Aislinn's turn to shake her head. "I can't imagine having that many kids."

"Start young, yes." Augusta assumed an expression of innocent questioning. "When you going to start?"

Aislinn ducked behind the counter for a bag. "There aren't many opportunities around here." She packed the groceries and handed them to Wil.

"You don't like loggers?" Wil asked.

"Nothing wrong with them I guess, except they're all married. Didn't you hear? Sewell & Bunting moved all the single loggers out, locked up the bunkhouses. It's just a matter of time . . . this place is going to be a ghost town. Just me and the old folks."

Wil looked straight at her. "It should have happened long time ago . . . they take too much, too many trees . . . change everything that's been here longer than people. They don't know this place."

Aislinn had no answer for him. When he talked like this, as he often did to her grandfather, she felt the forest's restless, secretive breathing. Walking down the overgrown logging roads, she sometimes had the feeling that the trees, the bush, all the green life held its breath waiting for her to go away so it could get on with its healing.

Augusta plucked at Wil's sleeve. "Come on, you can talk about the trees to Shea. I got something I want to show Teo." Augusta had her hand on the doorknob. "See you tonight, yes?"

"Yes," Aislinn said to the blind that flapped like a hand waving goodbye from the closed door.

Fern was laying in wait for Aislinn when she got home for lunch. Sally Chambers had not only talked most of the morning, but her sole source of conversation was her granddaughter: the Dairy Princess, Miss P.N.E., now a fashion model and on TV too. All this before she was twenty-three, Aislinn's age.

Without acknowledging Aislinn's greeting, Fern opened her mouth. The words came as if she were choking on them. "Why don't you take care of yourself? I taught you how. Look at you . . . dressed like a boy, blue jeans all the time and you walk like a man, sit like a man too, your legs wide open . . . maybe it's a blessing you don't wear dresses. I told your father he'd ruin you . . . treating you like a son. And you going along with him, letting him enter you in those loggers' contests. Shame on you, a young woman out there competing against all those men."

Aislinn put the kettle on. Her relationship with her father was well-trodden ground she tended to side-step. "So, how are you feeling?"

"I'd have felt a lot better if Clara had been here. At least she lets me finish a sentence or two."

"Mrs. Chambers forgets about your speech." Aislinn opened a package of Pop Tarts.

"How could she remember, she's too busy chattering. It's my daughter this, my granddaughter that, as if the world revolves around her family." Fern broke her Pop Tart apart with her fingers.

"Yeah, you should see her diningroom. It's full of photographs in fancy plastic frames. Most of them are of Miss

Downisland Guernsey." Aislinn spread a thick slab of peanut butter on half an apple.

"She said you'd make a good model, tall like you are and muscular. Imagine her saying in that piping voice of hers, 'They like women to have muscles now.' What does she know?" Fern stared at the mashed pastry on the plate in front of her.

"Me, a model? That's a laugh." Aislinn put down her apple and spooned up a fragment of fruit and crust for her mother.

"It wouldn't be if you started behaving like a young woman. I've seen pictures of that granddaughter of hers. She's got nothing on you except she knows how to act like a lady." Fern continued to stare at the plate, ignoring the spoon.

"What difference does it make how I behave up here?" Aislinn rubbed the palm of her free hand against the corner of the table.

"I didn't raise you to be a backwoods hick." The almost continuous tremors which electrified Fern's body made her look as if she were shivering with distaste at the thought.

Aislinn dropped the spoon on the plate, scattering sugar-coated flakes of pastry across the table. "What do you want from me?"

"Nothing . . . my tea." Fern wiped the sugar from her fingers.

Aislinn hadn't been back in the store long after lunch when she heard Linda's crackling laughter. The door hinges whined and her friend appeared with her two-year-old balanced on her hip. Corrine and Tracey came in with their assortment of children, a miniature circus of mismatched clothes and stuffed animals. The rubber smell of wet sneakers and a slug line of damp across Aislinn's clean floor meant they had met as usual in the Company Park at the end of Centre Street. She could see the kids pretending their toes were fish on the bottom of the wading pool while her friends talked about children, gardens, houses, husbands, but mostly jobs . . . the prime topic in Tanis Bay. The only real industry left was reforestation. The harvesting, the replanting, were the short, easy part. The bush would recycle the town before anyone came back to cut trees. At times, especially when the women and kids crowded into the backroom of the store for coffee, Aislinn felt the bush pushing at the town, forcing it inch by inch toward the cliff where the wind would lift it like a piece of scrap lumber and toss it into the Strait. The sense of waiting was that strong. People had always waited here: waited for supplies to come in, the mail, sitting on the landing when Aislinn was very young waiting for the steamboat to bring someone or take someone away. Waiting had been a way of life accomplished with leisurely grace, but the old rhythm was gone, winding down to the finish. It had not been her rhythm for years. Her wait held no grace, it would take a death to release her.

Aislinn put the coffee pot on the hotplate and opened the back door to the porch and untamed backlot. The children were easily drawn away from their mothers' voices by whispers in the bush. They had mapped the tangle of backlot growth that was taller than most of them, knowing only too well that this jungle harboured wild animals escaped from inside the TV.

The women sat on boxes of canned goods and toilet paper, one eye on the wilderness outside the back door.

Aislinn poured coffee into the mugs her friends brought with them. "Any word from Sewell?"

"Nothing, not a whisper," Corrine said.

"Not even a fart to show which way the wind blows," Linda added, dropping a couple of Sweet 'n' Low tablets in her coffee.

The other women laughed, a wry, knowing sound, more derisive than humorous. They tossed the conversation back and forth between the four of them as if it were a bruised apple no one was willing to eat or throw away.

"Just watch, the company will wait to the last minute. Keep the men off guard. I've seen it before."

"Yeah, keep them wondering, so they'll accept anything the bastards offer."

"Even if it means moving their families to the moon."

"There's no trees on the moon."

"Yeah, Sewell's been there too."

"God, I hate the thought of picking up and moving again. I was sure hoping we'd be here for awhile."

"Maybe you'll get lucky and end up in a real town with a movie theatre and a supermarket," Aislinn said.

"Not bloody likely. Tanis Bay is as good as it gets the way things are right now." Linda tucked a leg up under her so she could see past the porch railing to the end of the lot where a clash of red hair marked her five-year-old son.

Aislinn stared out the back door with the rest of them. "Isn't it funny, you want to stay here and I want to get out," she said. There was silence. She always managed to destroy the delicate balance. She spoke quickly, throwing words like small weights onto the scale. "Hell, I don't know what I'd do if I did get downisland, anyway. Sally Chambers tried to tell my mom this morning that I'd make a good fashion model. Can you imagine me prancing around on some stage dressed to the teeth? I've had dress shoes on twice in my life and those were flats."

"I can see why," Linda said.

"What are you, 5'10"? You're tall enough to model." Tracey flicked an ash off the end of her cigarette and studied Aislinn critically.

"What did your mother say about the idea?" Only Corrine would think to ask this question.

Aislinn was quick to answer, her voice high and bright. "It's a joke to her. I should have been a boy as far as she's concerned. Maybe I should get one of those sex-change operations."

"How would they get rid of those tits? No, you're definitely a woman." Encouraged by the laughter of her audience, Linda rose, arms folded across her chest in contemplation, and circled

Aislinn. From behind, Linda swept Aislinn's long black hair up dramatically, twisting it into a knot on top of her head. "Why don't we show your mom how good you can look?" Linda said.

"What do you mean?" Aislinn reached up to loosen Linda's grip on her hair.

"Tracey can run home and get her Avon samples and we'll make up your face." Linda slapped Aislinn's hand away from the knot of hair she was tightening.

"Hell no, I don't want that crap on my face." Aislinn almost stood up in response to Linda's tug on her hair. "Sorry Tracey, I didn't mean it that way. I've always hated the feel of cosmetics on my face, it's like a mask that's going to crack."

"The new products feel real natural, you won't know you got it on."

"Until I rub my eyes."

"Ah, come on. It's not going to kill you. You might like it and maybe your mom will too." Linda dropped the tail of hair and it spread out like a fine silk fan.

"Okay, but I don't want to look like Twisted Sister."

It was hard to know when Fern was surprised. Her face was as smooth as an egg on which raised eyebrows had been painted . . . Parkinson's mask. She really only had words themselves.

"What have you done to yourself . . . made up like a whore?" Fern laid her hand flat on the cover of the magazine as if she didn't want the woman there to see her daughter.

"Well, if anyone knows what a . . ."

Fern cut Aislinn off, "Don't you dare, you have no right . . ."

"I wasn't deaf when I was a kid, I heard you and dad fighting at night." The crash would wake her with a start and her eyes would follow the sound of the bottle rolling across the floor of the room above hers. Then came the slurred Jesus Christs, God damns, and her mother's 'for crying out loud, Francis.' Her mother never cried out loud, not even when he swore at her instead of the empty rum bottle rocking under the dresser. Some nights their words pinned her lids open like butterfly wings and she knew he cried out loud.

Fern strained to raise her voice and her neck stood out hard and white as carved stone. "You know nothing, you hear, nothing and neither did your father. Jealous, he was always green-eyed jealous and worse when he was drunk. No woman should have to put up with what I put up with."

Aislinn turned away and banged the pots out of the cupboard. She knew where the argument was going. She knew all about how much her mother had sacrificed to keep the family together for the sake of her and her brother and sister. Aislinn rubbed her eye and her fingers returned to the handle of the saucepan marked with the same colours that exploded in her head. Anger flared the way coloured paper did in the fireplace, quick and hot, but the ashes were always grey and dry inside her.

"Let me have a look at you again," Fern said, quietly.

"Just forget it. I hate the stuff, anyway. I'll wash it off while supper's on." It was no longer the make-up she felt, but the parched words on her tongue. She put her mouth under a trickle from the cold tap.

"Suit yourself. You could use a bit of colour . . . not a whole paint pot full, but . . ."

"Why don't you drop it." Aislinn slammed down the hall to the bathroom. She ran the water in the sink without looking in the mirror. What difference does it make? she thought. Women put this stuff on to impress men; who the hell was she going to impress around here? The newly wed and nearly dead, that was it. Aislinn raised her head and laughed, catching a gleam of white surrounded by red. The polished skin and outlined eyes belonged to someone else, a person who could imagine herself in exciting places, who could go out and find them. Someone who made the face fit the dream. She pulled the plug and the drain gulped down clean water.

Aislinn had settled her mother in bed for the night and arrived at her grandparents' house in time for Indian berrycakes and tea. She stood in the door for a moment, aware of the kerosene light that compassed the old folks in a yellow half-circle of warmth. They sat around the table within the glowing island while the rest of the room hung back in the shadows. The four of them seemed luminous, reminding her of the greased paper some of the old woodsmen used in their cabin windows instead of glass. If the rest of the room hadn't been in darkness behind them, she could have looked right through the old men and women sitting there. Her gran was right, electric light was too cold for evenings together.

As if reading her thoughts, Teodora turned and smiled. "Aislinn, child, come in. With all our talk, we didn't hear the door open."

Augusta looked up into Aislinn's face, her old eyes birdquick. "Child, Teo? She's no child. She wears a woman's mask, yes."

Teodora stood to look more closely. "Paint. Are you not visiting with us tonight, granddaughter?" She went to the stove for the kettle.

Aislinn pulled a chair up to the table between Wil and her grandfather. "Of course I'm staying, I've come to capture the hearts of your husbands. Wil, tell this good-looking man beside me how beautiful I look tonight."

Wil Charlie studied his hands and smiled at how unaware of herself Aislinn was. She had grown into a woman he could have carved in wood when he was a young man. She would suit wood; she was like the trees themselves: tall and sturdy, yet curved and crowned. He saw a raven on her shoulder. Although she was joking, he wanted somehow to show her that she was truly handsome. But his tongue had never been as good as his hands. "Shea, this girl of yours gone and grown up. And ... I'd say she's handsome."

Aislinn looked dismayed. "Men are handsome, women should be beautiful."

Wil realized that she didn't understand. "No, anybody can be beautiful, men and women, get some paint like you, nice clothes maybe ... that's not handsome." Wil knew the others were alert to his seriousness, watched him wrestle with the words. "When I was young apprentice learning to carve masks, we taught to look for the spirit behind the skin and bone and hair. The spirit we make out of cedar wood."

Tears crept under the thick stroke of eye-liner and invaded the powdery layer of blue around Aislinn's eyes. A liquid sky hung in her eyelashes. She was not used to the gentle, appreciative touch of Wil's words. They forced her to examine herself and that was dangerous territory, as risky as her daydreams.

Augusta saw tears as blue as trade beads on Aislinn's lashes and felt her struggle to keep her face from dissolving. She picked up the teapot and had them pass their cups to her. She talked as she poured. "Among our people we used to have Clown Women who showed people what they were doing wrong. A Clown Woman didn't speak, no, she didn't have to. All she had to do was mimic people's bad ways. When they saw themselves in her, they were ashamed. Clown Women were people with much spirit showing through their skin, yes. And it was the Clown Woman's strong spirit that made other people's weak spirit look silly. So Wil Charlie, when he was a little boy, he carved the faces of two Clown Women. That's how he got apprenticed to a carver."

Wil's face had changed as he listened to Augusta. It became solid, the eyes angry, the mouth sad. "That was before all the good carving trees in the north were chewed up by the mills," he said.

Shea knew this was meant for him. Although they had been friends for more than forty years, Wil would never forget that it was Shea who had surveyed the Atlakim Valley for Sewell & Bunting. According to Wil, logging in the north was Shea's fault; he had opened the door. "You know as well as I do, Wil, that there's more to be done with trees than carving them. People need houses, they don't need statues . . . even your people." He sat with his arms folded, the fingers of one hand harassing the edges of a small hole in an elbow of his sweater.

"We always had good houses and we had our poles too." Wil's voice came from deep within his chest, a low, hard sound. "We didn't take more than we needed, so the young trees they always grew up for us. Now the Whites have to do the forest's job and plant trees where they have taken everything."

Augusta would not let the poles go undefended. As far as she was concerned, people had to treat the spirit with more care than the body. "The body needs a roof, yes, the spirit needs food." Augusta spoke slowly as if she were explaining the obvious to a child.

Shea leaned forward in the rocker, agitated more by Augusta's tone than Wil's anger. "Yes, the human spirit is powerful. How could I have lived with Teodora all these years and not know that? But don't you see, the human spirit seeks change, finds new ways for the body to live . . . better ways." Shea turned slightly, his head lifted to direct his ears instead of his eyes. "Wil, you don't want anything to change and that's no good for people."

Wil glanced at Shea's out-thrust head and shoulders, his expectant grip on the arms of the chair. His old friend looked to be steeling himself against a blow. Wil's voice softened slightly, taking on the cadence of a storyteller. "Since the first man and woman came here, my people have found new ways to live . . . some good that we remember, some not so good that we forget. This is change, change we made with the blessing of the other world. The forest and animal spirits knew we would not abuse them with our new knowledge. Your kind of change is selfish."

Shea's head jerked back at Wil's last words. "My kind of change has saved countless lives in dried-up countries, my kind of change has brought food and medicine to people in remote jungle villages. You call these things selfish?"

Wil seemed reluctant to go on, but Augusta ignored the shrill note in Shea's voice and challenged his view of himself. "Sure, the dams and roads you built helped some people, Shea. Yes, we know. We also know that you helped build big guns to kill many people at once. So your change has two faces, yes, one good . . . one bad."

Aislinn felt hurt and confused. She hurt for her grandad, his old friends against him, but she could not take his side entirely. She sensed that the Charlies were right in a way, yet their ideas were jumbled up with her feelings. Aislinn turned to her gran, who had a way of putting all the sides of an argument together so you could see the whole problem like a picture flashed on a screen. "What do you think, gran?" she asked.

Teodora looked at Shea and then at Wil and Augusta, giving them time to lay aside the words waiting on their tongues. "Change walks on a slippery log across a fast running river. If he keeps his balance, he gets to the other side where he can eat the new berries. If he slips, he is carried away in tumbling water that may spill his brains out on a rock. Change when left to himself has pretty good balance . . . it's people that don't understand balance too well. It seems to me that people, especially white people, knew too many ways of doing before they knew about balance."

Spittle showed through the grey stubble at the corners of Shea's mouth. "That's right, Teodora, take their side against me. It always comes down to White and Indian."

Aislinn was close to tears again. Her grandparents' home had always been her refuge from the constant battles between her parents. Her old folks had been together for so long, how could they fail to understand each other? "Ah, grandad . . . gran isn't taking sides. All she's saying is that people have to think more about the things they do and what the outcome will be," she said.

Shea was beyond hearing Aislinn's plea. His temper was there in the red blotches on his face. "Augusta Charlie, you can't talk to me of killing, your people fought the other tribes all up and down this coast and you not only killed but you took slaves to do your dirty, heavy work. We invented machines to do our work, so people could be free." Shea slowly pulled himself up and out of the rocker by holding onto the edge of the table. His angry effort vibrated the table and the lid of the teapot chattered. "I'm going to bed," he said. "Aislinn, give me your arm."

The night rain had begun before Teodora was asleep, replacing the sound of others breathing in the house. It talked on the roof and kept her thoughts from turning into dreams. What Augusta had said during the argument had started Teodora thinking about Shea and the fighting in Mexico. He had often told her that he joined the Mexican Revolution because Pancho Villa was doing the right thing; Shea knew what it was to live in a country where the land had been taken from the people and they starved. At the time they met, he said this to her as if she couldn't understand all that it meant. But her people had been fighting for their land from the time the conquistadors came looking for slaves in the Yaqui Valley. She knew all the reasons, had seen the injustice, but she had also seen the suffering and death that came with war. How could killing make things right? Greed gave birth to war; sharing could be done peacefully. Look at how well she and her friends with all their children had shared a small house, food and work in Chihuahua City. They made life go on while the men fought.

She remembered the night General Villa announced that the army would march on Mexico City. The troops turned into wild men in the streets of Chihuahua. She had to avoid the central squares and main routes; it took her hours to get home. The dark walls in the back streets undulated with the shadows of revellers on roof-tops and in the plazas lit by torches. Teodora might have danced with the drunken shadows, she had good news for the women and children, but she couldn't celebrate more killing.

She reached the courtyard of her house with only the fumes of pulque, tequila, aquardiente clinging to her clothes. The drunks she had met in the back streets were there because they could do nothing more than sleep and clutch at her swishing skirts in their dreams. She entered the house where the women sat in semi-darkness, burning a small candle that would not attract attention from the street. "Sitting in the dark is no way to celebrate," Teodora teased.

Mamacita spoke from a chair by the stove, "Celebrate... they are not celebrating out there in the plaza ... they are praying."

"Prayer?" Teodora asked, bemused.

Mamacita's voice was hard, her words angular, her eyes angry. "Yes, they are blessing themselves with the water of forgetfulness, so they will forget to fear death."

Teodora spoke quickly so the other women could not continue with Mamacita's bitter pronouncements and ruin Teodora's surprise. "I have news," she said.

Rosa's voice was flat and apathetic, tired at the thought of riding on the boxcars all the way to Mexico City. "We know. General Villa is ..."

"I don't mean the march south." Teodora was becoming exasperated with them. "The General is going to leave a storehouse of food for those women who will stay in Chihuahua City." She lit a fat candle squatting on the table.

The women forgot the street full of drunken soldiers outside their door and rushed Teodora, cheering, clapping, talking.

Teodora hugged them all, then held up her hand for quiet. "But, we must convince the other viejitas that it is good to stay behind. The General will take away the food if too few women remain."

They all stood thinking about this chance to continue living within four walls in peace. They had noticed the change in their children since moving into the abandoned government house. There were fewer nightmares, fewer sleepless nights. Their children laughed. But their husbands might forget to come back for their families. It was easy for a man to start a new family these days. Dominga voiced their conclusions. "Most of the viejitas have children. They will stay for the sake of the little ones. The others are soldaderas and the General does not consider anyone who carries a rifle for him a burden. They will probably go with the army, anyway." She produced a bottle of pulque from behind a tall set of kitchen cupboards. "We have something to celebrate now," she said.

The women finished the fermented maguey juice by passing the bottle around the room a couple of times, so Leya contributed some homemade beer she had been saving for her man's return. The liquor made the women restless.

They could no longer hear the faint vibrations of guitars and violins in the streets, so they climbed to the second floor of the house in search of the music. Leya took down the crossbars on the wide windows that faced the Plaza Hidalgo and the wooden shutters swung into the room, carried by their own weight. The music drifted above the rows of walls and, carried on the smoke of the torches, penetrated the fancy ironwork grilles covering the windows. "Las Espuelas"—its fast, insistent rhythm reached the second-floor bedroom. At the sound of "The Spurs," Mamacita grabbed a hairbrush off the top of a chest of drawers and stood in the middle of the room, knees bent and the brush raised in her right hand as if to quirt the thin air that she rode. Leya, with the edge of her skirt raised delicately, stepped behind Mamacita and placed her right hand on the older woman's thick waist. Together they swung into a trot, their bare feet softly sucking the polished wood. Picking up speed, they stepped right, then left, rocking right and left, striking the left heel on the floor after four steps—a horse touching ground in loping stride. They danced together to the music diluted by the streets between them and the Plaza.

"Señor, what a fine horse you have . . . perhaps a little underfed," called Rosa above the clapping.

The dancers went about the room in a figure eight and broke into a gallop by rising on their toes, bending their knees, rising on toes and lowering heels, up down, up down, clicking heels together, producing the dense sound of solid flesh and bone instead of the smart click of leather boots and spurs.

"Señorita, beware of a man with no moustache," Dominga taunted.

"Yes, especially one that rides a starving horse," continued Rosa.

"If he starves his horse, he will starve his wife," Teodora joined in.

"And not even a moustache to tickle your bones . . . you'll be doubly starved and twice as thin as your married friends." Dominga shook a warning finger at the galloping Leya.

The riders moved from side to side, stepping left and right, faster and faster, the music lost in the slap of their feet and the friction of their skirts, until a great shout rose from the cowboy and his lady, and Mamacita and Leya collapsed on the bed, gasping, their arms around each other.

Tears pushed aside the beads of sweat on Mamacita's cheeks. She pulled her skirt up to hide her face. "Tomás, my Tomás so slim in your chamois charro pants . . . all the silver buttons adding a little music to the tinkle of your spurs and the click of your boots. My sister braided double rainbows into my hair . . . I was a girl. Gone now . . . dead and gone, my Tomás."

The women sat around Mamacita on the feather bed. Into the

silent room, warm night air brought the new songs of the Revolution. One by one the women fell asleep to the sound of "Adelita," "Jesucita," "La Cucaracha." And one by one, as sleep evaporated the liquor they had drunk, leaving a residue of fouled breath, they left the soft bed for the comfort of the floor, wrapping themselves in shawls and blankets.

She could sleep in those days, Teodora thought. She slept on top of moving boxcars, in ditches at the side of the tracks, in mountain snow curled close to rob the heat from her dying horse. Now, night was a time of remembering instead of dreaming. Fingering the black cord of knots looped around her neck, she felt an urgent need to put all the events of her life together, fitting the pieces into one large circle like the Sun Stones. To see her whole life, her path, and to know she had not abandoned the land of her ancestors. The viejitas would not accuse her of betrayal. Any one of them would have crossed the border if they could have. Crossed the border into Arizona or New Mexico to wait and return when the fighting was over, return home. No, they would return only if they had men to return to. Their lives were connected to men first, at least before the land, if not before their children.

This northern island had become her husband's home and hers, but she sometimes regretted not returning to the Yaqui Valley in the '40s to help her people rebuild the Eight Sacred Towns. To have added a brick for her father to the church at Pótam, and to have given tall, thick candles for her mother and sister might have eased her mind now.

Shea rolled over on his back beside her. "Teo, I'm sorry. . . ." He waited for her forgiving reply. "Are you awake?"

"Yes," she answered in the dark.

- 2 -

Aɪsʟɪɴɴ ʜᴀᴅ ʜᴏᴘᴇᴅ the clouds would keep the sun at bay until she finished, but the blood on her hands was becoming increasingly sticky and there wasn't a dry place on her jeans to wipe them. As the damp ground beyond the shadows steamed, she noticed the shade deepen around her. Winterborn flies had warmed enough to gather on small pools of blood that had spurted beyond the sheltered chopping block. She glanced at the coop. There were two left. Linda had already gone up to the house to make sandwiches. If the kids behaved a little longer, Corrine and Tracey would have these last birds plucked, cleaned and cooling in the water-filled plastic wading pool before Linda's old man got home.

Finished, the women washed up under the garden tap. Aislinn sat on the porch steps, dried chicken blood making cardboard out of her blue jeans. The others brought their drinks and chairs down onto the lawn in front of her.

"I'm glad that's over," Corrine said. "Chickens are such pathetic birds."

"Yeah, but whose fault is that? My gran says we steal the spirit from animals, then despise them for being spiritless."

Aislinn looked past Corrine to check on the dogs in the yard. "What's going on down at the coop?" she asked. "Tracey, the dogs are chasing your kid."

"What now?" Tracey turned around to see. "What's he got in his mouth?"

"Oh, my god," Linda said. "The little bugger's got a chicken head between his teeth."

Tracey bolted down the yard. Startled by her yell, her son and the dogs fled. She swept the small boy up and the dogs closed around them. She plucked the head out, cockscomb flapping, and threw it at the dogs. Returning up the yard, she wiped the boy's mouth roughly with the tail of her shirt.

Linda's husband, Earl, came around the corner of the house and stepped up to the porch. "Shit, what have you women been doing? You stink like a bunch of wet pillows." He bent down to undo the long laces of his calk boots.

Aislinn pointed to her stained jeans. "Fowl murders." She got no response from him.

Earl slumped into an old leatherette recliner in a corner of the porch. "Looks like the beginning of the end." He shook his head.

Linda handed him her drink. "What's up, Earl?"

He raised the glass but didn't drink. "We heard today the company's got a downisland contractor with a crew of planters coming up." He drained half the glass. "Tree planters, can you picture it? The word is that most of these guys are tightass university kids, to boot."

Corrine came up onto the porch where she could see Earl. "What does it mean?" Her voice low, cautious.

Earl reached for a refill from Linda. "Shit, who knows. I figure it's a sign things are really done up here." He waved aside the Coke Linda was trying to add to the Southern Comfort in his glass.

Tracey came up the stairs and put her glass on the table. "Did you hear anything else?" she asked Earl.

"Hell, no. They'll let us chew on this for awhile." Earl shot the recliner back so that his dirty, grey work socks rose above the porch floor toward the women. "Those city kids won't last long up here. That's back-breaking, dirty work."

"I don't envy them," Aislinn said as she got up to go.

The planters had arrived early one morning, were issued rain gear, dibble sticks, nylon tree bags, and immediately flown to a remote clearcut. Outside of that first appearance, they hadn't been seen in two weeks. But they became part of the talk, woven imaginatively into speculation, accusation, then unravelling into hysteria. They existed in many guises, in many minds, and Aislinn was as curious as everyone else when they materialized in the pub Friday afternoon.

She made her way down to The Lighthouse early that evening. The regulars were already loud, their noise intended to cover their interest in what looked to her like a group of ordinary guys. Sweatshirts instead of the uniform plaid shirts marked them as different, along with hair cut shorter than that riding up on flannel collars, but they were part of the wider male fraternity nonetheless. Their rowdiness showed they belonged to the men's club. Aislinn noticed the stiff movements of the planters taking turns at the dartboard. They grimaced when they lifted an arm to throw darts or swill beer. She thought she could see blisters and dirty nails. When the loggers started coming in, the air seemed to go out of the place, so that the darts dragged through what remained before hitting the board with a dull thud.

Earl, Doug and Tim were drinking and watching, standing at the end of the bar sizing up the bush crew. Linda, Tracey and Corrine had come over to sit at the table with Aislinn.

Corrine lowered her voice and leaned into the table. "Look at Tim and those guys." She nodded toward the bar. "You'd think this was Dodge City or something with them standing there like a bunch of gunfighters ready for a shoot-out."

Linda glanced at Earl. He was leaning back with both elbows propped up on the dark oak bar, his feet crossed casually in front of him and his eyes narrowed as he watched the planters up at the dartboard. "They look like they're planning something," she said. "God, I hope they don't get into a fight."

Tracey's smile was sweet and sly. "It wouldn't be much of a fight. Might make our guys feel better, though."

Linda gave Tracey a look of disgust. "You just like to see men bash each others' brains in . . . it gives you a kick, doesn't it?"

Tracey pushed back her chair to stand. It made an angry scraping sound and heads turned. Pulling Tracey back down into her seat, Aislinn held her there. "If you want to fight, go after Sewell, it hired those guys. Probably told the contractor squat about what's going on up here."

Tracey shook off Aislinn's hand. "I can see why you're so keen . . . beggars can't be choosers."

Aislinn placed her large, strong hand over Tracey's fingers clutching the arm of the chair. She squeezed with a grip that always surprised newcomers who had never seen her compete with an axe and saw at the annual fair. "Tracey, sometimes you're a stupid bitch . . ."

Linda cut in with a hiss, "Oh, shit, look. . . ." She pointed across the room to where Earl, Doug and Tim stood talking to the planters playing darts.

Aislinn released Tracey's hand and they turned to listen, as had everyone in the pub. Earl was doing the talking. "You guys are real hot shots, why don't you give us a game . . . our best against your best?"

One of the planters smiled. "We're not any good . . . we're just having some fun." His tone was friendly, but his eyes checked the room. He sensed people were more than curious now.

Doug stepped in. "What's a matter, aren't we good enough to play darts with?"

"No, hell. I didn't mean anything like that. All I meant was we wouldn't give you much of a game, we're pretty beat up from work," the planter said, his face showing real concern at the misunderstanding.

Earl nodded at this admission, but he wasn't about to lose the chance to take on one of these guys. "Nothing serious, what do you say?"

The planter smiled again. "Sure, sounds like fun."

"Fun." Earl drew out the word. "Yeah, best two out of three. I'll get my beer, you get your man."

Aislinn shifted in her chair to watch the planters as they went over to the table where the rest of the bush crew sat. They laughed and shoved each other until a fellow was nudged out to the open playing area. His workmates whistled from the table, giving him the victory sign while he waited for his opponent. When Earl stepped away from the bar to meet him, he was heralded by the noise of wood on wood as the spectators turned their chairs to face the action.

The planter introduced himself, "Hi, I'm Hugh Chan." He offered his hand. Earl took it reluctantly. He looked uncomfortable saying his name out loud in the silent, watchful room.

The planter threw first and his friends broke the sound barrier shouting, "Opening double, way to go, man!" Earl's double got the rest of the pub clapping and stamping their feet. Aislinn noticed the first few throws were cautious. Both men worked on the inside ring and came up with a number of triples. As they made modest inroads on 500, the talk around her faltered on who was the best player. It appeared an even match. Five hundred points dwindled a little faster than the pints of beer. The audience was more concerned with studying player technique than discovering the bottoms of their beer mugs. Toward the end of the first game, Earl and the planter were dancing a close waltz: they both needed doubles. The men in front of Aislinn sat straight up in their chairs, their heads thrust forward, right arms slightly raised in a ritual of sympathetic magic. The planter grazed the wire for 22; Earl threw a single 10. The bush crew cheered, the men with their backs to her slumped forward and ordered more beer.

The second game was closer still as both players picked up more triples. The beery loggers held their breath for each dart raised and went crazy between throws. The pub undulated like a giant water animal on land. It came down to the last throw again and for the first time the planter threw a single and Earl made his mark in the double's ring. Aislinn wondered if there wasn't some hustling going on.

Now the money hit the tables faster than the beer. The opponents were warmed up, so hot, in fact, they stunned their audience into a new respect for the damp bills lying in the middle of most tables. The planter and Earl both opened with double 20s and consistently bombarded the inside red slot under the wire 20. Earl was leading until his last three darts but he missed his final double. The planter came up with the two triple 20s and the double he needed to make zero.

The Lighthouse Pub went strangely quiet for a second before the bush crew let out a roar that turned into beer for everyone. The beer mugs hitting the counter was the overriding sound until the pub owner had pulled the last pint.

Aislinn turned her chair back to the table. "Come on, pay up."

Linda grumbled, "It's not fair . . . I had to bet on Earl."

"Just think of it as the price you pay for being married," Aislinn laughed, glad to be able to turn the tables in a small way. She knew they felt sorry for her.

Tracey crumpled up the bills and threw them at Aislinn. "Traitor." Tracey left to join her husband, drinking with the other men.

"It was just a game," Aislinn said to the others at the table.

They sat in silence, avoiding each others' eyes. Their meditation was broken by the drunken voice of Tracey's husband.

"Here's your fucking money." Doug pressed in on Hugh Chan, forcing him to take a step back. "I got a good mind to shove it up your yellow ass," he shouted, stumbling toward the table where the other planters were caught in a toast. "You don't belong up here. . . ."

The pub owner took Doug by the elbow. "That's enough, you've had your say." He spoke firmly and clapped his other meaty arm over the logger's shoulder. "Come on, it's getting late." The ex-longshoreman manoeuvred his drunken customer toward the door, hoping the others would follow. "Drink up, we're calling it an early night," he said to the rest of the room.

The patrons groaned until the owner swung around like a hog on a hook to glare at them. His whole face, including his eyes, turned red when he got mad. This was the signal. They had witnessed his temper, seen him turn into a meat grinder. They did as they were told. The bush crew hadn't stayed around to protest.

It was noon and Aislinn was getting ready to close and go home to Fern when most of the planters, including the dart champ, came in. This unlikely bush crew in clean jeans and tennis shirts grinned at one another when they saw her behind the counter. They said "Hi" almost in unison as if they were a boys' choir warming up. Expectant, they stood for a moment looking around, then fanned out among the shelves. Eventually they regrouped at the magazine rack and then drifted up to the counter one or two at a time to pay for the cookies, chocolate bars, toothpaste, toilet paper, comics and *Playboy*s they had gathered up. One of them asked, "So what's to do around here on a Saturday night?"

Aislinn paused with her hand on the handle of the adding

machine. She looked up at the clean-shaven, open face. She couldn't decide whether his eyes were laughing at her or just laughing. "Play darts in the pub," she said, watching to see if the cockiness faded. She noticed he had tried to clean his fingernails.

He smiled. "Oh, ho, we did that last night. We thought a dance or something might be less . . . challenging." He turned to the dart champ who was still at the magazine rack. "What do you say, Hugh?"

Hugh Chan didn't look up. "Sorry, I missed that?" He pushed his glasses up on the bridge of his nose.

"Never mind, Mr. Coppola." The fellow leaned on the counter toward Aislinn, keeping one eye on Hugh and speaking out of the side of his mouth to her. "He's got a thing about cameras, even brought one up here. Says he's going to be a great filmmaker some day."

This downislander's a real smartass, Aislinn thought. A city boy, any bet, probably goes to university. And what was that crack about bringing a camera up here? N.F.B. sent a camera crew to Tanis Bay for a week. Her face solidified as she straightened up to her full height. "$10.50," she said, her voice crunching down hard on the numbers, imitating the handcrank on her old adding machine.

The laughter retreated in the planter's eyes. He watched her with cautious curiosity until Hugh wandered up to the counter, his bony face still bent over the pages of the magazine. The fellow picked up his package and gave Hugh a nudge as he left.

Hugh lifted his head slowly and looked around as if he had just broken the surface after a long dive. "Okay, I'm coming." He put the magazine on the counter, open at the page he had been reading, and turned it toward Aislinn. "Anyways, have you seen this incredible shot? Geez, look at the tail of flame from those torches and those guys with their white clothes against the black sky. They look like they're in a trance, running down to hell."

Aislinn stared at the magazine, drawn to it by his enthusiasm. "Who are they?" She hadn't meant to say anything to the dart champ. Although she had won her bet on him, Aislinn figured he was a hustler. He had Earl the whole time and was so cool you would think he was an innocent kid having beginner's luck.

"The caption says they're Indians that live in the mountains of Mexico. They play some kind of game where they run for days kicking a ball in front of them. Hell, I wonder if they've tried any of these guys in the Olympics?" Hugh paused and shook his head. "Anyways, I'd sure like to shoot one of those mountain races. You could do a whole documentary on the games of mountain people all over the world. God, would that be something." He looked at Aislinn for confirmation, instead he saw angry eyes appraising him. Her look snapped him out of his speculation. "What's wrong?" He looked around. He was the only one in the store.

"$3.25," Aislinn said, not taking her eyes off his face.

"Yeah, sure. I was going to pay for the magazine." He fumbled the money out of the pocket of his jeans.

"I'm closing for lunch." Aislinn locked the cash drawer with a key dangling from her wrist.

"Hey, did I say something? I get a little crazy when I get into these magazines, but . . ."

Aislinn came around the counter to the front door. "I was supposed to close a half hour ago."

"Sorry," Hugh said.

Aislinn locked the door behind him and pulled the blind down on a bewildered backward glance. She went out the back door and down the lane toward home. The wild grass and tall weeds swayed into the lane, lured by the open space; Aislinn swiped at their heads. They ripped through her fist, leaving green sap on her hand.

Who did he think he was, she thought, looking at the stain on her palm. Talking about shooting documentaries . . . all over the world, no less. Acting like it happened every day. You just get on a plane and fly away. 'Games of mountain people' . . . what a fool. She could tell him a few things about those mountain Indians. Things he wouldn't have a clue about.

She stood in the lane, pulling up grass. Both hands attacked the slim stalks, tugging up white sinews clinging to balls of soil. "Fly away . . . just fly away. Rich bastard, everything going for him. Comes up here and . . ." She stopped fighting the grass and dropped to her knees in the shredded green bed. "Damn, damn it . . . I'm going nowhere . . . hell, even the days have somewhere to go. Do I have to wait for it all to die around me? Is that how it happens?" Tears broke her anger and scattered it over the dying grass.

Aislinn stayed home from the pub. She was tired of listening to her friends and their husbands complain, especially after they had spent a few hours in The Lighthouse. Saturday nights were worse still; they let loose and did what everyone agreed was some serious drinking.

Her mother had gone to bed without too much trouble and the house was so quiet it could have been abandoned. She left the TV off in case it disturbed Fern; without its company she found herself wandering from room to room tidying up. There wasn't much to do. Fern's domain had shrunk to the kitchen, and Aislinn's bedroom was the only place between four walls that contained anything of her.

In her room she picked a couple of sweaters up off a chair and folded them. They were bulky winter sweaters and she couldn't find space for them in the dresser. She looked around the room trying to remember where she had stored them last spring. She decided they had come from the battered bureau shoved against the back wall of her closet. The bottom drawer she was tugging on slid, then stuck. Inside there was a noise similar to marbles rolling on a hardwood floor. She had forgotten what was hidden there and the sound was no clue. She was rocking the drawer, trying to ease the swollen wood, when it dropped open. As the drawer gave way, she remembered it held what was left of her childhood: wild birds' eggs, special stones, burls that resembled faces, one of her father's flannel shirts. All the rest got packed up or thrown away when she asked for a pink room on her fifteenth birthday. A room where her girlfriends could come to play records and daydream about boys, rings and wedding dresses. It hadn't taken long for the boys to become a reality. The rings and a few white dresses came later. For her it was Billy, two grades older, just about out of school. He was already looking down the highway. Mind you, Billy wasn't a reality. She was the kid next door. Linny who could handle a hammer better than he could. He once said she should have been his father's son. To her girlfriends, marriage licences had been tickets out of Tanis Bay. They joked about the male train, twisting a phrase from a song.

She unwrapped Kleenex from around two small eggs, one the creamy colour of old lace, the other pale blue. They were perfect, fine and cool in her palm, still here and miraculously whole among the stones. She should put them in the pocket of the flannel shirt and fold it around their delicate shells. Save the eggs and the last of her dad's shirts, for what, she didn't know. His other shirts she had worn to rags gathering medicine plants with her gran, but those days were pretty much gone.

Aislinn hadn't really looked at her room for years, caught up as she was in the routine of caring for Fern and running the store. At one time she'd had the best collection of David Bowie posters in town. Her sister, working downisland for a hairdresser, went through all the movie and rock magazines in the shop and lifted the pictures for her. The walls were limp with them now, the glossy paper sagging or torn along the magazine creases. The faces, all belonging to one person, seemed to have nothing in common. Looking at the wall was like looking at old family photos. She felt remotely curious, wondering if she'd see a hint of herself in their reflections. What had mattered to her about this face of faces? Remembering the picture of Bowie she'd taped to the ceiling above her bed, she looked up. All that was left were four sticky dark rectangles on the plaster that reminded her of the black bands they used to cover the eyes of people in the tabloids. But she had made that face descend to hers, breathing on her lips, her neck, her breasts. That face had given her the big stuffed unicorn in the corner and the bouquet pinned to its head. Had sent her the postcards of sunsets and beaches, sunsets and islands, sunsets and ruins, the messages written in red ink and bleeding words such as *forever, pressed, warm, soft, love and kisses* into the corkboard. These had been her new totems. It didn't matter that they were homemade. Once they were dedicated to Bowie, it was forgotten, perhaps until now, that she had won the toy unicorn at the fair. The crispy brown bouquet was Kathy's. They had grown up together. Kathy had given her the bouquet instead of throwing it to the other girls outside the church. The postcards were from the rack in the Cleary store.

Aislinn caught sight of herself in the dresser mirror, standing still and wary as if listening for danger, the room part of her image in the glass. She turned away and went down the hall to the kitchen. Returning with a plastic garbage bag, she started on the postcards. The tacks popped out on the floor, the cards went into the bag, but they left their presence checkering the corkboard in faded and unfaded squares. Aislinn unhooked the board and put it in the bag too. Everything on the walls went in the garbage. And from the dresser disappeared the empty perfume bottles with their evaporated memories. But the snapshots tucked around the mirror stalled her, the free sides curled up like babies' fists protecting the soft flesh of what she was then. Instead of pulling a photo out of the frame, she tried to flatten the curled edge. Pressing the corners against the mirror, she found her dad holding a kid in two good arms. He wasn't smiling at the camera; he was smiling down at her. Who was behind the camera, her mom? For a moment she could feel his arms around her. He never hugged her after his accident. Released, the snapshot curled up like a grey slug. She left it alone. Grabbing the unicorn she thought of her sister's kids, but wanted things gone and quickly put it in the garbage bag with the rest.

Looking at it, she felt embarrassed by the room with its naïve pastel pink frills. It still wasn't naked enough. She took the stiff lace shade off the bedside lamp, exposing the bald light bulb, and ripped away the matching skirt from the night table. She had forgotten the table was a packing crate, but seeing the rough box under the cloth pleased her; it contributed to her sense of returning the room to reality. Using a fingernail file she removed the staples clutching bits of pink lace that ringed the top of the crate. Then she stripped away the rosy bedspread, leaving the grey C.P.R. blanket in place. Aislinn climbed on the bed in order to reach the ceiling bulb and remove the plastic cover that hung on its hips like a dusty crinoline.

She surveyed the room. There was the mat beside the bed; she picked up a corner, then remembered her mother had hooked its garish pink roses for her. She looked at the linoleum floor, feeling December in the shiny surface, and left the mat in place. It was the one anomaly in a room that resembled a cell. It was pure now, purged.

Aislinn hauled the garbage bag out to the back bin. She dropped it in, banged the lid down. It vibrated, a scolding noise like the tin lid off a jar dropped on the kitchen floor. She picked up a stick from the lane and beat the lid. It complained to the moon, but there was no help there, no hero among the stars, no god between the clouds to come to the rescue. The sooner that was understood, the better. There was only the dark under the trees.

Aislinn remembered her mother asleep in the house and retreated into the bush on the other side of the lane. She stood watching the house. No light. Sitting under a fir, her back against the rough trunk, she looked up through the branches and remembered the red, yellow and blue fish sailing across the sky. Her dad had hung it in a tree in the back yard. She saw it that night when she came up the lane from a school concert. Big brother Colin had sent it from Hawaii. He called it a windsock, she called it a mystery. Silk and fire against the stars. It meant good luck but it couldn't swim in the rain, so the wind tore it apart. That happened to bright things. She didn't have to worry.

She closed her eyes against the image of luck. It didn't stay with her long. Someone opened a window in the neighbouring house and she slipped away down the lane, sure Sam Stone was watching her. When she got to her grandparents' house, she knocked on the door before lifting the latch.

Teodora looked up from the steaming pot she was stirring. "Granddaughter . . . why aren't you out with your friends?"

Aislinn came over to the table and kissed her grandad on the cheek. "I came to see my best boyfriend," she said.

From her place at the stove, Teodora studied Aislinn, her slim, taut body bent over Shea's chair. The girl's bones pushed at the material of her jeans and sweater in knobs and ridges. Teodora shook her head, feeling the sadness that came from her granddaughter. Teodora could see that Aislinn was strung as tight as a new clothesline. She lowered her eyes from the girl's face to the spot above her heart. For a moment she sought the core of Aislinn's discontent. She sent warmth to soothe the anger there.

Aislinn took a mug down from a hook above the stove and poured herself a coffee. "What are you doing?" she asked Teodora.

"I'm making a lambsquarter poultice for the old man's swollen joints. Last time Augusta was here, she put honey with the warm leaves. Says the honey saps the medicine out of the plants. Figures it's the best remedy so far for the arthritis. We been trying it out on Shea, since he's in the worst shape of all of us. Isn't that so, old man?"

Alerted, Shea raised his head as if to protest to an audience just below the ceiling. "I'm also a helluva lot older than you and the Charlies . . . so don't speak to me of worst shape." He turned his head toward the sound of Aislinn slipping into a chair beside him at the table. "See, I told you she's just keeping me alive to use as a guinea pig. It's a miracle she hasn't killed me off with one of her mistakes."

Teodora tapped the spoon on the rim of the pot. "Mistakes, you say. I've only made one mistake, old man, and you know what that was."

"You could have left any time." Shea folded his arms across his chest. He meant to look stern; instead it appeared he was hugging his frail bones against a sudden draft.

To Aislinn he could have been a sparrow bunched against a window.

"And spent the rest of my life feeling sorry for a helpless thing like you." Teodora shook her head, a look of mock sorrow on her face. "No, I'm a feeling woman, that's my downfall." Teodora stood for a moment as if mystified, then smiled at Aislinn. "Don't you have any news for us tonight, granddaughter?"

"No, nothing special," Aislinn said.

Teodora poured the contents of the pot through a strainer. It smelled like the upturned earth of the garden after a hot summer rain. She spoke through the fragrant steam. "How's your mother today?"

"The same," Aislinn said. She watched her gran form some of the soft leaves into a small, flat poultice. She wondered at the toughened old hands that could handle the hot, wet pulp.

"Okay, old man, put your hands flat on the table."

When Teodora approached, Shea unfolded his arms and did what he was told. "Everything alright at the store?" he asked Aislinn, as Teodora quickly spooned honey onto one side of the poultice and laid it across the fingers of Shea's right hand.

It was Aislinn's turn to fold her arms over her chest, to hold her disgust inside. "Sure, it's all the same. Everything's the same. This damn town's the same as it was fifty years ago."

Shea had missed the angry edge to his granddaughter's words. He spoke in his telling voice. "No, you can't say that . . ."

Aislinn cut in on what she knew would be a 'good old days' in Tanis Bay story. She didn't want to hear about the sacrifices the settlers made to carve out the town. "No, your old buddies would never have dreamed that university students would be planting trees on the mountains they logged."

Teodora applied a poultice to Shea's other hand. "How are those downisland boys doing, anyway?" she asked.

"They were in the store this morning. Didn't seem too bushed." Aislinn got up from the table to pour more coffee. "Mind you, it's hard to tell. I think one of them is crazy, for sure. You should see this guy. He walks around in another world like he's spaced out."

"He takes drugs?" Shea asked.

"I don't know, he's just weird. Showed me this picture in a photography magazine . . . he thought it was the greatest thing in the world. Some Indians running and kicking a ball in front of them down a path"—Aislinn glanced at her gran, a conniving light in her sullen eyes—"in the mountains . . . in Mexico."

Shea spoke first. "It is a great sight . . . the Tarahumara foot races."

"Tell me about the Tarahumara," Aislinn asked.

Shea's face took on the withdrawn look of the storyteller, the memoryspeaker who is feeling the winds of another time brush his cheek. "We were taking a chance going back over the Sierra Madre in October, but General Villa figured he had no choice.

He had to get an army into Sonora to deal with that turncoat, Obregon." Shea paused, his old head nodding on its column of gaunt muscle and loose skin.

"And you got lost in a storm and nearly froze to death before the Indians found you." Aislinn prodded her grandad ahead in the story. "But what I want to know is what were they like, the Tarahumara you stayed with?"

"You should ask your grandmother. She was with them longer than I was. But you're missing out on the best part of the story." Shea shook his head. "One thing I will say about those Indians, they were untouched. Not a sniff of the white world."

"You mean they kept to their old ways?" Aislinn asked.

"It was more than that." Shea searched for the right words. "They believed as they always had. Wouldn't you say so, Teodora?"

Teodora dried her hands, poured a cup of coffee and sat down at the table. Her silver-white hair stole the light, leaving her face in shadow. "The Tarahumara had never forgotten the other world that lives beside the one we know. The force that keeps things stuck together in the shapes we see, they knew it. The old woman who healed us had great spirit power. She was a spirit-helper to me. I called her Waiting Woman because I had seen her in a vision two years before."

Aislinn poured a spoonful of sugar onto the table and pushed it about with her fingers, shaping it like a sand sculpture. It wasn't the spirit woman that she wanted to hear about. She wanted to know how they lived.

Teodora ignored Aislinn's fidgeting. She would tell the girl what she needed to know. "It happened when I was riding through the Sierra Tarahumara. I had left my village to heal the leader of the Yaqui mountain fighters where he hid from the rural police. I went because I was told I could return home when he was well enough to travel to Chihuahua to join Villa. But one of his men tied me to a horse and took me over the mountains with them. The men didn't want to go to war without a healing woman. So I gave the landmarks along the trail names and strung them together into a song that would take me home." Teodora paused to see if her coffee was lukewarm the way she liked it.

"How did they look?" Aislinn asked, still concentrating on the sugar as if she could form the Tarahumara there as her grandmother spoke. "Did the men always wear white?"

"In the summer, the Tarahumara live in caves high up in the cliffs of their mountains." Teodora placed her hand over the mouth of her coffee cup to keep the warm breath inside while she continued the story. "When the mountain fighters passed through Tarahumara country, the cavedwellers came out on the cliffs to watch us. Their clothes were red and white, and they seemed like flowers growing high among the rocks. They were quiet as flowers. When I looked up to see them, the sun made water stand in my eyes and for a moment a grey mist took the place of the stinging light. And in that mist I saw an old woman sitting inside a cave with a rock wall shielding the opening. The woman glanced up at the cave entrance and the sun reappeared in my eyes. I felt she expected me, so in my map song I named the place Old Woman Waiting."

Aislinn swept her palm across the pile of crystals. "And it was this old woman who took care of you and then grandad when you came back through the mountains in the storm." She drew a question mark in the grit. Where was her gran's story going? There were other things she wanted to know.

"Yes, this old woman was the village curandera. You still know the word?"

"Medicine woman." Aislinn hid the sugar under her hand. It had been a long time since her gran used that tone with her.

Shea's head sank to his chest and a rasping snore escaped his open mouth. Teodora looked at him, her eyes full of remembering, full of wonder at what had brought them together. Her expression made Aislinn regret the mess on the table. Who was she to be impatient?

Aislinn tried to regain the thread for Teodora. "Do you think that when you first saw the old woman she knew you would have an accident and be brought to her?"

"No, she had only a glimpse of me as well, but she had enough power to know we would come together."

"What kind of power?"

"Medicine power. Granddaughter . . . Waiting Woman healed my body only after she had taken me to meet Death's bird and bone creature."

"What?"

"Listen to me." Teodora leaned forward. Her eyes reflected bars of kerosene light that trapped Aislinn's gaze. "The spirit world is not unknown to you. I have taught you how to call on the spirits of the plants we use to heal our ills. Augusta has given you her people's dances. The spirit world is made of forces felt by us, but not easily understood. Death is the most powerful teacher. You can ask anyone . . . if they have come close to Death, they are changed." Teodora paused. "The Old Ones have met Death . . . often more than once . . . and learned about the forces that are life. When the Old Ones combine the power of this world and the world beyond . . . it is strong medicine."

"And you are this kind of healer?" Aislinn asked. In all the years her gran had been telling her about healing plants and even when Teodora and Augusta had trained her to join the Woman's Clan, her gran had never seemed mysterious. She thought she knew her old woman, but there was more, more she didn't know.

"I once brought back to this world a piece of Death. Here"— Teodora unwrapped her shawl and rolled up the left sleeve of her cotton blouse—"feel my arm between the elbow and wrist. Right there, that's it."

"It's a lump," Aislinn said. She'd felt it when she was a kid.

"Press around it with your finger," Teodora directed.

"It's like there's something hard under the skin." Aislinn took her hand away.

"Yes, something hard, a bone, an extra bone." Teodora rubbed the protrusion and the loose skin wrinkled like crêpe paper. "All I remember of the accident in the mountains is the horse slipping on the ice. I don't recall falling into the ravine. What I remember is singing my map song and the words that came from my mouth lifted me into the air, taking me from place to place. The song was taking me home and I was content to float and watch green meadows cling and climb like moss up the stone legs of the mountain gods. There was no snow and ice where I was in my song.

"When I reached the cliffs of the Tarahumara, I couldn't remember what came next in the song. I stopped singing, expecting to fall out of the sky. Instead a rush of air sucked me into Waiting Woman's cave. 'It is a good day to arrive,' she said to me. I was confused. I couldn't see her at first. All I saw was my breath in the cold air. I said, 'This is not my village. I'm on my way home.' When she spoke again, my eyes followed the sound and I saw her outline against the back of the cave. She said, 'You are closer to home here than anywhere else in the wide world.' But in my mind I saw the stone houses of my village, the faces of my People, and I refused to understand her. 'That cannot be,' I said.

"She ignored my words and ordered me to sit beside her on a mat. When I sat down, Waiting Woman placed her hand on mine where it rested on my knee. With the touch of that old claw, I became rigid. There was a pain deep inside me as if a pine torch had suddenly been lit there. My eyes filled with red tears and through the scalding blur I watched the flesh melt from my bones. Waiting Woman pulled my bones apart at the joints and piled them in a corner of the cave. They lay there all mixed up, except for my head that was still on the mat, watching. I knew I didn't have the power to put them back together and I cried. When my tears hit the ground, they turned into black scavenger beetles that swarmed over my bones, stripping away the tatters of flesh down to the white.

"Waiting Woman kicked my head and it rolled toward the bone pile. Slowly, the old one put all my bones and my head in a sack. She walked with me on her back, the sack like a huge pouch filled with the carved bones my people used to play a guessing game. I was finally dumped out on the ground in front of a great bird head with a black curved beak and feathers the colour of oil on water. . . . I had seen him once before. He was the sound of death. Made of bones and teeth, his body rattled as he picked over my bones looking for one more to add to his noise. As I watched, I realized he would claim my spirit with the bone he took."

Aislinn had been wiping her hands up and down her jeans trying to rid herself of the sugar between her fingers. She abruptly stopped and pressed the palm of one hand against the corner of the table and rubbed.

Teodora recognized the action. It had always signalled the girl's fear, the way sweat gave others away. "I cried again, sticky tears that smelled of blood. The bird and bone creature laughed at me spilling my life force on the ground. But I couldn't stop and the red tears flowed over my bones. Still hunting through the pile, Death's creature shifted the bloodied bones and the pieces of my left hand came together. It seized the bird's sorting hand. Surprised, the huge head cocked to one side, directing the gaze of a shiny eye at me. The bird pulled away and there it was—the last joint of his fleshless middle finger in my left hand. Angry, the bird and bone creature kicked the pile of bones and they clicked together, joining so quickly I couldn't see what was happening. All I know is I stood whole in front of Death's creature with a bone of his pressing sharply into the flesh of my palm, and where it pressed I felt my pulse and the courage to sing out my map song. So I began to sing again." Teodora paused. She turned to look at her granddaughter.

Aislinn's eyes were lowered, examining her grandmother's story as if the words were sprinkled among the crumbs and spilt tea on the kitchen table. She would not raise her eyes to be read. Instead she directed her question to the intricate pattern of living, stained into the table top. "What happened to the bone?"

Teodora lifted Aislinn's hand off the table and placed it on the lump in her arm, holding it there.

Aislinn glanced from her grandmother's face to the strongly knit hand covering her own. Suddenly she was cold, as if she had sat too long without shifting position and her blood was slow-moving slush. Her mouth tasted bitter. She could not pull her hand back from that place of raised flesh, not even when her gran took her old hand away. Frozen where she sat, she finally met her grandmother's eyes. The golden flecks in the brown irises released her into warmth. Her mind clicked over, but she could not find words for the new questions that replaced the old familiarity.

Teodora continued with her story. "I remember opening my eyes to a room filled with smoke and living fog that came from dark figures huddled against cold that not even the hearth fire could chase out. I thought I was in another cave, this time with Death's soldiers. I screamed and the dark bundles went silent and turned toward me. I thought to myself, 'You fool. You've done it now, screaming like that.' The bodies shifted and Waiting Woman came out of the fog and knelt beside me. I closed my eyes, expecting her to take my body apart again. Instead, she poked me, saying, 'You make us wait a long time before you come back.' Then the Old One lowered her voice and asked if I still had the creature bone. I tried to raise my hand to my face, to see, but Waiting Woman caught my arm and held it down. 'I fixed,' she said. 'You broke, I fixed.'

"She had put the split body of a lizard on my broken arm.

This is Tarahumara medicine; the Yaquis don't use the yellow lizard.

"Anyway, Waiting Woman told me I must hold the creature bone in my fist until my arm healed. I was hurt on the inside too and had to lie on the floor of the hut for a long time while the Old One tended me. And day by day the bone in my closed hand grew smaller until one morning I awoke and it was gone.

"On this day Waiting Woman took the dried-up lizard off my arm and felt along it with her thumb, pausing for only a moment at the lump. Then she worked the arm gently back and forth at the elbow. She seemed as pleased as a doll-carver holding her work." Teodora flexed her arm for Aislinn, illustrating the movement Waiting Woman had produced. The stringy tendons were like the controlling cords of a puppet arm. Teodora rolled the sleeve of her dress down and buttoned the cuff. She was suddenly absorbed in the small act.

Rearranging her shawl seemed to take forever and presented Aislinn with an odd sight: her gran uneasy. Aislinn thought those old, deft hands incapable of a wasted action.

Teodora picked up her coffee cup as if to rise and refill it, then let it rest in the cradle of her fingers while she spoke. "That meeting with Death showed me something. It showed me all forces live inside people. And each one of us, you, me, everybody, controls the forces of life and death within ourselves. Yes, even death. We may not know the moment of our death . . . but we should know the sound of dying in every breath. You have to understand this. If you don't, you can't guide the forces that move your life."

"Move," Shea mumbled.

Teodora and Aislinn turned to the sleeping, forgotten man.

Shea kicked out in a dream fall, shaking the table and rattling the women. His voice was querulous with sleep. "Move, move over, Teo. You're lying on my hands. Come on old woman, get off my hands."

Teodora and Aislinn looked at Shea's hands and their loud laughter woke him.

Bewildered, he turned his head from the sound of one to the other, then went to raise a hand in protest. But his hand would not come off the table where it lay embedded like a giant leaf in amber. The honey spooned over the leafy green poultice had hardened on Shea's hands, sticking them to the top of the table.

"Damn it woman, stop that racket and unglue me." Sleep had been replaced with indignation. "You did this on purpose . . . some joke, some joke." His eyes narrowed as he suppressed the laughter that was moving his lips and puffing out his cheeks. The laugh exploded popping his eyes open, round with the humour of his entrapment.

Teodora went to the sink for warm water and a cloth to soften the mess.

Once released, Shea flexed his fingers as if doubting that they still worked. He found the joints less stiff where old age left its deposits, the pain nagging instead of insistent. He rubbed his hands together and this action combined with an expression of wonder on his face made him look like a man who had just discovered the mother lode. "Well, old woman, at last you've found something that works. I just might rest tonight."

"The way you snore, it doesn't sound to me like you lose much sleep." Teodora dried her hands on her apron.

Shea rose slowly from his chair. "There's sleep and then there's sleep and it's the sleep of a young man that I want. That would be true magic."

Teodora took him by the arm. "To sleep like a young man you must have the dreams of a young man. Can you dream like a young one, old man?" Teodora moved Shea forward as she spoke.

Shea stopped, his six-foot frame straightening slightly, tickling a spine that had dutifully curved like a shell over a soft inner body. He put his free hand over Teodora's where she held his arm. "I never stopped dreaming like a young man . . . over all these years."

"Yes?" Teodora knew what his hands told his eyes about her.

Aislinn turned away to the sink full of dishes. She pulled on the tap. The water covered the dishes, the noise covered the sob that was quivering in her chest as it rose to her throat. If the love in her grandad's voice was part of her gran's magic, she only wished that Teodora had worked some of that magic on her dad and mom. Then, maybe, her dad would still be here to help her.

The sob expanded and burst like the soap bubble foaming under the tap. Her gran talked of being in control of life. Parkinson's Disease was in charge of her mother's life and hers. It was the force, death in every moving minute for both of them.

When Teodora returned from the bedroom, the dishes were done and Aislinn was putting on her coat.

"Granddaughter, don't go so soon. Stay and have a cup with me," Teodora said.

Aislinn remained near the door out of the light. "Thanks, gran, but I'm tired." She yawned to disguise her wavering voice.

"Yes, you sound tired," Teodora dissembled. It was best to let the girl escape with her tears unseen. She would be back with dry eyes and then Teodora would use warm words to dissolve a little more of what trapped Aislinn far more than her mother's sickness.

No matter what she did that night when she got home, Aislinn couldn't get her hands warm. In bed under the pillow or finally between thighs tucked up in a foetal curl, they were still ice when she fell asleep. Fingers too stiff to stroke the tiny head pushing through a chipped hole in the eggshell. She tried to free the chick, but her fingers wouldn't bend enough to crack the shell. The curved beak, like two ancient yellowed fingernails, opened and closed as if gasping for air, but there was no sound. The ragged edges of the shell were tight around the red-feathered neck. She cried when the egg rolled away from her useless hands. Tears filled the space around her as her spine curved drawing her in, her legs and arms folded close to her body. The egg floated by and the chick's long curved beak cut a cord near her. She stopped breathing.

Aislinn woke into the small light of the coming dawn. She lay very still, one part of her remembering, the other listening to see if she had disturbed her mother. Under the C.P.R. blanket, the cold lay on her like a dead skin. She needed to move, to get her blood going. Dressed in a sweater and jeans, she carried her sneakers to the kitchen door. Outside she breathed deeply.

In first light, the path away from town was dark under her feet, but she knew it the way her fingers knew the faded buttons on the store's adding machine. Where the path forked to Devil's Tongue Falls, Aislinn kept right and continued on to North Point.

The trees gradually thinned, grudgingly making way for the wind off the ocean. Those that resisted lay about like a giant game of pick-up-sticks. The trees opened onto jade islands strung on blue thread. Aislinn sat on a stump on the wind-cleared tip of the headland, waiting for the sun to push above the trees behind her and choke the Strait with colour.

It was just light enough to see the coast north where a couple of boats lay anchored offshore, and south as far as the old landing dock which was shrinking away from the town, curling in on itself as if it were a discarded orange peel on top of the water. South Point was a black shadow behind the dock, pulsing at the edge of Aislinn's vision. Out across the waves, the islands cut the mainland into fragments. The greenblack islands and grey coastal mountains resembled puzzle pieces laid out on a blue tablecloth. Mary Cleary LaCroix lived on a grey piece to the south that had to be imagined from Tanis Bay. Aislinn didn't have many images for her sister's present, she tended to remember Mary as fearless, her protector, her tormentor. She could still hear Mary calling her 'Mommy's little mistake.' She was wondering if her sister considered any of her brood the Pope's fault, when her thoughts were ambushed by the sound of leather scraping on bark. Tanis Bay locals knew the path through the wind-blow. Only a stranger would go to the hard work of climbing over downed trees.

Aislinn turned to survey the open headland. A man, his face undiscernible in the early light, was hauling himself and a bag over a prostrate oak. Then he picked up a rifle resting on the tree he had just crossed over. Aislinn slid down behind the stump she had been sitting on, aware that the top of her head showed above the ragged remains of the tree. It seemed reactionary to lie full out on her belly like a commando, but she didn't want to be discovered before she could see the man's face.

The noise of his struggle was gradually becoming intelligible. The curse words were familiar, the voice was not. He must have short legs, Aislinn decided, if he was having so much trouble straddling the lay-about trees. She cautiously raised her head above the edge of the stump so she could have another look. Against a lighter pre-dawn sky, Aislinn recognized the dark head and slight shoulders of the dart champ. It wasn't a rifle he was carrying, it was a tripod.

Aislinn turned her back on his slow crawl and sat on the damp ground, the stump supporting her. She almost wished it had been someone with a gun, at least her solitude would have been broken by some excitement. Damn! She had come out on North Point to think, not to talk to some idiot with a camera.

His strained breathing was almost in her ear. She sat very still. He was so busy making it hard for himself, she was sure he hadn't seen her. It was light enough to see the path, but still he sanded the last log with the seat of his pants before stepping up behind her stump.

She could sense him looking out over her head at the water

and the salmon glow on the mountain peaks. "Nice, eh?" She shot the words up to him without turning her head. She hoped he would jump out of his skin, maybe drop his camera and scamper back over the deadfall, clawing at the decaying bark in terror.

"Yes, it's going to be a great sunrise," he said, putting down his camera bag and opening his tripod.

She got to her feet quickly, aware that the wet had seeped coldly through the seat of her jeans while she had sat on the ground waiting for him. She stood, her hands behind her assessing the wet patch, her eyes lighting spotfires on his back as he bent over his camera case.

He picked up his camera with familiar care and set it on the tripod. "You like sunrises too, huh?"

"I like peace and quiet," she snapped and turned to leave.

He stopped adjusting the camera to look at her. "I'm sorry, I didn't expect to find anyone out here so early."

Again, he had done the unexpected. She had been rude and he had responded with an apology. "You sure like to do things the hard way. You know, there's a path as plain as the nose on your face through the deadfall," she said, going toward the foot-flattened grass.

He was still looking at her, wondering about the hunched shoulders in the man's sweater. "Yeah, I saw it once it got a bit light out, but I only had a few more logs to go. Anyways, I figured you'd hear me coming over the trees."

She wheeled around on the path. "I heard you, alright. I heard you coming for miles."

He noticed fists where they stretched the pockets of her jeans. "Good, I didn't want to startle you."

"You, you . . ." Her dark eyes stared. "You didn't want to . . . Shit, I live here. I grew up here. Cougars don't startle me, how could something like you?"

Instead of rising to the insult, she watched his eyes widen as he sent furtive glances among the dead trees. She couldn't tell if his expression was real or he was clowning, but it didn't matter. Those pathetic eyes eased the tension in her chest, releasing her as if tuning pins inside a piano had been loosened. Unstrung laughter vibrated free as she straightened her shoulders.

He laughed into the sun rising behind her.

She came back and sat on the stump while he clicked his appreciation of the Strait waters running red.

"Sun fish," he muttered, "I'll call this one Sunfish."

The mountains ate his sunfish dribbling red down themselves.

Within minutes the sunrise faded, replaced by the sober colours of day. The warmth went out of the sky, but some of it remained with her where the laughter had rubbed away care. She was reluctant to turn and face the dart champ. What could she say to him?

Neither of them spoke or moved. They blinked as if the house lights in a theatre had suddenly come on . . . aware of each other in the new light.

He surprised the silence when he extended his hand and said, "Hi, I'm Hugh Chan."

- 3 -

THE WIND WAS A MIDNIGHT BIRD on the roof, flapping hard wings against the tin as if the house were a drum. Aislinn could see the demon wind, wings out like a skirt, whirling on the peak and convulsing the trees. Bold in the dark. Lately it had grown confident during the day. It could be seen around town pecking in the dirt at people's feet, hissing into lethargic ears, stirring a dreadful kind of calm in Tanis Bay. And when the men got in the crumbies and drove down from the mountain, it flew up behind the vans, put its dusty ear to the roofs and listened to the talk inside. They talked now instead of nodding off or playing tricks on each other. When the crews hit the pub, everyone could tell they had started blowing off as soon as the crumbies hit the road.

The wind, the town were making her restless. For the last five mornings she had taken the drumming in her head out to North Point. There at dawn the new sun revealed mountain range and strait as if uncovering a cross and the noise left her on black wings. Things were right for a moment in the red-gold light, before the day turned real and grey, leaving her empty again.

Looking across the Strait to the mainland from North Point always made her think of her sister. Mary, out there living in the world. Mary, who was swollen, soft motherhood, rounded out by five children and sixty pounds of cradling flesh. The ten years between her and her sister were swollen too, stretched so that Mary seemed more like Aislinn's mother than anything.

She hardly thought of their older brother Colin. He had been gone so long and travelled so much that she couldn't imagine how he must have changed. What she remembered about Colin was that when they were young, he was tall enough to kill spiders lurking on the ceiling without having to stand on a chair. A skinny spiderman. The only thing their mother feared in those days was spiders. So there was a killing technique handed down in the Cleary family. Colin always said the skill was in the flick of the wrist which killed or maimed, but did not mash. The spider should fall to the floor so that it could be swept out the door, otherwise, tall or not, you had to get a chair, a piece of toilet paper, and wipe the spot off the ceiling. Before Aislinn, Mary had hunted the black ovals pressed to the white ceiling, their many languid legs like thin cracks in the plaster, and before Mary it had been Colin, but who had done it before Colin or on the days their father was at work and they were all in school? She had always assumed her mother was helpless when hunger drove the spiders out from behind the walls. Fern didn't seem to notice them these days. What lived inside her had longer, stronger legs.

Things had changed utterly and not at all since the Clearys were together at home. The place that stored their memories and housed their dead was itself dying. Tanis Bay, her grandad's town, was wrapped in fear as it waited for the deathrattle to sound in Sewell's throat. The animosity born of that fear blanketed the town the way sour smoke off the mill stacks used to. The town was dying and that meant more to her than it did to the loggers—they could get out; yet she could not join in their constant derision of the bush crew. It wasn't their fault. They were just kids doing a job. Probably okay kids, at that.

The weird one, the dart champ, had proven to be not so bad, after all. The other morning, sitting here together on the Point, he had paid attention when she told him about the Tarahumara. He had actually seemed interested, asking why her grandfather had gone to fight for Villa. Did her grandmother miss her homeland? His grandmother missed China. He puzzled her. She had been nasty to him when they met. Most men would have got mad at her needling and jabbed back or sulked off. But Hugh had laughed with her and talked to her as if, as if what? As if she knew something and he could learn from her. His unpredictable behaviour had her studying him, replaying in her mind his brief appearance in town.

It wasn't the wind that woke Fern in the dark, early morning; it was Aislinn passing her door on the way out. Fern half-wondered if her daughter was meeting a man, but the morning hardly seemed a likely time for a tryst. No, it was more of Aislinn's erratic behaviour. The girl was her father's daughter and her grandmother's shadow. According to Aislinn, her beloved gran had special powers; as far as Fern was concerned the woman was an old fraud using a few simple remedies and far-fetched stories to win the girl over. There was a time, the most desperate time, early in her illness, when she believed Teodora had put a curse on her. Later, she thought her mother-in-law might use her herb knowledge to cure the Parkinson's. Teodora had made medicine for her, but it was so foul that she stopped taking it after a few unchanged days. The Clearys had never given her anything of consequence. They were takers, the whole family, and they had made sure they left her with nothing. Francis had more than made sure. All those years of grief after his accident with him drinking up his compensation cheques. Then drying out just long enough to make a fool of them all at the loggers' fairs. The One-Armed Logger and His Girl, more like the One-Armed Clown and His Daughter, the Amazon, such an embarrassment. . . .

The worn kaleidoscope of thoughts tumbled in Fern's head, keeping her awake and waiting for Aislinn to come in. It wasn't enough that the interminable rain woke her as if it were driven through the closed window, forcing her to pick up sharp bits of reflection, but now her daughter's morning escapades were waking her out of what little peace she had.

The kitchen door opened. Fern was alert, her eyes alive. She had heard. There were footsteps in the hall. She strained to send her words through the closed bedroom door. "Aislinn, Aislinn come in here."

The door opened slowly. Aislinn usually burst through the door as if she had to take a run at it to make herself go through. She must be guilty of something, Fern thought. "What have you been up to? Going out to meet some man, I bet . . . ," Fern said, as the door swung inward revealing Teodora in the entrance.

With the blinds down, Fern could not see her mother-in-law's face clearly, except for Teodora's eyes which always seemed unnaturally bright. "What are you doing here?" Fern's voice was full of accusation. "Go away." She couldn't tolerate those eyes.

"I'm glad to see you too, daughter-in-law." Teodora stayed in the doorway so Fern could not see the sadness she felt. What a waste, she thought. All those unfulfilled desires had turned against her son's wife. The energy she had put into being disappointed had left her body exhausted and sick.

Fern addressed the silence. "I don't want you here."

It amazed Teodora how Fern could hate. After all these years and with Francis gone, she still resented this place. Certainly for the isolation but also because it wasn't isolated enough. Francis had had a past here, a family, which meant she hadn't been his whole world. Teodora was sure, even now, that Fern still hated Quan'i, a girl she had never met, a girl long dead, because she had been someone in Francis' life. "I came to see Aislinn."

Teodora hoped that's why she had come.

"She's not here."

"Where is she?"

"Why ask me? You're the one that knows everything."

"When did she leave?" Teodora ignored Fern's gibe.

"Not long ago, twenty minutes, maybe."

Teodora disappeared out of the doorway before Fern could say more. She must get to Aislinn. How stupid Fern was. How could she forget that it was in the hour before a new day that Francis had left this house for the last time? Now Aislinn was taking the same path.

Teodora walked the slick grass trail with the certainty of someone who has learned to let her feet take her without being hindered by her eyes. She moved quickly, making her fear run out front like a tracking dog so that she was alone with the voice in her head. Time was short. She would have to listen and make the right choice when she reached the place where the path branched off to North Point.

As she neared the spot, she became quiet and her feet carried her down the north fork away from the dark trail to South Point. She was strangely relieved, although cliffs were cliffs and she didn't slow her pace toward North Point.

She broke out of the trees and threaded her way through the deadfall. As she drew near the Point, she could see a figure standing beyond the stumps among the naked rocks edging the cliff.

Teodora approached silently at first, then, when close enough to shout if she must, she stumbled stones underfoot.

Aislinn turned. "Who ... gran, what are you doing out here?"

Teodora noticed that Aislinn looked bewildered and that was all. "Following you," she said. "I was up tending your grandad's cough when I heard someone pass by the house." Teodora kept her voice neutral.

But Aislinn had already noticed the urgency of her

grandmother's walk, the forward thrust of her head. "Did you go to South Point first, looking for me?" she asked.

Teodora climbed up among the rocks beside Aislinn. "No, I knew you were here."

"But you were still worried?" Aislinn watched her grandmother closely. Although she didn't know what kind of sign she was looking for, her gran had never lied to her.

"Yes." Teodora watched the suspicion in Aislinn's face turn to pain.

"Like father, like daughter?" Aislinn's eyes were quick with anger.

"I thought it, yes, but my heart would not believe it. You are stronger than your father and not as unhappy." Teodora had never fully understood her son's unhappiness. It was as if he were always looking over his shoulder at something gone by. But his girl, she looked forward. Aislinn was caught in time, as Francis had been, but hers was yet to come and there was hope.

"Not as unhappy, no, I guess not." Aislinn wondered how her gran could be so sure.

"Men don't change to meet the world as easily as women do. Many men think it is only their two hands that can do good work." Teodora saw Francis stroking the curved and polished arm of a chair he had made.

Aislinn, who had always believed her gran knew everything, was struck by the look of vulnerability on that strong face. "You didn't expect dad to do it, not that way, did you? You thought he might drink himself to death."

"No, I didn't see death standing behind him. But, then, we don't, love keeps us from seeing what we would recognize in a stranger." Teodora paused to examine the image of Francis before her. "Your father was different when he came back from the war . . . I expected that. But I didn't know how much. I do now."

"Then it wasn't just the logging accident that did it? It wasn't losing his arm and getting into the drink like mom says?"

"No, when he got back from across the ocean, he couldn't seem to get death out of his eyes. It didn't leave when your mother came over either . . . it didn't leave when you children came along. I should have known."

"Known what?" Aislinn felt something tighten her chest and squeeze the air from her lungs. Why was her gran talking like an ordinary person?

Teodora heard the catch in Aislinn's voice and turned to face eyes that could have been her son's, her own. "Your father knew how easy it is to die," she said.

At this moment, Aislinn thought she knew how hopeless her father must have felt. She sat down on a flat rock. "Would he have gone on living if he could have done something, been useful?"

Teodora sat too and reached an arm around Aislinn's waist, patting her gently as she had done when she was a child. "I don't know. He didn't talk about the fighting he had done, but he seemed to be grieving . . . for friends, maybe, or himself. . . ."

"Or people?" Aislinn brought her knees up and hugged them to her chest. It seemed to ease her breathing.

"Yes, people, the hurt, the grief we cause . . . yes, people." Teodora leaned into Aislinn and felt her granddaughter's arms relax slightly.

"You haven't hurt anyone, gran." Aislinn searched the small, brown face resting against her shoulder. She wanted to be reassured that this was her wise grandmother.

"I haven't always been old and tame, granddaughter. I was once young and thought only of myself. But my uncle cured me. He sent me away to die."

Aislinn let her knees drop. "Gran, you're always saying things that make my heart jump."

"Why should your heart jump? I was the one sent out into the wildlands." Teodora removed her arm from around Aislinn's waist.

"See, you did it again," Aislinn complained.

Teodora settled herself by pulling her shawl tighter. She hadn't taken time that morning to tie it in proper Yaqui fashion. "Like your father, I was full of grief," she said.

"For your family killed in the landslide?" These people were her gran's family; she found it hard to think of them as her great-grandparents and her great-aunt.

"Yes, for my family, but more for myself abandoned by them, forced to live with my uncle. I was a girl growing up. My uncle was outside of life. He knew so much and people needed him so much. They feared him." Teodora could see that Aislinn was forgetting her own pain for the moment.

"I thought he cured people, like you do. Why would they fear him?" Aislinn asked.

"Because power is power. If he has the power to cure, he can have the power to harm. And they were right. Power doesn't care about good and bad, it's just the forces at work. When a person can speak to those forces, he decides the work they do. My uncle was not a witch, but I didn't want to be part of the village's fear of him. I was, though, and I made myself sick with sadness." Teodora noticed that when she spoke of power and her past these days, Aislinn lowered her head as if to meditate or retreat.

"You were ill and he sent you away? How could he do that?" Aislinn raised her head, indignant.

Teodora smiled. Any minute now, her granddaughter would tuck her old grandmother safely under one of her big, young wings. "Because he wanted me to be whole," Teodora said without the smile, "he wanted me to respect life, he wanted me to know that it is easy to die but better to live."

"Okay, you must of . . . wait, you said the other night you had two meetings with that bird creature. Was this the first one?" Aislinn couldn't decide whether she wanted her gran to answer yes or no.

Teodora contemplated the eager note in Aislinn's voice. Was she keen for knowledge or just for another of her grandmother's strange stories? Teodora's casual storytelling tone sharpened to a new edge of seriousness. "My uncle told me I was robbing his medicine of power. I was no longer putting energy back into the world. He found when he ground medicine plants gathered and dried by me, they turned to powder so fine it disappeared with the breeze. And when I filled the clay water jar from the stream and put it on its tripod of sticks in the shade, it did not sweat a cooling rash of moisture as it should. Instead the water became warm and stagnant. I hadn't even noticed. I was too busy feeling sorry for myself."

Suspicious, Aislinn glanced at her gran. She had heard the 'sorry for myself' phrase before.

"He talked to me in his quiet, patient way about the job of human beings to feed the wider spirit of the world. He said that because people had the gift of feeling and knowing beyond the belly's hunger, the tongue's thirst, it was our duty to share this inner energy. Otherwise humans were just thieves. I remember, as he talked, I didn't even have enough sense to be embarrassed. I was thinking how unfair he was. And he knew what I was thinking.

"Then he said . . . I can still hear his words . . . 'If you will not let me help you heal your spirit, you will have to go away from here.'

"I was ready with my answer. I said, 'I'll go back to live in the village.'

"He stared at me for a long time, as if he couldn't believe we shared the same blood. Finally, he said, 'Don't you understand? The spirit you give off is bad. It makes a place unfit to live in. You cannot return . . . unless you care not at all for our people.'

"For a moment everything stood still. There was no sun's glare, no breeze, no scratch of small animals, the rocks held their breath. I understood what I must say, but I didn't expect to act on my words. I thought the lesson was in the talk. I said, 'Then I must go where I cause no harm.' He didn't answer.

"I was such a stupid child. I thought my uncle just meant to scare me. So I turned and walked toward the high mountains beyond the plateau his house sat on. I kept waiting for him to call me back, but he didn't. As I walked the day away, I thought: he's going to wait until dark and give me a fright. By this time, I was angry, so I decided not to stop. There was a full moon and I kept travelling so he couldn't sneak up on me. I was going to make him do some walking.

"When I finally lay down among the rocks, I was two days' walk into the backcountry. I was too stunned and tired to even feel sorry for myself. I had been asleep a short time when coyotes let out a wail that almost lifted me to my feet. In the darkness they surrounded me, their voices as close as the smell of their meat-eating breath. They circled and howled and it seemed as if the rocks I was sitting on were trying to push me off them. I didn't wait for first light, I left that place." Teodora wondered what her granddaughter was thinking. Could Aislinn see this land that was like sun on skin?

"I just kept moving. The ravines and arroyos all became one to me. I was almost to the top of a mesa before I realized I had been climbing. The spindling trees and bushes up there were black and the rock floor was as broken up as a dropped water jug. This place so close to the sky was dead. It had been hit by lightning. I'm not sure I realized that when I started to pile the shattered bits of rock up in a circle around me. By now, I thought I knew why my uncle felt I brought misfortune to him. God was still punishing me. Taking my family was not enough. He was driving me away from my people and my closest relative. Even the wilderness shunned me." Teodora paused, resting herself and the story.

Sitting with her back against a rock, Aislinn had barely moved since her grandmother had started to talk. As always, her gran's voice had such a soothing quality that everything stopped for Aislinn and she was lost in time. But the word "God" had struck her as odd. When her gran talked of such things, she always spoke of the Great Mother or the gods. "Gran," Aislinn said, as if her grandmother was walking quickly ahead of her. "What god are you talking about?"

Teodora stared at Aislinn. "Father Valenzuela's god," she said.

Aislinn shook her head. "Who is Father Valenzuela?"

"He was the village priest. He sent me to the convent at Hermosillo." Teodora looked puzzled. "Haven't I told you about Father Valenzuela, about him fetching me home to the mountains from the convent?" Teodora smiled at the thought of her girlself and the young village priest on that narrow path. Old age, she thought, was like standing at the opposite end of a dangerous rope bridge: she looked back and couldn't believe she had dared come that way.

"No," Aislinn said, "you haven't. But before you get sidetracked, are you telling me you thought God, the Catholic version, had caused the landslide that buried your family in order to punish you? To punish you for what? For not becoming a nun?"

"In a way, yes. You see, I left the convent because I wanted to be the bride of a priest, not the bride of Christ." Teodora remembered how sure she had been that God would understand her love.

"But grandad says you left the convent because you were homesick." Aislinn's eyebrows drew together in confusion, creating a thick, dark line across her forehead that was almost menacing.

Teodora laughed. "Homesick and lovesick. I had this wonderful plan for helping my people and getting the man I desired. Father Valenzuela wasn't like the other priests. He lived with us in the mountains. He knew we suffered without land

and he believed we should be given back the Yaqui Valley. But he wanted us to fight with words, not guns. In the villages where he was welcomed as a friend, he set up schools, not just for children, but for men and women as well. I thought he loved people more than God, and I loved him more than anyone.

"My plan was for us to marry, to teach my people together and maybe, someday, lead them to the President of the whole of Mexico. There we would speak with our hearts and tell in the right words of the injustice done in Sonora and all would be changed instantly." Teodora laughed again, a little at herself, but more at Aislinn's fisheyed stare. "You're not shocked, are you, granddaughter? I won't say any more. It would be painful if you stopped blinking for good."

"No, don't stop. What happened?" Aislinn blinked rapidly to encourage her grandmother to continue.

"So, on the journey back to the mountains from the convent, I tempted the man away from his God. Father Valenzuela was horrified when I hugged him and then kissed him on the mouth. He called me names. But I was young and although I was hurt, I was sure I could win him over. All the way home I tried, and he continually told me that God would punish me.

"Two days after I arrived home, the rocks came down on my father's house and I was the only one not at home. I was away at the school still trying to change Father Valenzuela's mind. Later, when I saw that pile of rubble where our house had been, I knew he had been right and their deaths were my punishment." Teodora sat quietly, looking across the Strait and seeing the Bacatete Mountains of Sonora. That spine of red rock had not protected her people. Many died before the Yaquis returned to their valley on the coast.

"Hell, gran, what a thing to live with. No wonder you didn't know what you were doing. You should have told your uncle what was bothering you." Aislinn followed Teodora's distant gaze out over the water to the greying mountains. She knew without turning around that the sun was climbing up the limbs of the trees behind them.

Teodora shrugged off the image of the red mountains, as if she could afford to dismiss the memory forever. She realized Aislinn was waiting for a reply. "No, I couldn't tell him. The priests were his enemies. He said their god was evil . . . 'a hungry, human-eating beast' is what he called it. Anyway, as far as my uncle was concerned, the nuns had ruined me. That was the problem." Teodora noticed the light on the water. She broke off the story by returning her voice to its everyday pitch. "We should go, your mother will be worried."

Aislinn shivered. In the presence of a struggling sun, the remaining night air seemed colder. "You haven't told me what happened on top of the mesa," she protested.

"I'll tell you another day," Teodora said.

"No, please finish. You can tell on the way back, we'll walk slow."

Aislinn steadied Teodora down off the boulders. They walked side by side where the deadfall allowed. On the narrow trail through the living trees, Teodora walked behind, her voice raised to reach Aislinn.

"Well, I kept piling rocks up until it got dark. I suppose I was doing it to keep out of the wind, although by then I think I had accepted my fate. So, I wasn't surprised when the wind blew clouds over the moon and stars. Then, thunder tumbled off the mountains and there was a buzzing in the air. My hair stood out from my head and I remember thinking, 'God has sent St. Elmo for me.' And he had. Right then, I was hit by lightning." Teodora was reliving the fear and relief she had felt while enclosed in the electricity of St. Elmo's Fire. She didn't see Aislinn stop on the path ahead.

Aislinn turned to her gran in time to catch her in her arms as Teodora bumped into her. "Whoa, who's chasing you?"

"Why did you stop?" Teodora said in surprise.

"Why did you stay?" Aislinn responded. "When you heard the thunder, why didn't you get down off that mesa? Did you want to die?"

"I didn't think I had a choice." Teodora prodded Aislinn into motion again. "Later, I learned that I did. While I lay there burned as black as the skeleton trees, a monk stood over me, the cowl of his brown habit hiding his face. A hoarse, rasping voice came from the dark hole in his hood. 'Your arrogance is disgraceful,' he said to me. Then he lifted his arms in the long, full sleeves of his robe. Moving them like the wings of a great bird, he created a fierce wind that pulled me into the air and tumbled my rigid body like a dry twig over and over in the darkness above the mountain.

"He closed his arms, the wind stopped and I fell out of the air, landing at the foot of the mesa. As if the earth were quaking, the loose rocks I lay on kept pushing up, lifting me off them, while others leapt from the mountain, burying me.

"Where I lay buried, the rocks kept shifting as if they couldn't bear to be near me. I was completely covered except for my face. My burns caused such agony, but I couldn't move, not even to lick the dust from my lips.

"Then the sky filled with colour and I watched as the colours separated, moving above me in a crazy dance. Suddenly, the pieces of colour collided, vibrating into a picture. In the sky was St. Francis and the birds from the stained-glass window of the convent chapel. I forgot my pain until thunder made the window shudder and explode.

"It rained bright glass slivers that stuck like needles into my face. The sun filled the hole in the stained-glass sky and the light glinted off the glass slivers in my flesh, burning my eyes. My lids wouldn't close; my mouth wouldn't open to let out a scream."

Aislinn felt a tingle in her arms and her hand itched. She held her breath against the sensation, her fingernails dug into her palm, into her gran's pain.

"A shadow stepped in front of the sun and the monk's voice found my ears beneath the rocks. It was like a small rush of air between the stones. The air tickled while the words bruised. He said, 'Such arrogance to think your love for a priest is worth the lives of your father, mother and sister. What a truly ignorant child you are. Your agony is your own fault. The four powers that have touched you here, do so at your bidding. Your poor treatment of your own spirit has harmed the Great Mother's spirit. By wasting your inner energies, you have weakened all energies. Your bed of rocks, your broken sky are your own doing.'

"The monk stood aside so the sun could melt the needles of coloured glass in my face. This wet my lips so I could speak. 'Who are you?' I said. And at the sound of my voice, the rocks jumped up off me and rolled away.

"The monk lifted his cowl and let it fall to his shoulders and I saw a black beak, yellow eyes and iridescent feathers that lay flat against his bird skull. He walked away and his robe fell, exposing bones of every kind: human, bird, fish, animal . . . of every kind. That doll of the dead held a bone finger out to me and, despite my fear, I tried to reach it. At my touch, the bird's head with its rattling body and enormous necklace of dangling bones was sucked up like a puppet through the hole in the sky.

"When I looked again, my uncle's face was there peering down at me. He unfolded his medicine bundle and without a word he put dried tobacco leaf powder on my burns.

"I whispered, more to myself than to him, 'You were right about the world.' I couldn't stop staring at the perfect sky. There wasn't even the ragged edge of a cloud to mark where the hole must have been.

"As he worked his healing on me, my uncle asked in his quiet way, 'How do you know this?'

" 'A bird creature told me,' I answered. 'He offered me a finger bone.'

"My uncle stopped and looked at me closely. He asked, 'Do you have it?'

"I said, 'No, I only touched it.'

"He went on with his medicine, saying, 'Touched death's finger . . . well, your time will come.'

" 'Come for what?' I asked.

" 'This was your first lesson,' he said. 'Every act, every action you perform has an effect on this world for good or bad.'

"Burning pain was flooding back. Pain seemed to be raining out of the tranquil sky and with it came fear. 'What's going to happen to me?' My words were clumsy with panic.

" 'Don't worry, Teodorita,' my uncle said. 'You are very lucky. There will come a time when you will take what was offered today.' "

The sun was warming the earth outside Teodora's door when she and Aislinn arrived back. Teodora was silent now. Yes, her time had come; she had taken the bone. But there was more. After all these years there was still a time to come for her when she would absorb the knowledge of Death's bird and bone creature.

Aislinn raised a hand to shield her eyes from the sun as she turned and looked down into her grandmother's face. Something had occurred to her as she walked and listened on the way home from North Point. "Gran, why haven't I heard these stories before?" Aislinn asked.

"There's a time for everything." Teodora's voice was neutral, almost casual.

"And what time is it now?"

"It's a time of testing for you, granddaughter."

Aislinn started to speak and Teodora held up her hand.

"Aislinn, I know, you think you are too young to be tested. You haven't had time to live. But remember what I said the other night . . . all forces live inside us, the world around us does not control us, it is just there . . . good and bad. . . . Feeling sorry for yourself changes nothing. Find another way to feel."

"It's that easy, is it?" Anger splintered Aislinn's voice like a hammer finding glass.

"No, not easy, but possible. And necessary. Granddaughter, would I say things to hurt you? Is that what you think of your old grandmother?" Teodora filled the space between them with her hand.

Aislinn enclosed her grandmother's hand. Its small bones with their small strength made her want to weep. Instead she hugged her old gran, entangling her young fingers in the silver braid loosened by the morning wind off the Point.

Aislinn entered her mother's kitchen. Deep in thought, she pried her right sneaker off with the toe of the left, then bent to undo the left one so she could slip it off. The room seemed soft in the diffused light that filtered down through the firs to the windows.

She stood very still in the doorway, no longer thinking. It was as if there was nothing inside her and the air in the kitchen was moving toward her to fill the void. Instead of becoming frightened and shaking the feeling off, she waited.

The quiet crept over her and she felt as she did just before she drifted off to sleep. Her inner voice was speechless; it couldn't argue with the soothing light and peaceful air. That constant voice was no longer in control and that was a relief, not the terror she had imagined.

Her skin was so sensitive that she felt the hum of the refrigerator through the soles of her bare feet. It sent a small electric thrill through her body. She could have stood there forever, her heart enticed to beat by the vibrations sent out across the timerippled linoleum from the refrigerator.

She barely heard her mother calling through the thrumming of air and blood in her ears. When Fern's voice broke through, Aislinn shivered, agitating the air and the light suspended in it so that the room filled with hard, bright edges.

Aislinn entered her mother's bedroom, bringing some of the feel of the kitchen with her. Once over the threshold, she usually got straight to the business of dressing her mother; this morning she sat on the end of the bed.

This departure from routine stopped Fern in mid-sentence and suddenly she was remembering the young warmth of a small daughter who shared her mother's bed when her father was away fishing. When had she lost that daughter? It had started when Francis couldn't fish anymore, or work, or love. . . . He didn't lose an arm to that choker cable, he lost nerve. She saw before her a bundle of long, blue-grey wires being pulled through her husband's heart and out his shoulder. Exposed, they pulsed on the end of the severed arm, then died. He had been stripped of feeling. If he were alive, they would make a good couple now. Francis numb from the inside out and she from the outside in. Her tremors intensified as she shook her head for him.

Aislinn had been watching her mother's eyes change and change again in her smooth unwrinkled face. "What's wrong, mom?" she asked in a voice whose softness belonged to a time past.

Fern attempted to control her trembling by focusing her eyes on a spot behind Aislinn's head. "Nothing," she said.

The bed was hard and Aislinn was sliding toward the edge; she put a hand on the bedstead, to rise.

Fern spoke to keep her there. "It's too late now. You see, nothing is wrong now, because there's nothing left to go wrong. It's all been done." She paused. "You know, there's something to be said for that."

Aislinn rose and went to the window. Instead of letting the blind roll up with a slap, she guided it up the frame. She turned to look at her mother in the light.

Fern was staring straight ahead to where Aislinn had sat on the end of her bed. "I really mean that. There's a kind of relief in knowing there's nothing left." Consciously willing the action, slowly she turned her head to look at her daughter. "I lost you a long time ago, before I was ready to let you go. Now, I can't let go. Life is strange, isn't it?" Fern's voice fell flat on the light note she had hoped for. To her own ears, she sounded like a pathetic old woman.

"You never lost me, mom. Things changed . . . I tried to help dad, that's all, like I'm helping you now." Aislinn's shoulders slumped as if she were trying to reduce her frame to the size it had been in the years before things had changed.

Fern saw how unprotected her tall, thin daughter was, despite the masculine muscle and tough ways her father had developed in her. "Yes, you were always willing to help. Maybe we took advantage of that willingness. With so many years between you and Mary and Colin, well, they were gone by the time things changed around here and a lot of it fell to you. We never meant it to happen that way . . . it just did. Bad luck, I guess."

"Yeah, things just happened. It's nobody's fault," Aislinn said. Bad luck, she thought, that's not what her gran would call it. It was just the forces out there swirling around, but damn it, it was bad. Getting mauled by a logging chain was bad, suicide was bad, disease was bad . . . they all made her suffer. How could that be good? She felt her hands itch with frustration. She rubbed a palm on the corner of a dresser. Over the years she had rubbed the paint off just about every sharp corner in the house trying to satisfy that itch. Finally she said, "I guess we better get going here or it'll be noon before the store opens."

Aislinn was late and arrived just as the tribe was wandering up the street for coffee in the backroom of the store. She watched them from the porch; the children seemed subdued, staying close to their mothers, holding a hand where they could. Sewell's silence was exacting a toll, whether the company meant it to or not. It looked as though it was going to be another sullen gathering. For an instant she was tempted to rush inside the store, lock the door again, leave the blind down and the GONE FISHIN' sign in the window. Then she had an idea.

She was in the door before her friends had advanced two more steps. Aislinn swept down the aisles grabbing up party favours, candles, a frozen cake. She decorated the backroom by throwing a roll of floral toilet paper over the rafters, working her way back and forth across the small room. Two-ply streamers billowed down between the beams. The party hats and whistles were laid out on the table. She just had time to stick a few pink candles in the softening ice-cream cake and touch the match to the wicks.

When Linda parted the curtains to the backroom, Aislinn let loose on a snake whistle that screamed as its paper tongue unfurled in Linda's face. Everyone stood in the doorway. The children looked from the room to their mothers' faces for clues.

Aislinn took the whistle out of her mouth and its tongue curled back up, neatly. "Surprise! It's Seesaw Day and we're here to celebrate." Her voice was the voice of television, a game-show host's exaggerated joy.

Linda's colour was coming back now that the snake's tongue was tucked up and she spoke out of relief more than surprise. "It's what? What the hell are you talking about, woman?" Then she burst out laughing. She had just focused her attention enough to see the bedecked room and the conical foil hat Aislinn had perched on her head.

Linda came up to Aislinn and snapped the hat's thin elastic hooked under her chin. "You dingbat," Linda said.

"Well, that's how much you know about anything. We're talking history here," Aislinn objected. "Just ask my grandad. They always used to celebrate Seesaw Day in Tanis Bay. It's a great northern tradition, it even has its own motto . . . carved each year in a living tree"—her voice became church solemn—"carved in Latin, so only those that knew, the true northerners, would recognize it. Now"—she pointed up—"those trees are gone, logged off, of course, Latin words and all . . . and the celebration's kind of been forgotten along with the motto . . . except by a very few who belong here. And we've handed it down through generations, guarding it with all the care . . ."

Corrine broke in on the lecture. "Did you know your cake's melting?" she asked.

"Oh hell." Aislinn turned to see the candles sputtering and sinking into a dark chocolate hole. "Quick, kids, get a spoon, no plates, just spoons, so dig in." She shoved plastic spoons at them.

Corrine took a spoon and went to work with the kids. "So what's this motto?" she asked, shifting a lump of ice cream to a cheek that bulged like a pack-rat's.

"Damn, Corrine, you had to ask, didn't you?" Tracey said. "Now we'll never get any coffee."

Aislinn took the hint and put the kettle on the hotplate. "I'm glad you asked that. There's a lot of history behind that motto," she said, looking the part of a strange orator with a shrunken dunce cap.

"No bullshit history, just spit out the motto," Linda put in.

"Okay, okay, if you're not open to a little education. . . . Anyway the motto is made up of the first words spoken by the first logger to ever bring a Swedesaw into the virgin timber of this island wilderness. He said with a tear in his eye, a lump in his throat, and as he puffed out his chest, 'I come, I see, I saw.' "

The women grabbed rolls of toilet paper stacked on a shelf and hurled them at Aislinn as she retreated out the back door. They locked the door, leaving her to bang on the peeling paint and then slink around to the front entrance.

Aislinn pulled back the curtain and stood in the doorway with her pointed party hat down on her forehead like a unicorn's horn. "So, you feel better, do you?" she asked through the laughter.

Corrine swallowed the hiccups that always erupted when she laughed too hard and said, "I guess we've been pretty down lately."

"I hardly noticed," Aislinn said, removing, with relief, the garrotting hat elastic from under her chin.

Tracey took the kettle off, pouring hot water into mugs of instant coffee. "We have a right to be." She slammed the kettle down on the hotplate.

Aislinn came over to help her pass around the mugs. "Yeah, don't I know. Whatever happens, at least none of you will be caught in a dead town waiting for the old folks to leave one way or another. You can take your families and move to where life's going on." The tears came so fast that Aislinn didn't have time to will them back. "Cripes, I'm scared. What am I going to do when you all leave?"

The silence in the room let in the sounds of the children playing in the backyard. Their noise inside that small space had an unreal quality as if it were being broadcast over a loud-speaker.

Linda jumped down from where she sat on a carton of paper towels. "We're going to have a party tonight. To hell with this being down in the dumps. It's not the end of the world." She looked around at the others. "What do you say?"

Corrine, whose head barely reached Aislinn's shoulder, hugged her tall friend and said, "We'll have it at my house. It's my turn. Everybody come over after supper . . . we'll put all the kids to bed in the spare room."

When Aislinn got home from the store, her mother was unusual-ly quiet. Fern seemed almost shy. She didn't natter and nag through supper, instead she made small requests much as a child does to forestall bedtime. Rather than bustle her mother off to her room, Aislinn lingered over the supper dishes in the sink.

Neither of them said much. It was as if they occasionally opened their mouths to taste the air, wondering whether any of the rarefied atmosphere of the morning had remained. It was a good kind of silence, without argument. Aislinn let it be.

It was dark when Aislinn finally started for the company side of town. She passed Sewell's community hall where some teenage boys were swinging on the heavy fire door. With every outward arc of the door, rock music broke out into the night. She couldn't help but laugh at the boys dancing with the door to avoid dancing with the girls inside the hall. Their shyness would turn into bluster as they got older. But they would never be as infuriatingly confident as the university guys on the bush crew. She couldn't decide which was worst. Why couldn't they just be people, be themselves without all the posturing? It must be the genes or hormones or something.

Her friends' husbands were blusterers. Most of it was talk. What would they be like if she couldn't hear their words? Because of her mother, she spent most evenings with the sound on the TV turned down and she had noticed that you could learn a lot from just watching. Words, like sleights-of-hand, tended to distract a person's eye from the human being behind the mask.

Aislinn was late, the party was well under way. Instead of going in, she stopped in the street to watch what was happening behind Corrine and Tim's livingroom window. From where she stood in the dark, it was like looking at a movie screen, the actors framed by light, separate from the dark. Doors and windows were open, releasing a buzz of music and noise to her in the green, silent night.

At the centre were Earl and Tim, each with a foot on the coffee table and their banjos propped against raised thighs. They were both bent low over their instruments, playing with concentrated fury the follow-the-leader music of "Duelling Banjos." There was a frantic quality to the scene like the old silent movies where the music never kept up with the cranking camera. The music from inside the house was delayed in coming to her, trailing too far to be real behind their fingers. A bad dubbing job.

"Duelling Banjos" turned into a piece of square-dance music that shuffled the feet of a few couples who only had room to swing in tight circles radiating out from their locked elbows. Promenade they could not, so they whirled, changing direction by unlocking and locking opposite elbows. As Aislinn approached the house, she could hear the dancers' stamping feet, a demand for freedom from the small room, its carpet and solid furniture.

She entered the light by opening the screen door and was welcomed by wailing from a room at the back of the house. Linda hollered at Earl to hold it down while they got the kids back to sleep. Someone put a beer in Aislinn's hand. Earl put his banjo down, reached for his guitar and said something about being "folky" to Tim. The dancing feet retreated to the kitchen for more beer, then came back to rest on the crushed shag of the carpet.

Earl began. "Four strong winds that blow lonely, seven seas that run high." His voice was too husky for the words. Tim joined in, his voice soft but with ragged edges like torn flannelette. "All those things that don't change come what may. But our good times are all gone and I'm bound for moving on." The dancers became singers. "I'll look for you if I'm ever back this way." Tracey and Corrine could be heard in the kitchen. They stirred the song into the pots of chili on the stove. Aislinn gulped down her beer.

Tim set his banjo carefully in its upright stand and left Earl to finish the last chorus. Others drifted with Tim out to the refrigerator. He opened more beer by pitting the teeth of one beer cap against the teeth of another. The last, his own, he opened on his back molars. Within the strobe light of the fridge door opening and closing, Tim's neighbour was giving the beer drinkers the lowdown on his bandaged hand. The loggers were having a laugh on him, his mishap and his Scot's accent. To them he was something of a greenhorn in the bush, so it wasn't surprising he'd get it on a sharp piece of cable.

"Didn't see the damn jagger, till I felt it. I was setting the choker cables real fast," he said, "and at the same time swatting the noseeums away from the rip in the seat of my trousers."

Someone mimicked, "Trousers. What's trousers? I wear jeans."

"Yeah, shit, I got this bloody big tear you could drive a truck through. Besides the noseeums, every fucking mosquito for miles around wants a taste of my arse."

"The smell should've been enough to knock 'em dead on the spot." The fellow next to the Scot slapped him on the back.

"Look who's talking, the genius here. Do you want to show them your new tattoo the way you showed the van driver this morning? Let me tell you, this lad dumped a full cup of coffee all over his boots. Do you want to tell it?"

"No."

"Okay, it happens like this. He puts his arm straight out to the driver, coffee and all, then turns it over to show the naked girlie he's got tattooed there on his forearm. Whoosh, no more coffee. No coffee, no reason to stay awake. So he dozes off, his lunch pail between his feet, see. We undo his laces, he's still snoring, string 'em through the handle of his lunch box and tie 'em together. When we got to the job, he just about broke his nose getting up. Curse, you should've . . ." Encouraged by the laughter, the neighbour continued, his accent burring like a rip-saw missing several teeth.

The kitchen was cramped and hot; Aislinn let herself out the screen door to the back porch. Sitting on the top step, she lifted her heavy hair off the back of her neck. The night air touched the sweat on her uncovered nape and she shivered. Taking an elastic band from her pocket, she tied the hair back in a ponytail. She heard from behind the wire net of the screen door, ". . . stuck his head in the tiger's mouth. Bravest, bravest . . . Don't do it Marvel . . . not your willy . . . you'll bleed to death . . . you're the very bravest . . ."

She imagined the words straining to come to her through the small pores of the screen, pushed through by waves of laughter like grains of sugar in a sieve. Her ears licked them up, missing as many as she got. She liked the jumble of crackerjack words and suds in her head, the beer foamed and kept everything bubbling. The crystalline words she missed went into the sky and crackled in starfire like burnt sugar. She watched the stars brighten on the sweet fuel. Caught up in her private circus, she didn't hear Tim step through the door.

His eyes were on the sky too and, unseeing, he stumbled into Aislinn.

"Shit. Hey, whatcha doing out here?" Tim looked a little closer to make sure who it was.

Aislinn couldn't decide whether he sounded surprised or indignant. "Cooling off," she answered.

"Yeah, a hot party . . ." His voice started loud and trailed off. "We're known for hot parties . . . ," he tried again.

"Especially in the summer," Aislinn replied. Unsure of Tim's intent, she didn't emphasize the humour in her statement.

"Yeah." Tim jumped from the porch, landing on all fours on the lawn. He pulled himself up unsteadily, using a nearby tricycle as a crutch. He pushed the kid's trike in the direction of the boat shed at the end of the yard and followed. Then he turned back to Aislinn sitting on the stairs. "You wanna come see my baby?" Walking backwards, he stumbled over the tricycle.

Aislinn followed Tim down the yard. He was already inside the boat shed when she entered. He hadn't switched on a light, so the interior was a deeper shade of the outside grey—the nightfiltered light of a fat moon. He was sitting inside the half-finished cabin cruiser he had worked on all winter.

Aislinn straddled a sawhorse yellowed by the castoff light of the kitchen coming in through the open door.

"So, what do you think?" Tim asked as he rolled a half-bottle of rye back and forth across the planking between his outstretched legs.

Aislinn disliked the limping sound of a rolling bottle on a wood floor. She spoke low, hoping he would have to stop to hear her. "Looks good to me. What you going to call her?"

"Call her . . . ? Unfinished, that's what I call her, 'cause she won't be anything else . . . until . . . You know, we were going to take a trip in this baby. Down the coast, show the kid how to fish . . . Corrine's a real good fisherman, she can even handle the big salmon, you wouldn't think so just looking at her. She's a midget compared to you, but she's real wiry, I can say that for her. We haven't had a Christly holiday since the kid was born. We were going to make up for lost time." Tim paused.

Aislinn could hear the lame thud of the rolling bottle again. It echoed in the silent boat shed. She wondered why the sound didn't lose itself in the soft, moist sawdust she could smell. Her eyes, adjusted now to the moongrey, saw tools neatly arranged on the walls. The floor was swept, the sawdust heaped in one corner. The wall above a plain workbench was hung with calendars displaying gorgeous ocean sunsets. She felt she should whisper. Tim's voice startled her.

"My old man was crazy about boats. We built one together once. Never got a chance to sail it though. This would have been a real trip, this one with Corrine and the kid. You know, I hate loggin', never liked the damn bush. It crowds me, like the kitchen tonight, makes me feel like I'm suffocating. I should've gone in for fishing . . . out there you breathe and see . . . it's all open, so you know. Not like the bush where you're always watching out, waiting to get taken out by . . . God, by just about everything that moves and things not meant to move. Always lookin' out for what's above." Tim unscrewed the bottle and raised it above his head in salute.

"No," Aislinn said. "Instead you got to watch out for seagulls shittin' out of the sky on you." She was trying to lighten up the conversation. She'd never known Tim to be a talker. His sudden openness made her uneasy.

Aislinn realized he hadn't laughed at what she said. The bottle was between his legs once more. He continued on almost as if she weren't there, although she could see him plainly and he her if he raised his eyes from the perpetual motion of the bottle, the foaming waves within.

"Can't do it now. Fishin's as bad off as loggin'. Too many boats out there now, not enough fish to go around. No one's making a living, no more. Sure wish I could get out of the bush . . . don't know much else, though." Tim looked up, directing his gaze over Aislinn's head and out the door. The light reflected golden in his eyes. "You know, I been to university . . . took music, philosophy, literature, stuff like that. Didn't last out the first year. I was too busy building that boat with my old man. Built others since then, you know. It all comes down to a bloody boat. It all comes down to this bloody hunk of wood . . . and it doesn't make a fucking bit of difference, not now when it should. You know?"

A shadow replaced the light in his eyes as Corrine stepped out the kitchen door onto the back porch.

"Tim," Corrine called. "Tim, you out there? Come and eat."

Aislinn swung her leg over the sawhorse. "Coming, Tim?"

"Yeah, go on. I'm coming."

Aislinn turned in the doorway in time to see a plume of rye spray from Tim's mouth over the ribs of the boat. She heard him say, "I christen you, The Fool." He raised the bottle and took another mouthful.

She continued up the yard toward the house. In the treeshadowed yard, her foot found the tricycle Tim had pushed aside. She grabbed it by the handlebars to haul it up to the back porch. Instead she raised a foot onto the little runningboard covering the back axle and pushed off with the other. The rubber pedals on either side of the front wheel whirled frantically, trying to keep up with her push. She circled the yard, in and out of the dark side of the trees. Around and around, she thought, they all went around and around, pedalling as fast as they could to keep up with the push from behind.

The flicker of black and grey stripes on the lawn mesmerized her. Aislinn was on a track of tarred timbers and grey gravel, a circular track with no beginning and no end. Around and around, was it whim that got you on the track? Is that how it happened, a playful trick?

She was puffing hard, coming up the slope of the yard one more time, when the front wheel of the trike wobbled, then spun away free. Aislinn went down with the handlebars until the twin forks that had supported the front wheel impaled a grey shadow to the lawn. Abruptly halted, poised on the handlebars, one leg caught in a propelling kick, she felt like an acrobat balancing for a handstand. Then, she fell over on her side, as if in slow motion. A giggle came up from the black shadow that had caught her. "So that's how you get off the track," she said to the disabled trike.

Inside the house, everyone was collecting around the stove for another helping of chili. The kitchen talk centred on the delightful damage red chili peppers could inflict. The real kind such as Anchos that lifted the skin off your tongue just as surely as if you had placed that warm, moist slab of speech against a frozen pipe in the middle of winter. Aislinn filled her bowl from one of the pots on the stove. She was trying to think how she would explain the trike to Corrine. She'd get it fixed, of course, but maybe she would just say she tripped over it in the dark.

Returning the ladle to the pot, she heard someone behind her remark that she had guts spooning up a big helping of the hot stuff with the jalapeno peppers. "That'll make your hair curl from the roots out." She didn't realize there was a difference between the two pots on the stove. Hesitating, she looked out the kitchen window into the darkened yard. She remembered Tim just as she saw movement down near the boat shed. Her concentration was suspended between the discomfort of the hot bowl in her hands and what her eyes were recording. The thought came to her that Tim was spraying rye again, this time over the walls of the shed. Except, the bottle he threw away under the trees was the size of a gas can. She thought her imagination must have lit the match between his fingers, because the flame burst in her mind before it illuminated the thumb that had scratched the sulphurous head.

Aislinn breathed, "No, my God, Tim." She shouted, "No, Tim, no." Dropping the hot bowl into the pot, she banged out the screen door, only to be stopped on the porch by the deliberate fall of the match into a pool of gasoline that grew into a red balloon sucking up air. Aislinn held her breath as if to deprive the gasping ball of her air. But it didn't need her. It didn't need Tim either. He had fallen to his knees.

Others were on the porch now and for a moment they shared the unspoken feeling that the fire was right and they should not interfere. They had blundered onto something private they should leave alone.

The fire was singing. Tim turned his smiling face to the house. His beard, the lick of hair on his forehead were black where they should have been brown. This realization broke the trance and Aislinn ran for the garden hose wrapped around the outside tap. The green hose snaked alive as she turned the water on full and drenched Tim, still kneeling. She tried to direct him to his feet with the force of the water.

Now Corrine was there pulling at Tim.

Aislinn looked to the fire and saw the sparks floating up and, like bright fish, many were caught in the net-like limbs of the cedars. But they couldn't be held there and, freed, they dropped onto the roof of the house. Aislinn turned the water on the moss-bearded shake roof. When the roof shone in the twin light of fire and moon, she stretched the thin, inadequate rubber tube as far as she could to jab a needle of water into the ribs of the boat shed.

Corrine's hair was crinkling into scorched curls as she watched Earl lift Tim across his shoulder and carry him away.

The others were passing pots and buckets of water from the kitchen down the yard. The fire went on singing from the centre of the shed; the boat lay at the heart of the song. The hose and the buckets made up a hissing chorus at the outer edge of the flames.

Into the night they watched the fire, as Aislinn sprayed the house and trees with water. Tim was passed out on the lawn, his arm thrown over his eyes and the idiot smile still on his lips.

- 4 -

AISLINN HEARD HER MOTHER TAPPING on the wall. She got dressed quickly and didn't bother to make her bed.

Fern spoke as soon as the door opened on the darkened room. "What time did you get home? Late last night sometime, I'd say. And dead to the world this morning. Sleeping it off and the store waiting to be opened."

Aislinn snapped the blind up and a strong finger of sun pierced the white room as if it were the shell of an egg.

"It must be noon already," Fern continued, stopping only to catch her breath when the light struck the glossy wall beside her bed. "I smell smoke, you didn't light the wood stove on a day . . . my God, what have you done to yourself?"

"Done? What are you talking about, mom?" Aislinn went to the dresser. "Which housedress do you want to wear?"

"Aislinn, your hair. You cut your hair."

"No I didn't." Aislinn looked up into the dusty mirror over the dresser as she pulled a pair of knickers out of a drawer. She dodged the reflected sunlight and strained toward the mirror. She couldn't see herself. Looking down to close the drawer, she discovered the white dresser cloth was peppered with broken bits of black hair. Then she shook her head and the dresser top turned into a barber shop floor.

"Hell," she whispered. Aislinn held the underwear up to screen the sun from a corner of the mirror. "Holy hell, my hair."

"What is it?" Fern asked.

"It looks like I've got a freaking brush cut."

"Aislinn, mind your mouth."

She looked again and snorted. "All I need now is a safety pin through my nose."

"Talk sense."

"I've finally done something with my hair, mother." She ran the palm of her hand over the fringe of short, spiky stubble that extended in a swath back from forehead to crown. "It got burned."

"Burned? You were drunk."

"No, I was stone sober, fire has that effect on most people . . . except Tim, maybe."

"What are you babbling about?" Fern had the stringy neck and bulging-eye intensity of a baby bird.

"My hair got singed, mom. Tim's boat shed burned down last night. I was helping put out the fire." Aislinn pulled a brush through her hair again and again, while the linoleum floor's faded pattern was sprinkled with new outlines. Her long hair flowed away from the trimmed border around her face and the flat avenue that ran front to back. "It was the ponytail, that's what saved the rest of my hair."

"My God, where were the men?"

"The men were there. We all fought the fire." Aislinn put down the brush and moved to the closet for Fern's housedress.

"How did it happen? Was anyone hurt?" Fern said, as Aislinn buttoned the front of her dress.

"No one was hurt. Tim lost his boat." Aislinn lifted her mother off the bed.

Fern's arms went around her daughter's neck and her slow-moving lips were beside Aislinn's ear as she carried her to the kitchen. "I could see something like this happening to that know-it-all Doug, with his bad temper, but Tim's so quiet and careful. How could it happen to him?"

"We're not sure . . . it was an accident."

Fern allowed herself to be rushed through breakfast, although she never stopped lamenting Aislinn's hair and her reckless habit of jumping into the forefront of any situation. One of the men surely could have handled the hose.

As Aislinn approached the store along the lane, she could see the town's teenagers pushing each other off her front porch. At the sight of this group she felt a surge of the self-consciousness that had been born on the first day of grade nine when she entered a new classroom with her botched home perm. Her mother had left the curling solution on too long and her hair had coiled as tight as watch springs. Her nickname that year was poodle and the boys barked at her.

She went in through the back door and stood quietly in the storeroom, unwilling to turn the sign in the window and unlock the front door. She tried to convince her reflection in the small mirror over the sink that it wasn't too bad. If she evened out the burnt patches so the hair was all one length, it might be less noticeable. The large utility scissors were awkward to handle and she ended up cutting off more than she intended. The hair around her face and on top of her head stuck up in short tufts.

The kids were banging on the front door. Finally, she turned the sign and the lock, allowing the restless tribe to push inside. They stared. She carefully ignored them from behind the counter. They came closer for a better look. "Wow, real punk, electric," they said. She was surprised into silence.

"How you doing, Tim?" Aislinn asked from outside the gate.

He sat on his front porch, staring at the trees beyond the road. His hair was still blackened, his face smudged. He didn't answer.

His eyes didn't move to include her.

Aislinn went around to the back of the house and knocked on the screen door. "Corrine, are you in?"

"Come on in." Corrine sat at the kitchen table, a cup of coffee going cold in front of her.

Aislinn noticed from across the table that Corrine's fair eyelashes were like the short, sharp hairs of a caterpillar. Her eyebrows were extinct, singed out of being. "Are you alright?" Aislinn asked.

"Yeah, I'll live." Corrine got up and dumped her coffee down the sink. She poured a fresh cup and one for Aislinn.

"Has Tim been sitting out there all night?" Aislinn inhaled the steam coming off the coffee and with it came conflicting smells. The odour from the sodden, smouldering remains in the yard was challenged by scorched spices and charred meat. The chili pots were soaking in the sink.

"He's been out there since five this morning." Corrine turned the cup around on the table as if inspecting the design painted on the rim, but she wasn't noticing the faded carousel horses. "Slept it off on the cot in the back porch." She finally lifted the cup to her mouth. "Hasn't said one word, nothing all day."

"He's probably afraid to come in. I know I would be." Aislinn smiled and touched her friend's hand.

"He did this once before. When his dad died, he sat in the garage for days, sat and stared at the wall, didn't move, didn't talk, nothing."

"He needs time to think. I know how that is."

"It's like he sinks a little deeper into quicksand. When something happens, he takes it inside him and it's like a god-damn weight, you know." Corrine looked past Aislinn, out the kitchen window and down the yard. "Just thankful the house didn't go up."

"Yeah, but it must be hard to lose something you put so much work into. He must have been some pissed off at the world last night."

"The world, maybe, more likely himself. He doesn't know what he wants . . . been letting things drift for the last few years. Who am I to talk? I don't know." Corrine looked at Aislinn, seeing her almost for the first time since she had entered the kitchen. "Hey, why have you got a scarf on?"

Aislinn pulled the edge of the scarf a little farther down on her forehead. "I slept in . . . didn't have time to wash my hair this morning."

Corrine rose to get the coffee pot and leaned over the table to pour. "You smell funny." She raised her hand to touch with a fingertip points of hair so short and sharp that they pierced the cotton weave. "Oh, Aislinn, your beautiful hair. It got burnt." Corrine withdrew her hand, standing over the table with the coffee pot held up as if it were a lantern. "Show me . . . please."

Aislinn reached back and undid the scarf.

Corrine emptied her lungs of air in a long sigh that sounded more exasperated than surprised. The tears rolled down her cheeks and instead of catching the drops with her tongue as usual, she started to laugh. Aislinn's first impulse was to cover her head with the scarf again, but Corrine was such a funny picture herself that Aislinn balled up the scarf and threw it at her. She took Corrine's hand and led her into the hall where they both stood in front of the mirror and laughed until they slid down the wall to the floor, weak and gasping.

"I'm really sorry about your hair." Now Corrine looked grief-stricken.

"Will you cut it off at the back for me?"

"Oh, no. You don't want to do that, the rest will grow out."

"Come on, I'm due for a change."

As Aislinn approached her grandparents' house, she heard more than two voices behind the door and a nervous hand tugged down the edges of the scarf. Aislinn entered, knocking on the door as she went. Augusta and Wil Charlie sat at the kitchen table with her old folks.

Augusta's smile was broad and cracked, her chipped teeth old porcelain yellow in the kerosene light. "A gypsy girl comes, yes," she said.

Teodora took up Augusta's teasing tone. "Comes to read our palms, tell our futures."

"Wasting her time, she is, yes," Augusta said. "No future in these old hands."

"Let me see," Aislinn demanded, pulling Augusta's swollen right hand across the table and under the light. "The lines here tell much. I see a girl, small but strong and handsome." Aislinn glanced up at Wil. "Oh yes, handsome. Whose shining smile turned men into . . . into bright-eyed birds hopping and flapping about her, except for one . . . a hunchbacked raven that always looked sideways as if he knew her secrets." She winked at Wil. "And it says here that there were lots of secrets, for sure, because this girl became a Woman of the Clan. Now, a gathering of the Women's Clan had a way of scattering the men like seagulls complaining across the sky. But not the Raven, he loved the handsome girl and had much respect for the Clan's ancient wisdom."

"Raven?" Augusta chuckled. "Blackhearted crow!" She curled her puffy fingers up stiffly. "You see the past, yes. Easy to see back, not easy see forward."

Aislinn gently uncurled Augusta's fingers and looked closely at the crumpled brown palm. She was about to say something such as, 'You have a stubborn life line, it runs forever,' but instead she heard herself say, "You have much to do yet, a promise to keep." Aislinn stared at the brown leaf of a hand resting in hers. It seemed to invite her to stroke it with the fingertips of her free hand, to feel its warmth and resilience even in age.

Augusta and Teodora had raised their heads as if Aislinn's words were a cue. Their eyes met in recognition before they turned their gaze on their granddaughter.

Wil saw this exchange and remained silent.

Shea sensed a special quiet and his eyes under their drooping lids moved as if he were looking from one to another around the table. His impatience at not knowing made him demand words. "Enough tomfoolery. I've not had a hug and kiss from my granddaughter." Shea turned his head. "Age before beauty, Augusta," he said in her direction.

With her free hand, Aislinn covered Augusta's entrapped hand for a second before returning its brown warmth to Augusta's lap. Aislinn circled the table to reach her grandfather. She put her long arms around his thin shoulders and kissed his cheek.

Shea pulled back from her embrace. "Aislinn, what have you been doing?"

Aislinn straightened, standing behind her grandfather. "Tim's boat shed burned down last night," she said. "He lost the boat he was building." She untied the scarf. "I lost some hair."

The wrinkles around Wil's eyes began a twitching dance.

Teodora turned to look up at Aislinn. "Are you burnt?" Teodora was on her feet, alarmed.

"No, gran, no. Don't worry. I'm just short on eyebrows and eyelashes . . . and, well, a bit on top, too." Aislinn bent down and placed Shea's hand on her head.

"By God, you're as bristled as boot brush," Shea said.

"And I expected sympathy from you guys," Aislinn complained, supressing a grin.

Augusta came around the table to get a better look at the ruin. "No one got hurt, yes?"

"No, Tim was the only one near the fire and we got him away." Aislinn patted the top of her head. "Is there something I can put on it?" she asked.

Wil spoke from behind his cup. "A hat, maybe."

Aislinn broke in on their laughter. "Go ahead, make jokes. I'm used to it with you . . . you old farts."

"Ah, Wil, you've made her call us names," Shea said, "poor girl."

Augusta touched Aislinn's hair. "We get some soap plant to wash it in, yes. Better than stuff in the bottle you got in the store. Using that bottle stuff like putting a paintbrush in gasoline," Augusta chuckled.

"First, rub olive oil into the scorched parts," Teodora added. "Sit down, we'll do it now and you can wash with my white clematis hair soap. Otherwise, I'll make you sit in the corner near the door."

"Why?" Aislinn settled into Teodora's chair at the table.

Teodora paused and glanced at Shea. "Because I hate the smell of burnt hair." Teodora dropped a tea towel over Aislinn's shoulders.

"How did the fire start?" Wil asked.

Aislinn wanted to shake her head, but Teodora was keeping her still by clutching the ragged tail of hair Corrine had left at the back. Finally, she said, "Tim set fire to the shed."

"Deliberately?" Shea questioned.

"Yeah, but he was drunk."

Wil lifted his shoulders. "Drink can do that," he said.

"It wasn't the booze," Aislinn replied. "He was mad. They're all mad . . . and scared. Scared they're going to get shafted by the company. And the company's not talking, so they're chewing on their moustaches and building it out of shape." Aislinn laid her open hands palms up on the table. The gesture had her father in it. "I'm just surprised things didn't blow before now, but it's started. This is the beginning, for sure."

Augusta watched Wil turn the teaspoon over and over in his hand weighing its usefulness as he did with most things that came into his hands. She said, "Wil got mad like that once, yes.

Now we live on little Klaskish Island."

Aislinn's dark eyes searched Wil's long fingers with their many scars for signs of past anger. All she saw was the respectful caress of a strong finger along a silver edge. She looked to Augusta.

"Those hands of Wil's used to haul in the fishes, yes, in big nets, off a good boat. A long time he worked wages, day in, day out, to get the good boat with big motor. By that time we have only one daughter left, no sons to help him pull the nets, no. But our daughter healthy, strong girl and like to fish." Augusta stopped to pour some tea in her cup.

Aislinn wrapped a towel around her head. "You mean Quan'i?" The name hung in the air.

Augusta continued, "Fishes were selling good for the Charlies then, 'cause all the young mens were away fighting in the big war, yes."

"My dad too," said Aislinn.

"Sure, him too. He not gone very long. So Wil and Quan'i fished hard, staying out as long as they could, yes. Everything was okey-dokey, we have lots of money and good boat. But Wil, he got mad at that good boat and big motor. He take that big motor apart piece by piece, yes, and throw it into the water. He put the anchor down in the baywater outside our village and he leave that good boat to the ocean. He go to the village and carve a canoe that takes us to Klaskish by ourselves. This time we stay for good." Augusta tasted her tea.

Aislinn adjusted the towel to keep it from slipping off. "But why leave the boat?"

Wil spoke, "It was not a good boat for an Indian." He looked down at his tea.

Aislinn turned to Augusta.

"Something go wrong with that big motor," Augusta said. "Something go wrong when Wil and Quan'i fishing far out, yes. Quan'i not feeling too good that morning, but she go out on boat anyway. She's going to have a baby and she figures she just feeling baby sickness and it go away in a few hours. Instead, the baby starts to come out too early . . . the baby only five months inside. Wil makes the motor go a little then it stop, go a little, stop. Quan'i bleeding too much." Augusta paused to look at Teodora.

Aislinn wondered at this look which seemed to ask a question, but the talk went on.

"So Wil and me, we went to Klaskish, yes. Not one of our people touched that good boat of his. Wil was proud of that good boat, but it rotted and broke up on the water. The village was glad when it washed away, yes, it was a bad thing."

Aislinn examined the faces of the old folks sitting in silence around the table. There was greater grief here than she could understand and it made her want to back out the door and run down the path. Instead, she got up, ran water into the kitchen sink and unwrapped the towel from around her head. She felt sad, sadder than she should, and she tried to attach the feeling to a source: Augusta and Wil. But it was more than them and their daughter, it was her old folks, her mom, Tim, her friends, her . . . There it was again, the panic, the flutter that had begun when her dad died, that fear of tomorrow.

Walking up the street toward the pub, Aislinn was facing into the sun, low in the west but still shimmering with heat waves. The sweat ran down inside her thin blouse, tickling her back. She could feel beads of moisture on her upper lip; she ran her tongue over them. An old habit from the days of sawing logs with her dad. The rhythm going back and forth between them without pause because neither wanted to be the first to take a break. He may not have worked in the bush after the accident, but he worked hard at odd jobs, determined to prove he could do them faster, better than anyone. She never heard him complain, not when he was sober. When he drank, he got angry enough to cry. A night of booze and tears made him quiet and tense the next day and she would have to throw challenges at him to make him notice her. "I bet I can finish breakfast before you. I'll race you to the store. Beat you down to the dock." His restless frustration was there when they sat silent in the evening or walked the beach. She always associated that feeling with the first time she went into the bush with her dad. She was young and he was telling her about the trees, their names, what they were good for, how to tell a spruce from a fir.

"Here, roll a spruce needle between your thumb and forefinger. Now do the same with the fir needle. So, what do you feel? That's right, the spruce needle has corners. It's square, not flat like the fir."

"S for spruce, S for square," she said.

"Say, that's good kiddo, good for you, Linny."

Or, he'd tell her how you had to be careful if you were scrambling on logged cedar. Even if it had just been felled, it could be rotten inside. Rotten to the core, just a husk pretending to be a tree. You could get a real surprise if you broke through the bark skin; yellowjackets like to nest inside deadwood. The whole horde would come out of the log like a shotgun blast right in the face. She stepped carefully these days, aware of the restless energy under the town's skin.

After the hot street, the pub was a cool hiding place. Inside the door she shivered and in the dark passage, before her eyes adjusted, she stumbled down the two stairs to the entrance, blundering into the noise. Earl saw her come in and hollered at Mad Dog to set up a round on Aislinn.

As she approached the table, Doug flicked a burning match at her. "Hot enough for you?"

"Yeah, and getting hotter." Aislinn sat down.

Doug struck another match and tossed it across the table at her. She knocked it away with her hand and it landed in Tim's lap. "Hey, you trying to make an ash of me?" he asked Aislinn.

She gave Doug a hard look. "Little boys shouldn't play with fire."

"Drink up," Earl said. "I need your beer mugs."

Linda nudged him. "No, Earl, you'll get us thrown out again."

Earl lined up six heavy glass mugs on the table in front of him. "Mad Dog won't even notice. He's too busy." He picked over the others and pushed aside those with rounded bottoms.

"This town needs some entertainment," Aislinn said, nursing her beer and fingering the flat base of the mug.

Corrine, sitting across from Earl, moved her chair back from the table. "We should see about bringing in some movies to the community hall."

Tracey slid her mug over to Earl. "Sewell's community hall?"

Corrine couldn't ignore the sneering tone. "Damn it, have you got a better idea?"

Doug looked at her as if she had thrown the challenge directly in his face. "Sure, we should get Mad Dog to bring in a couple of strippers and turn the place into a night club. Christ, yeah, a white girl and a black girl. Salt and pepper. The spice of life," he mused.

"Here." Tracey threw the salt and pepper shakers across the table at Doug. "That's all the spice you're going to get . . . black or white."

Doug winged the salt shaker back at her, but it went off to one side and Tim caught it.

"Hey, I don't need any more bad luck," Tim said. He carefully gathered up the grains of salt that had sprinkled on the table in front of him, and threw them over his shoulder.

"Bad luck, Tim? Yeah, I guess so," Earl said. "We'll just have to keep you away from the rye in future." He added the last mug to level five of his transparent pyramid. He looked at Aislinn. "The apex is yours."

"I'm not finished my beer." She felt like making him wait.

Aislinn saw a burst of yellow before the match hit her in the forehead. She threw her beer at Doug. He jumped, kicking a table leg. The shining monument toppled, shooting mugs onto the floor. It happened so fast no one even tried to catch the mugs. The whole pub went quiet, waiting for the wrath of Dog to descend on the builder.

A broom handle came down hard on the table again and again, smashing the rest of the beer mugs. Mad Dog pushed the end of the handle into Earl's chest. "You owe me. Pay up and get out."

Aislinn turned and left the pub, the red spot on her forehead alive, burning with anger. She shoved her hands in her pockets and jangled her keys as she walked fast down Centre Street toward the dock. She shouted out across the water, "Bastards." The tide thumped against the pier. The steps to the beach swayed under her weight; she took them two at a time, reckless with the decaying handrail. The rocks jabbed her through the soft soles of her sneakers. She walked harder, striking the barnacle-encrusted stones with keen satisfaction. The wind raised the hair on her bare arms. Hugging herself, she turned back up the beach. There was no way to get enough distance between her and those idiots, between her and everyone and everything.

Turning again, she walked down the beach into the water. It tugged at her legs, inviting her to lie down, to be rocked in the tide cradle. Cold washed over her as she stepped off the shelf that ended the rocky bench. She rose to the surface gasping, treading water. Across the Strait, the mountains stood like high, dark waves on the horizon. The current would carry her south to Mary. Even now it was pulling her away. She looked back at the beach translucent in the moonlight. She was drifting toward South Point. Her arms flailed out; no, not South Beach. She swam back.

Trailing up the beach near the spot where she had entered the water, she slumped down with her back against a log. There must be a way out, a hole down which she could disappear. What magic had Mary performed? She had cut off her ponytail and the next day she was gone. That was the answer: she made herself different. Aislinn felt in her pocket for her dad's penknife on her key ring. It was slippery and hard to open, the blade cold grey in the light. She lifted the hair that lay over her shoulder like a wet rope and began to saw through with the knife. There was too much. Separating it into smaller hanks, she chopped it off, dropping the pieces into her lap. She studied the pile of clinging black hair. Was there something special she should do with it? Teodora had warned her when she was a little girl not to let anyone keep her hair clippings. But she had let Corrine tie the pieces she had cut the other day to the fence around her garden. It was magic enough to keep the deer away. Then who should she honour with her hair? The ocean . . . always moving, always there. She gathered the hair up in her shirt and crawled down to the water's edge. Carefully she placed a handful on the rocks in reach of the tide. Other powers? The earth . . . changing, forever the same. She stood folding her shirt into a pouch and went toward the cliff where there were fewer rocks. Digging a hole with her hands, she buried most of what remained. The rest she gave to the sky, casting it into the wind.

Aislinn stood in the doorway watching the two old women dance, their skirts pulled back so they could see their feet.

"Right, left, right, left," Teodora commanded as they swayed on thin legs. "Strike your right heel on the floor. That's it. Now the left, then we go round the room making a big figure eight."

As they passed her, Aislinn clapped in time to their promenade. Shea whistled a tune she didn't recognize and Wil tapped a spoon on the kitchen table. The women returned to the centre of the room and Teodora began showing Augusta the next set of steps.

Aislinn joined the men at the table. "I see I'm going to have to spend Saturday nights here. You know how to party."

Shea stopped whistling. "Well, get over there, Teodora can teach you too."

"I came to ask the old women out." Aislinn turned her head. "Gran, Augusta, do you want to go to a fair?"

Still holding hands, the dancers approached the table. "What fair?" Teodora asked.

"I don't know what they call themselves, but this caravan pulled up to the store this morning to ask whether we had a field they could use."

"What kind of caravan . . . a circus?" Shea asked.

"No, nothing so good. This is a bunch of campers and converted school buses. From what the guy said, it's mostly artsy types selling crafts. There's supposed to be some music and a show for the kids."

"Sure, I'd like to see some of their handiwork," Teodora said. "How about you, Augusta?"

"I go get my sweater, you want that fancy shawl, yes?"

Teodora crossed the ends of the Mexican shawl over her chest, wrapping her waist and tying the tails at the back. Her long silver braid, still as thick as a girl's, lay against the red silk. Augusta pinned the neck of her pink cardigan together with a jade brooch that had belonged to Quan'i. She wore it on those occasions that deserved dressing up. Teodora had seen the brooch only a few times in the last forty years. And when she did, it always had the same effect on her—a picture of Francis in his army uniform filled her head. In the picture he was grinning as he pinned the brooch on Quan'i's sweater and kissed her good-bye.

Wil walked the women to the door. "Aislinn, I'm counting on you now. You keep these handsome women out of trouble."

"Trouble, yes. I seen enough trouble to last a whole long life," Augusta snorted. "I don't go looking anymore, no matter what kind it is."

Aislinn put a hand behind her back. "I've got a big stick here, to beat away the men. So don't worry."

Shea spoke from his rocker by the table. "And who is going to watch out for you, granddaughter?"

"No problem, grandad. I'm not wearing my headscarf."

Augusta pushed Aislinn out the door. "Get a move on, if we're going."

As they rounded the corner of the school, the playground wavered like a mirage, heat and dust muting the colour and noise of the caravan. The first stall they came to was a miniature log house built on the back of a three-quarter-ton truck. Arranged on the tailgate were dusty green and greyish-black packets of teas and herbs. Teodora and Augusta stopped, Aislinn continued on to the next peddler. The man sitting in the open sidedoor of the van had his hair pulled back in a ponytail and tied with a leather shoelace. This gave him a showplace for his artwork. His right ear displayed five different silver earrings, the left was pierced with brass and feather creations. He watched Aislinn approach the table of jewellery in front of him. He watched her with his eyes, the rest of his body was inert as if it scorned commerce.

The eyes looked on, the mouth moved, the arms remained folded. "You might like those leather earrings with the silver studs. The big ones near the top of the tray."

"No, I don't think so." Aislinn stroked the blue eye of a peacock feather dangling at the end of a brass wire.

The mouth moved again. "What about the silver skull and crossbones? . . . not as heavy."

Aislinn looked at the man. "Not my style."

The eyes flicked, the man smiled.

Aislinn fluttered the peacock feather back to the black plush tray.

Aislinn caught up to Teodora at a tent with the canvas sign: POTS & PETTICOATS. Among the rough earthenware jugs and bowls were cotton blouses embroidered around the neck, granny-print quilted jackets and the thinnest, finest underthings Aislinn had ever seen. She picked up a pair of panties that slid through her fingers like a handful of pastry flour. The panties fell on top of a camisole of the same mysterious fabric.

Teodora was inspecting the cotton blouses and skirts; she was always glad to see cotton in this land of wool. She held a blouse up to Aislinn. "This would fit you?" she mused.

Aislinn glanced at the blouse, her fingertips buried in the wonderful camisole. "Yes, but I don't need a blouse," she said pragmatically.

Teodora looked at the white froth in Aislinn's hand and asked, "Would you like those underthings?"

"Well, no . . .," Aislinn said in surprise. "I mean I like them, they're beautiful, too beautiful to wear."

The seamstress contemplated Aislinn's hands barely touching her best work. "They would be perfect for a trousseau."

Aislinn laughed, a gruff sound she used around loggers. It was meant for the oldfashioned word, the oldfashioned idea in the mouth of this earth mother. Perhaps it was also for the image of herself in the trappings of marriage.

Teodora asked, "How much are they?"

The seamstress turned her attention to Teodora.

Teodora took the silks from Aislinn's hands, saying, "That's okay, I'll buy them."

"No, gran. You can't spend your money. Underthings like those don't belong with blue jeans and sweat shirts."

"Put them away, like the lady said." Teodora took the money from her skirt pocket.

Augusta was making her way toward a honey seller on the far side of the semi-circle of stalls when she noticed two chalk-white faces in the crowd. She stopped to watch as these men in black pants and shirts followed a group of teenage girls. The men put their heads together, pretending to whisper and giggle. Their jaws flexed non-stop as if they had wads of pink bubblegum in their mouths. Suddenly the white faces turned to follow two young men in black T-shirts, the short sleeves rolled up to the shoulder. Their blue jeans were so tight they had to carry their cigarette packs tucked up in rolled shirt sleeves. The mimics walked with a swagger, their heads tilted back. One pretended to comb his hair, the other picked his teeth. Augusta laughed and shook her head at the clowning. Aislinn and Teodora came up behind her.

"What's so funny?" Teodora asked.

Augusta nodded toward the shifting crowd. Aislinn caught sight of the white faces as the young guys turned around to see what was attracting so much attention. The mimes shook their heads, pointing at each other. Among the watchers, Aislinn recognized the straight black hair and slight shoulders of the dart champ, his face hidden behind a camera. The mimes found another subject and Hugh moved with the crowd, rarely taking the camera from his eye. He was heading toward a display of paintings hung on the side of an old milk van. In front of the gallery a man sat playing a guitar.

Aislinn turned to the old women. "Let's go listen to that guy."

As they reached the van, a fiddler and a banjo player joined the guitarist. Aislinn saw Hugh off to one side of the performers. When the fiddler struck up "The Orange Blossom Special," an audience began to gather. Wondering why Hugh would want photos of a hippie fair, she glanced at him again. He had the camera pointed at her. She stuck her tongue out. He lowered the camera and waved. Augusta noticed the exchange and gave Teodora a nudge. Hugh came through the audience and stood quietly beside Aislinn, waiting for the song to end.

When Teodora turned her head to look at the young man, air touched her face as if a drum had been struck nearby, a blue drum. She didn't hear what he said to Aislinn, but as he walked away she could see he trailed a thin thread of light. "Aislinn," she said, "that boy, he's not from around here?"

"No, he's one of the planters Sewell brought in."

"How do you know him?"

"He's been in the store."

"Just the store?"

"Why do you ask?" Aislinn turned to Teodora.

But Teodora was looking at Augusta. "He makes me think of water," Teodora said and Augusta nodded in agreement.

Aislinn shook her head. "Him . . . water?" The musicians were playing the opening chords to a piece she didn't know and she dropped the question. Listening closely, enjoying the music, she was surprised by booing from the back of the crowd.

Someone shouted, "Why don't you stop butchering that song?" The voice was thick with liquor. "Where did you get that banjo, a cereal box?"

The audience shushed the intruder. The trio kept on playing.

"Do you fuck as bad as you play?"

"Shut up," rang loud, above the music. This new voice was also near the back of the audience.

"What did you say, asshole?"

"You heard me, just keep your mouth shut . . . asshole," came the slow, measured reply.

"You going to make me, shithead?"

"Yeah . . . behind those buses, shithead."

Aislinn recognized the heckler's voice. Her friends must have come from the pub. At the back of the crowd, where the voices originated, she could hear a new audience gathering and moving off. Hugh darted by.

"I'll be back in a minute, gran," she said and slipped behind the milk van. The only person there was a woman struggling to get a garden hose hooked up to a grounds' tap inside a box sunk in the lawn. Aislinn could hear shouting from the other side of a big yellow school bus. Beyond the bus she found a gyrating circle of onlookers. She could hear the grunts of what must be a wrestling match, not a fistfight.

In several places she tried to breach the crowd in search of Corrine. Finally, she found Earl at the inner edge. She still couldn't see; there were a couple of loggers elbow to elbow with Earl in front of her.

Aislinn jabbed Earl hard in the back. "What the hell's got into Tim?" she shouted.

Earl glanced over his shoulder at her. "Rye," he bellowed.

"Stop him, Earl, drag him out of there."

Earl didn't answer and Aislinn thought her words had been lost in the uproar.

"Earl," she prodded.

"Not yet," Earl said, "he's holding his own. He's getting what he wants."

Aislinn stood on her toes to yell in his ear, "Where's Corrine?"

"Went home. Got mad at Tim. Him and Doug were razing the bush crew in The Lighthouse."

Aislinn caught a glimpse of the men on the ground. She didn't recognize the man sitting on Tim's chest, bashing away at his face.

"Shit, Earl, can't you . . ." Her plea was cut off by a jet of water that hit the basher full in the face.

It came from the top of the yellow school bus: the big woman with the garden hose.

Tim rolled his surprised opponent off. Trying to crawl into striking distance, both men slipped on the wet grass. The piercing stream struck back and forth from face to face, accompanied by a less fine spray of words.

"Get the hell out of here, you animals. I got kids trying to sleep in this bus. You filthy pigs, I don't need them watching this kind of stupidity. They get enough of that shit on TV."

Small heads could be seen framed by a wide window. They grinned when the crowd turned toward them, then ducked their heads below the sill.

Earl used the opportunity to grab Tim and push him toward a couple of sober workmates.

Red-faced, the woman threatened the crowd with her riot hose. "The show's over."

Aislinn watched Earl deliberately walk around the school bus while the woman climbed down the attached ladder from the roof. Aislinn stopped in the shadow of the milk van, curious about his motives.

Earl approached the woman, who aimed the hose at him.

"What do you want?" Her voice was pitched low and heavy with bluff.

Earl raised his hands, palms out as if he intended to wave with both. "Hey, no problem. I just wanted to thank you for breaking that up."

Aislinn was too surprised to snicker. What was going on here? This big mama wasn't Earl's type. Was she?

The woman threw down the hose with a belly grunt and rumbled over to the tap.

Earl followed. "That's a great bus you've got there. Your man fix it up?"

The woman contemplated Earl's midriff with a sideways look from where she bent over the water box. "Why?" was all she said as she straightened up and planted her hands on her wide hips.

Earl was as smooth as the silk in the brown bag Aislinn had pressed under her arm.

"Just interested," he said. "It's no mean trick to make a family comfortable in a house that size. There must be some fancy innovations . . . some thinking gone into it." He looked the woman in the eye for a second, then turned his gaze to the bus leaking yellow light from the kids' bedroom.

The woman followed his gaze and noticed the light trapped but not disguised under thin summer blankets. "Come have a look while I settle those little beggars down." She led the way with a possessive stride.

Aislinn could see Earl poking around. She kept him in view until Teodora touched her on the shoulder from behind. Aislinn gasped . . . she had barely been breathing, waiting, holding on.

"What's going on back here?" Teodora asked.

"It's all over," Aislinn said.

- 5 -

Dust sanded the sides of the 1956 Ford half-ton rubbing at the faded R.C.M.P. logos on the rusty yellow doors. The old women in the cab bounced on the arthritic springs. Aislinn held tight to the steeringwheel to keep her head from putting one more dent in the roof. The bush on either side of the road to the lake seemed to hold its breath as they passed.

Teodora and Augusta held onto the dash. With their arms straight out, braced against the bounce of the old road and the older seat, they looked like children eager to get to a picnic. The ruts shook their words loose and they joined the rising and falling dust in the cab.

Augusta tried to talk without opening her mouth more than a crack. "Could be a bit early for them cattails, yes. Hard to tell with this hot weather." She hated eating dust.

For Teodora, the dust was a friend from another time. "We'll get reedgrass and bitter cherry anyway," she said. "We've got young, strong hands today."

Aislinn smiled at her old women, always in motion, as spendthrift with their energy as the dust devils spinning on the road behind the truck. They were going to make new mats for Augusta's house and both of them wanted new berrypicking baskets. If this fine weather held, Aislinn could see them sitting out in the yard, working their long, thin ironwood needles and mat creasers. And she was there, a girl, braiding the cattail leaves into selvage pieces to bind the edges of the mats. There was a place for her in their talk, a place for her sitting between the two of them. Unlike her parents, they wanted her to know their secrets. But she was no longer a carefree child and not the girl they had initiated into the Woman's Clan. That was part of another life, a past life. She knew there were still things they wanted to teach her, but there was no time now to go to First Woman's Island.

The dust subsided as the trees crowded in on the road, their lower branches blessing the roof of the truck. The dense growth, more green than the silver-grey they had left behind, flaunted its proximity to water. Here, in deference to waterbred fecundity, the road took a dog's-leg bend. They stopped in the crook of the dog's-leg, the marsh beside them. Outside Aislinn's window the marsh was edged with brown cattails twitching contently above the long, broad leaves the old women desired.

Dressed in castoff, cutdown work pants rolled up to the knee, Teodora and Augusta waded in, planting their bare feet firmly in the mud, to check the cattail leaves. Aislinn disturbed the pollen-dusted water standing in the ditch on the other side of the road. She tugged on a fistful of glossy, hollow reedgrass stems. They eased out of the water protesting with a sucking sound, but came up easily enough. The grass was ready to be the creamy white design on a basket. Aislinn took a green plastic garbage bag out of her pocket and shook it open, fanning the rank smell of trapped water. She would start with the reedgrass, it was a small job compared to the cattail leaves. Anyway, she enjoyed the tug of war with the reedgrass.

Teodora and Augusta had partly filled their garbage bags

when Aislinn joined them in the cattail field. "You two stay at the edge," Aislinn said. "I'll go farther in." She pushed among the sword-shaped leaves, gripping the muddy bottom with her bare toes. Her knife against a leaf was a blade on a blade, the leaves hard to the touch.

Teodora straightened to rest her back and stood watching Aislinn. "How does your new friend like working in the bush?" she asked.

"New friend?" Aislinn repeated, looking at Teodora for a clue. "Oh, you mean the shutterbug. I've hardly talked to him."

Augusta joined the conversation by raising her voice but not her head, so that her words came from behind a loosely woven green curtain. "He's your friend, yes. You don't need talk for that."

Aislinn turned to have a good look at the two conniving grey jays behind her. "Okay, you two, you can cut it out right now. There's nothing between me and that camera freak and there isn't going to be. So stop grinning like that."

"Maybe we know better," Teodora said.

"Yeah, yeah." Aislinn turned back to the cattails by loosening the grip her right toes had on a root. With the same foot, she stepped into a hole. She only just kept herself from a face-first dive by hugging the spiky green bed rising to meet her.

"See what happens when you turn your back on us. You should know better." Teodora's smile was as pointed as the leaves in her hand.

"What are you telling me?" Aislinn's voice was loud with aftershock and frustration. "Did you see something the other night?"

Augusta was standing, her hand massaging the small of her back. "The boy has blue around him, yes," she said.

"So, he has a blue aura?" Aislinn sliced through a leaf with enough forceful impatience that she severed the spine of the plant and the brown velvet tail fell into the water.

Teodora had become serious. "When he stood beside you, he turned you from red to purple."

Aislinn laughed. "Red and blue make purple. Yeah, I know, learned that in grade school."

Teodora straightened all at once as if she were threaded on a string and the end had been pulled through the top of her head. It seemed to Aislinn that she had heard rather than seen her grandmother snap into the single piece of brown agate that stood before her. She stopped laughing.

"You forget too much, granddaughter, and you remember the wrong things. You forget what surrounds you is not colour, it is your life sign, the being from within. That young man touched your life and changed it. Think of that."

"But I don't see why." Aislinn halted in confusion. "He'll leave here soon. He goes to university. He's . . ."

"Those things are just the outer appearance of life," Teodora said quietly. "They can and will be changed."

Aislinn felt the still water ripple against her bare leg. She looked down to the graceful arch of a small water snake conforming to the curve of her thigh. She wondered, had she felt its skin or just the touch of the water? "Gran, it's so easy for you to say that things change, but saying isn't any good for me. What difference does it make if Hugh turns my aura purple? He doesn't belong here and I can't leave."

Teodora bent to cut and rose again. "Your red self has shown since you were a child. It is stronger now because you've had to have courage. Your red courage comes from love, not pride. Purple shows power. It is the colour of unity."

Aislinn flexed her toes in the rich mud and watched for the bubbles released from the dark ooze to rise and break in the light. All these words, all these things she was supposed to be, when her gran forced them to the surface, disappeared as readily as those pockets of air she stirred up.

The moment was still. No breeze to fluster the mosquitoes.

The swarming noseeums formed nimbuses over Teodora and Augusta's heads. Their faces shone like chestnuts polished with sweat and light off the water. Augusta disturbed the attentive insects by shaking out a big red hanky to tie around her head.

As Augusta fastened the ends, she looked across to Aislinn. "You know when he carves, Wil's blue, yes. When he's busy making things, his life light makes more sky."

Aislinn stirred the water with her leg. "But what does it mean, really?"

"Really," Teodora said, shaking her head. "It means we should have taught you patience when you were a girl. What it means doesn't matter. It can mean anything you want. That it happened is what counts."

"We did." Augusta spoke to Teodora as if Aislinn wasn't there. Sideways talk was the way important things got said. "She got patience alright. Still here in this place, she is, yes. The problem, I say, 'cause she's been away too long from the little house on the island. She's forgotten how to see the world. She needs to find her vision again in the Clan house."

Teodora nodded. "But she would say she has no time to prepare. And she would be right, I guess. There's a lot she would have to learn again to make ready."

Aislinn went on cutting the firm cattail leaves. The pithy inner cells were slit where the knife left a line.

"Sad, so sad, yes. She is no more a friend to herself." Augusta shook her head.

Teodora stopped nodding and stood quite still, looking down into water that reflected the intense blue sky. There was a joining of water and sky, a blue balance, a blue peace. Yes, there had been union in Aislinn the other night when that boy was beside her. What she and Augusta had seen in that moment was what was missing, no, not lost, parted. The living thread that being is strung on, like a bead on a coloured neck string, was untied, the bead had slipped to the end of the thread where it dangled. What would it take to join Aislinn to herself again, so the bead balanced gracefully in the middle of the thread?

Aislinn couldn't ignore the pity in Augusta's voice. "What do you mean . . . no longer a friend? . . ."

"What she means, granddaughter," Teodora interjected, "is you've let your hurts go too deep. Now you fight yourself and there is no peace in you."

Teodora's words poked at Aislinn and warm tears spread down her cheeks, dropping into the sun stench of the pool. She wouldn't let them see her cry. She inhaled deeply and was stunned by the tepid air off the marsh. It knocked more tears out of her. It smelled so strongly of life, of uncompromising life that grew no matter. She was shrunken, as shrivelled and white as her feet, alien creatures transplanted in this green womb. Aislinn dug her toes into the rich bed, forcing them deeper. The mud was as thick as ropes of muscle between her toes. Her feet were sinking. And then, she lost her balance and fell hard, sweeping the cattails before her. They flattened under her weight, bent, then separated to let her through. Her eyes were open as she descended toward the water where she saw her face, saw that her mouth was open and she was falling into it. Under the surface, the water swirled with life, whole and living before her eyes, and she choked on it, swallowed. She breached the surface of the water, not as cleanly as a whale, but dragging up a fountain of water like the lady of the lake rising.

Teodora and Augusta looked on amazed, only to laugh when Aislinn shook herself as thoroughly as a dog in one long shiver.

Aislinn plunged past them, dragging her green garbage bag full of floating cattail leaves. Dropping the bag near the truck, she went around to the far side. Enveloped in the ripe stench of vitality and decay, she thought she was going to retch. But the water she swallowed would not resurface. It was hers.

There was a comb in the glove compartment. She sat on the tailgate of the truck to comb the tangles out of her hair. Her shorts and T-shirt mixed water with dust, turning the dents in the tailgate to miniature mud holes. Coming out with her old folks was supposed to be fun, a break from town. Instead they had stirred it all up again. There was no place for her to feel quiet. She trailed the pointed end of the comb through the mud holes on the tailgate, connecting them as if they were a child's dot drawing, except there was no picture when she was finished.

Augusta and Teodora had filled their bags and were wading out when Aislinn dumped the leaves she had gathered and spread them in the box of the truck to dry. The old women sat in the shade cast by the truck to rest and eat. Aislinn went back into the marsh to fill another bag.

The day piled up in the back of the truck, measured out in green garbage bags of reedgrass and cattail leaves. Aislinn had spent the last hour searching out a clearing that held good-sized bitter cherry trees. She sliced the smooth reddish-purple bark with her knife and peeled it off the trees in sheets. And now they all sat in the cab, smelling like garden soil and wet dogs.

Aislinn pointed at the loose skin on the old women's calves. "Your legs are as wrinkled as your faces," she laughed.

Teodora and Augusta looked at each other, looked down and laughed.

The truck sputtered to life with a jab of the key.

The backroom of the store was hot and smoky. Corrine had started back on cigarettes, giving Tracey an ally so that it was now a split democracy—two on two.

Linda got up to open the back door wider. "How was your day out with the old ladies?" she asked Aislinn.

Aislinn joined Linda near the door. "It was alright. They got their stuff and I got wet."

Aislinn and Linda stared at Tracey and Corrine with obvious disgust.

"Get off your high horse, Linda," Tracey drawled. "It wasn't so long ago you smoked."

"Yeah, and I had the good sense to quit. Look at the money I saved."

Corrine tried to head off the lecture. "How did you get wet, Aislinn?" she asked.

"I slipped in the marsh mud and went in head first."

"Ugh, into that horrible stinky water." Corrine made a face. "It's got bloodsuckers in it, hasn't it?"

"Not the marsh. The ditch on the other side of the road does, though."

"Speaking of bloodsuckers," Tracey said to Aislinn. "The ones we live with are up to something. Every night this week they've stopped for one beer after work, only one, then they beat it home for supper and disappear right after."

"Yeah." Corrine kept the conversation focused on Aislinn. "They turn up at my house. Don't come in, just whistle for Tim and they all head for the boat shed."

"The boat shed?" Aislinn asked.

"Yeah, they've just about got the burned stuff hauled away and the place cleaned down to the cement pad," Corrine said.

"And they're not talking," Linda put in, tired of being ignored. "Every time I ask Earl why they're cleaning up that mess, I get some smartass answer."

"At least you get an answer." Corrine butted her cigarette out hard. "Tim's not talking to me. Not that I'd talk to him, even if he was."

"Shit, you still mad?" Tracey asked.

"No, it's not that. Tim's punishing himself, so he's making himself miserable and me too." Corrine reached for another cigarette.

"He's punishing himself for the fight at the fair?" Tracey was incredulous.

"Hell no, for the boat. Getting his face bashed in made him feel better. And I'm still trying to get the blood out of the carpet where he passed out."

"Well, at least they're not making Mad Dog rich," Aislinn said. She opened a bag of cookies. Maybe they would eat instead of smoke.

"That would be a real bonus," Linda said, "if I didn't have the feeling we're going to pay for it. They're not staying away from the pub for nothing."

"Time will tell." Corrine had a cigarette in one hand and a cookie in the other.

Aislinn had been airing out the backroom of the store for two days but it still reeked of smoke. She figured it had got into the cardboard boxes. Every time she brought stock out of the back the smell made the trip as well. She would have to become a dictator and lay down the law. How could she sell scented feminine hygiene products when they smelled like the bottom of an ashtray?

She bent down to stock the lowest shelf of an aisle with boxes of Kotex. The rough wood floor left slivers in her jeans and aches in her knees. Straightening up, she realized that five shelves up at eye level was a shelf of mousetraps, insect repellent and light bulbs. Why was she on her knees every three weeks? Because her mother thought that female necessity should not offend the eye. The box of mousetraps and cans of insect repellent came off the shelf and joined her on the floor while she pulled out boxes of napkins.

The door opened as she stood with her arms full of Kotex for the upper shelf. It was Hugh and the bush crew. They smiled and nodded at her. The last man in had to duck coming through the door. It was Tim's basher. Hugh came and stood across from her on the other side of the bank of shelves.

"Hi." He paused, looking uncertain. "Good performance last Saturday night, eh?"

"Which one?" she asked. She didn't give him time to answer. "It looks like you got a new crewman."

Hugh turned toward the magazine rack where Aislinn was looking. "Oh, yeah, Ivan the Terrible came up last weekend. We're not getting the planting done fast enough, so the contractor got another pair of hands."

"Looks like the contractor got more than hands. Mind you, they seem to be talented hands. At least at nose-breaking." She was visually measuring the new man's shoulders, a jock, a football player, maybe.

"I take it you know the guy who was mouthing off," Hugh said. "What I meant was . . ."

"Yeah, Tim asked for it." Aislinn gave the big man one last look and turned a different gaze on Hugh. "But he's not a bad guy."

Hugh was quick to answer, "Sure, we all have our downside." He picked up a can of peaches and tossed it from hand to hand. "Anyways, were you with those older ladies at the fair the other night?"

Aislinn started. It ran through her mind that perhaps he had seen what her old women claimed to see. She examined him, wondering if he had the ability to see human light. She had seen the energy of the soul, could see it if she was meant to, so it was possible that Hugh was open to that energy as well.

She was on her guard. "Yeah, why?" she said.

"They're Indian, aren't they?"

What was he getting at? "Yeah, so?" she answered.

He quit juggling the canned fruit; his expression was serious. "It's just that their faces . . ."

Aislinn stopped throwing boxes on the shelf.

Hugh went on, "Hum, their faces have a special quality, an

inner strength . . . like my grandmother's. Anyways, I wondered if I could photograph them? Could you ask for me?"

His bloody picture-taking. "Well, it's hard to say." Aislinn paused. "You know Indians don't like having their pictures taken. They figure the camera steals their souls." She stroked pursed lips with a thumbnail.

"I thought that was just Hollywood stuff made up for cowboy movies?"

In Hugh's wide-eyed look, Aislinn could see the potential for some fun. Especially if the old folks were involved. "No harm in asking, I guess," she said. "But they speak mostly Indian, so it might be difficult for you."

"You could help, couldn't you?" His voice, instead of rising, became deep with excitement. "You speak their language?"

She could see he was getting ready to ask more questions when the door opened and they heard shouting from outside.

Aislinn's neighbour, Sam Stone, came in. "Linny," he said to her, "come have a look at this."

Coming up Centre Street was a strange parade led by Earl, all the lights on his truck flashing and a yellow warning light strobing from his roof. Behind him was a huge tow truck, the kind used for rescuing heavy machinery, lit up for the business of towing a faded orange school bus. Tim rode with the tow-truck driver and Doug followed the bus, his truck flashing yellow smiles.

Sam Stone turned to Aislinn. "What are they up to?"

"I don't know, Sam. They've been acting all mystery lately, not a word to their wives."

"What could they want with a brokendown school bus? It beats me," he said.

Aislinn had a flash of Earl inside the big woman's bus at the fair. She hadn't said anything to Linda about what she had seen that night, but she had watched for signs of discontent in her friend. She hadn't seen Earl all week, so she didn't know how he looked: guilty or innocent.

Almost to herself, she said, "Hell, I think they're going to convert it into a holiday wagon."

"Can't be." Sam's hearing was still good, it hadn't gone into retirement when his hands did. "The way things are around here, those boys can't be thinking of spending money right now."

"Doesn't seem likely, does it?" Aislinn said.

Earl stuck a bull horn out his truck window. "Hey, I got something to tell you." His amplified voice bounced around the street. "Everybody follow us down to the park."

They watched the parade grow longer as pickups and cars from around town fell in behind Doug. The kids ran for their bikes.

Aislinn went back inside the store. The bush crew was at the counter with their magazines and chocolate bars. The only one not buying was The Basher; he stood back and watched her. Hugh was the last one up with a copy of *Photo Canada*.

"So your name's Linny," Hugh said.

"No, my name's Aislinn."

"But, I heard that man say . . ."

"My dad called me Linny. Mr. Stone was my dad's best friend."

"Oh . . . well, Aislinn, you won't forget to ask your friends if I can photograph them sometime? Maybe you could let me know tomorrow. I could meet you here."

"That fast, huh. You don't waste any time, do you?"

"If that's a problem, I'll come into the store next Saturday?"

Aislinn thought she might like another look at The Basher, those shoulders, he might even be fun. "Where you guys hanging out tonight?"

"There's some kind of dance at the community hall tonight. I think we're going to check it out."

"That's a jailbait dance." Her smile was sardonic.

"A what?"

That's what she expected him to say. "The young stuff. The kids," she said with impatience.

"What can I say? I guess kids know how to dance."

"They sure do," she said. "I'll see you there at nine o'clock."

"Great," he smiled.

It was a warm smile and Aislinn remembered he was blue.

She was alone again among the mousetraps, bug dope and Kotex. Pushy little bugger, that Hugh, when he wanted something. She rubbed her palm on the corner of a shelf. Calling her Linny. The name still made her shrink inside. She still felt all her father's hurt as if it were her own. She could see herself hiding behind the kitchen door, listening in when she was supposed to be in bed. Sam was telling her grandad about the accident.

'You know, Shea, them heavy choker cables wrap around those cedar logs with the speed of a whip. Chokermen get caught all the time. And that's bad enough, except this time the log rolled and settled back. That's when Francis screamed. His arm, caught like it was between the choker cable and the log, got wrenched out of the socket, pulling him off his feet. He was dangling beside that bloody big tree by a scrap of skin and shirt. The cat operator and me were scrambling to get to him and all the time he's staring gape-eyed at the sky, his lips whispering. We got the cable cutters in there and when the cable let go, he fell like a rag doll to the ground. That's when he started cursing the clouds out of the sky. He kept trying to get up and I was telling him not to move, to lie down, so I could cut his shirt open and get a look at how bad it was. When I saw, I wrapped it real quick in the cat skinner's jacket. But I wasn't quick enough, Francis saw too. Something shifted in his eyes like a cloud passed overhead. The cursing stopped. He unwrapped the jacket. That arm was just hanging on the shoulder by a scrap of skin. Francis looked at it for the longest time, you'd think he was studying every scar, every hair. Then he got loud with cursing and his voice rose high and harsh above the treetops. He grabbed that mangled arm in his good hand and tore it away from the shoulder, flinging it toward the fallen trees.'

Aislinn had heard about the accident many times, never from her father. Everyone in Tanis Bay had their version. They said things like . . . 'he had guts,' 'he didn't want them trying to save it,' 'he knew it was useless,' or 'the air was blue and it wasn't diesel smoke neither.'

Mostly, they just shook their heads and kept shaking them until he threw his whole body off South Point onto the beach rocks below. The stories gathered again like storm clouds, rained and then dried to, 'Poor Francis, he was stumbling drunk as usual.' And all her mother could say was, 'He hardly drank more than a thimbleful, before.'

Aislinn was jarred by the sound of metal striking wood with a snap. She found herself shaking the open box of mousetraps, but instead of lining up neatly, the traps were jumping about, their wire jaws clacking. When she looked closely, she noticed many of the traps were set. How many visits had it taken the kids to set those mousetraps for buying fingers? How many dimes and quarters had been sacrificed on gumballs and licorice ropes to keep her occupied at the counter? She shook the box again. She would have to talk to Teodora and Augusta about a nice little live trap for the shutterbug. Her old folks were good at practical jokes.

Teodora and Augusta sat close to the house in the late afternoon sun, checking skeins of stinging nettle twine for untwisted strands. Aislinn sat crosslegged at their feet and they handed her loose lengths that she re-rolled between her thigh and her palm. "You know your blue boy," she said. "Well, he's taken quite a fancy to you two."

"That's no surprise," Teodora said.

Aislinn continued, "He was in the store today. He wants to take your pictures. I told him you were too shy, but he was determined I ask you."

"Two old women," Teodora said. "This boy wants pictures of two old women?"

"He should want you for a picture, yes," Augusta added.

"I told you he was weird," Aislinn teased, "even if he is blue."

They sat in silence, working and thinking.

"I told him you don't speak English," Aislinn said.

"What? What are you up to, granddaughter?" Teodora eyed Aislinn with suspicion.

"Well, he believes anything you tell him. He's seen Indians on television and in the movies. He probably thinks you're like them." Aislinn kept her eyes on the rough fibres rolling red marks on her skin. "We could show him what real Indians are like."

"And what are real Indians like, granddaughter?"

"Oh, well, kind of mysterious, you know, with all their chanting and drumming. Their strange clothes, weird food and funny ideas about medicine."

"How come we don't know any of these real Indians?" Augusta asked.

"'Cause you've never been to Hollywood," Aislinn answered.

"Where is that place?" Augusta looked unconcerned.

"So you want us to put on a show, granddaughter?"

"Something like that. Give him some real good pictures. Something he's never seen before."

"And never will again, likely." Teodora examined Aislinn closely. "After, you'll tell him it's a joke?"

"Yeah, when the time is right." Aislinn looked from Teodora to Augusta. "Will you play along?"

It was Augusta's turn to study Aislinn. "Why you want to be

mean to this boy?"

"I'm not being mean, I'm just having a little fun. He can take it. And you know you'll enjoy yourselves."

Teodora and Augusta nodded at this.

Teodora placed her completed skein in a basket. "You know, I sometimes forget every English word I ever learned."

"I'll tell him he can come next Sunday, okay?"

Aislinn got home just as Clara Stone was leaving Fern for the day. The stocky woman was squeezing through the unplanned opening in the hedge between the Cleary and Stone houses. Aislinn waited on the back stairs until a printblouse blossomed in the other yard, then called hello and got a wave.

Fern looked tired. Aislinn had noticed that her mother was getting weaker. She often asked to go to bed right after supper. When she was tired like this, the tremors were worse. The Kleenex box, which Aislinn had put new on the kitchen table that morning, sat empty. Wet tissues lay balled in Fern's lap and the wastepaper basket beside her chair was full.

Aislinn sat down at the table across from Fern. "Should we try the medicine again? I can call the doctor and check with him?"

"No, drooling's not as bad as vomiting. Give me a clean face cloth instead of these tissues."

Aislinn went to the linen closet and dug around for a fairly new, soft cloth. She placed it in Fern's hand and closed her fingers on it.

"I'll make a quick supper, so you can go to bed," Aislinn said.

"Are you going out tonight?"

"Not till later."

"Where are you going?"

"No place special."

"I hear from Clara that those friends of yours have bought

themselves a brokendown school bus." Fern stopped for breath. Her words came so slowly that it seemed to take forever to get a sentence out. "One would think they would be more careful with their money."

"Yeah, that kind of surprised me too," Aislinn said as she opened the refrigerator door. "But Earl's planned this big scavenger hunt. I heard he handed out lists at the park today. Pretty smart idea, to get folks to find the things the guys need to make the bus into a holiday wagon."

"Why would people want to do that?"

"There's a party and a prize. Whoever brings in the most items off their list gets to use the bus for their vacation."

"These men should be thinking about work, not vacations," Fern said.

"Maybe it'll keep them out of the booze and that's a saving." Aislinn took some salad greens from the crisper.

"Yes, don't we know."

"Ah, mom, don't start. Can't you remember the good times?"

"Good times," Fern repeated. "Name one." It sounded more like a plea than a demand.

"Ah, hell, how can I if you think none of it was any good?" Aislinn broke a head of lettuce apart and threw it in a colander. "What about the surprise party we had for dad? The look on his face when he came in, the house all decorated, folks packed into the kitchen and livingroom. Remember, Colin got so excited he yelled 'Merry Christmas' instead of 'Happy Birthday.' Mom, you listening to me?"

"Yes, you know, there was that time Francis went downisland and brought me back a silk dress and real silk stockings. It was a surprise, for no reason, it wasn't my birthday or Christmas. It was a beautiful dress. I didn't think he had it in him to choose such a wonderful pattern, navy blue background with small yellow dots he said looked like fat little bees to him. He probably bought it for those bees."

Fern talked on but the words came more slowly and the pauses increased until her head drooped on her chest. In sleep the tremors stopped.

Aislinn had given up her blue jeans for a cotton skirt and blouse. It would be cooler, she told herself. The community hall would be a sweathouse. While she was getting dressed, she had toyed with the idea of not wearing anything underneath. Naked in her room she had imagined the brush of her skirt when she danced, the breeze of it against skin. No elastic to bind and trap the sweat along red welts. But between her and the community hall was the street and the wind. Wouldn't that stop traffic? She was ready for it, but maybe the town wasn't. She settled for the silk dainties her gran had bought her. A dance on a hot summer night was a much better place for them than a hope chest—not that she had one.

It was still light outside when she stepped through the open door and walked down the dark passage to the hall. The music forced through the old P.A. system at top volume was bouncing off the walls in demonic distortion. She stood in the hall entrance, blinded by the splinters of light from a homemade light board.

There was more sitting than dancing. It was easier to conceal liquor bottles behind a barrier of legs underneath the tables. The bush crew had a table to themselves. Aislinn noticed that The Basher was up dancing; he was hard to miss, his fair hair was like a beacon above the heads bobbing on waves of music. He was with one of the teenie tribe who hung around the store, but there was something different about her. Aislinn looked around the room for the rest of the girl's gang; they went everywhere together. The other girls were probably sulking, jealous that their friend was dancing with an older guy. They were at a corner table and the sight of them set her back. Every one of them had cut their hair so short in front it stuck up in spikes. She hadn't heard from their mothers, so they must have done it tonight in the washroom.

Aislinn sat down beside Hugh. The fellows at the table looked more alarmed than surprised, as if they were minors in a club and she was the bouncer.

Hugh took on the duties of host. "Guys, this is Aislinn, from the store." He introduced the others by name. As she said each name in turn, they nodded and the place got comfortable again. There were cans of Coke on the table. Hugh offered her one. One of the guys offered to doctor it for her. But she wasn't ready to drink with them.

She turned to Hugh. "You can take your pictures next weekend, on Sunday . . . if you're still interested."

"Great, that's super . . . day or night? I mean what kind of light, inside, outside?"

"I don't know. They said something about having some kind of ceremony all day." Aislinn watched Hugh; he was slipping into high gear.

"You mean, I can shoot this ceremony?"

"I guess so. But you just better go easy at first. The old women are very secretive about this kind of stuff. They may not want you taking pictures of the actual ceremony. They do things like going into trances and that's pretty heavy if you're not used to it. They probably just want to show you their costumes before the ritual gets started."

Hugh was nodding his head at her, but his eyes were already checking his camera equipment, making adjustments. He didn't even blink when Ivan sat down across from him in his line of sight.

Aislinn was waiting for Hugh to introduce them. So was Ivan. When the waiting got tense, they both broke out at the same time. "Hi." "Hi." Ivan backed off and let Aislinn go first.

Then he extended a large hand with curiously fine fingers. "I'm John."

"I thought your name was Ivan, Ivan the . . ." Aislinn stopped short, brought up by his knowing smile rather than her near blundering out of his nickname.

"Ivan is Slavic for John, but you can call me whatever you like."

The smile was there again, playing games with his mouth and eyes. Playing games with her.

"I've been calling you The Basher, myself. I saw you at work last Saturday night." She couldn't be sure in the dark hall, but she thought she saw spots of red come up high on his cheeks.

He shrugged. "Some people ask for it."

"Do you always give people what they ask for?" Aislinn's smile wasn't showing.

The spots of colour on the wide cheekbones spread down over the jawline.

"It depends on how they ask," he said, bending an empty Coke can into various shapes.

"Not what they ask for?" she questioned. Aislinn had the tab top to the can Ivan was sculpting. Her fingers concentrated on bending the metal in half along a seam that wasn't there.

"Why don't you ask me to dance and find out?" He set what looked like an aluminum butterfly on the table.

Aislinn hadn't noticed until now that everyone at the table was listening to the exchange and watching them openly as if they were on stage. Beside her, Hugh appeared confused. "Do you want to dance . . ." Aislinn saw his hands go down to push back his chair. She finished the request with ". . . Basher?"

"Well, if you put it that way . . . sure." He was out of his chair.

The music was fast, the beat insistent, the singer throaty, raunchy, demanding. Through the thin soles of her sandals, Aislinn could feel the floor vibrate. She longed to take off her shoes. Music had a way of making her aware of her body, so aware that her eyelids lowered against the outside world. She sensed her partner with the surface of her body, as if his form across from her reshaped the music and sent it at her. And her body moved to catch and absorb those waves. She saw his movements, anticipated the vibrations he would send from a shoulder, a hip, and moved to meet them, but she didn't see him. Nor the look on his face. Her concentration was diffused throughout her body, transformed and delivered out from her skin. There was no focus; there was only pleasure.

She was shocked when the music slowed and he took her hand. They swayed, the music between them. He pulled her in closer, forcing the vibrating music out to surround them. The spell was broken. She was now aware of having to share the music, of having to compromise her rhythm to someone else's. Her feet could barely move. When they did, she realized he was doing the traditional waltz step and struggling to lead. She had learned that one, two, three, four box step in grade school, but there were never enough boys to go around and she was tall. She had learned to dance forward. She expected to watch and steer, not to dance backward, compliant and trusting. She was tall enough to see over his shoulder, to see their way.

They both moved forward on the one-count and Aislinn grazed her hip on his pelvis; two-count to the side brought their left hipbones together; there could be no three and four to complete the box. He took a step back to look at her. "Didn't you ever learn to follow?"

"No," she said.

"Well, let's do it the way they do." He gestured with a nod of his head to a couple wrapped together as tight as a flag around a pole that swayed in the wind.

Aislinn saw that smile again, so easy to read. It challenged her to get that close. Her hip still rang where the curve of her bone had sounded the bulge of his blue jeans. They moved together, forgetting the beat, the count, the steps. Her senses were on him, the music shut out, the rhythm overpowered by the weight of his arms around her waist, by the sharp scent of excitement that couldn't be masked by his shaving lotion. When she could no longer stand the heat and the exquisite tension between them, she pulled away and led him down the passage.

The full moon was a round window in a dark house, cool as glass. They wandered over to the swings in the community playground. Aislinn sat on a swing and started it gently in motion, skimming her feet over the trough worn in the grass below. "Are you from downisland?" she asked him as he sat on the next swing.

"Down island? Oh . . . no, I live on the mainland, the city." He wrapped his arms around the parallel lengths of chain from which the swing's seat was suspended. He joined his hands in front of him as if his arms were the parts of a vice meant to squeeze the two chains together.

"What do you do when you're in the city?" she asked. The light was grey on the band his arms formed; they seemed to be part of the chains holding him up.

"Go to school, university." He watched the grey dust puff up off the ground passing below her skirt.

"Like the others," she said. "Why didn't you come up with the rest of the bush crew?" She felt vaguely disappointed, as if somewhere in her mind she had been hoping he wasn't a student.

"I took a couple of courses in the spring semester." His tone was matter-of-fact.

"You must like it." Aislinn knew she sounded sour.

"Not enough to stay for five years. I'm trying to get my degree in four, so I can get out and work."

She watched him examine the V's of his elbows as if they were precise tools purposely designed to press down and draw in the resisting chains. What would he study? What was he working so hard to be? "What kind of job?" she asked.

"Electrical engineer," he answered, letting the tension go out of his arms so the force of the chain, stretched by his weight on the seat, sprang back against his biceps. "So, what about you? You grow up in Tanis Bay?"

"Yeah, does it show?" What was he trying to do? Make comparisons?

"Sure, the old folks in the store stay around to chat with you. Your last name's Cleary, right?"

"How did you know? I only told you my first name."

He laughed, "It's on the front of the store."

"Yeah, it's been there for a long time, too long to notice anymore."

"It must've been great growing up here. People know each other kind of like a big family of relatives, but you can go off fishing when you want to be alone. Best of both worlds."

Aislinn swung out just a little farther so she could see his face better. Was he being condescending? Making small talk because he suspected she didn't have much to tell about herself? "Most people don't feel that way about up here. The world stops long before you get to Tanis Bay. This is the boondocks."

"The world is too much with us. Now, who said that? Somebody famous. Somebody with his mind on a place like Tanis Bay."

The swings creaked, protesting against the night shift; they were day workers, she thought. The community hall door was thrown open hard, banging against the wrought-iron railing. They looked up to see Hugh and the others standing outside the door. One of them called down the yard, "Hey, Ivan, is that you? We're going over to the pub."

He turned to Aislinn. "Would you like to go for a beer?"

"No thanks. I have something I have to do." Aislinn got up from the swing and started toward the gate in the Frost fence. Her friends would be at The Lighthouse. She couldn't walk in with The Basher.

He came up beside her. "Can I see you next Saturday?" he asked.

"I'll be in the store." Aislinn knew what he meant, but she wanted to hear it.

That smiled tipped his mouth again.

"You know I mean Saturday night," he said.

Aislinn paused. To avoid his eyes without looking down, she glanced at his hair. It was curly, she didn't like curls on men, but on him it was right. It softened the angles and straight lines of his face.

"Sure." She looked over his shoulder. "Your friends are leaving, you better go. See you at the store on Saturday."

"Saturday night, then."

"Yes. Hey, what do I call you, John or Ivan?"

"Surprise me," he said.

Aislinn walked straight home, as if she had something to do there. She didn't notice the cold silence the way she normally did when she entered the house at night. Ivan's voice was in her ears, a reminder of his after-shave in her hair. She paced her bedroom; there was nothing there to divert her mind from their conversation. As she unbuttoned her blouse, she noticed in the dresser mirror how much darker her freckles appeared against the creamy camisole. She wondered how she looked to him. She hated it when her thoughts came to that question. The night's excitement dulled by every freckle, every protruding bone and bitten nail. Afraid she would see herself with his eyes, she moved away from the mirror to take off her skirt. Her eyes followed the strong upward curve of her legs from the pool of blue cotton around her feet to old lace and silk that was too light to disguise dark hair dominating white flesh.

She kicked aside the skirt and stood in front of the full-length mirror hanging on the back of the open closet door. With just the tips of her fingers, she traced a line from each lace shoulder strap down the V that directed her fingers like water down a fall to where they rested under her breasts. Although her fingers barely touched the magical material, they sensed the weight of her breasts . . . not a heaviness, a fullness. She disturbed the silk and it brushed her nipples. They hardened against the soft second skin.

She reached the lace on the panty band, her fingers moved to each hip. There was no elastic in the legs, just lace marking the opening that parted up the hip all the way to the band. She raised a leg and white silk fell away from the back of her thigh like a flag. The departing touch had been finer than the fingertips she slid along the outside of one thigh and up the curve of her hip. She was holding her breath, redirecting all her senses into her skin.

And then there was someone in the mirror. Watching her. She touched the corner of the closet door with her foot; it swung shut, harder than she had intended. She was surprised by a cry from the next room. Bile rose in her throat. She grasped a corner of the dresser to listen. But Fern was quiet now; she had succeeded, taken over the night.

- 6 -

"Look it, you asked for one, but I found two propane cylinders."
The man pressed Earl. "Do I get extra points?"

Earl was thoughtful. Finally he said, "I can't very well do
that, can I now? What if someone brought in two kitchen sinks
or two tables, we haven't got no use for two."

"But, you need . . ."

"Tell you what I'll do. If you tie with someone, I'll use the
extra cylinder as a tiebreaker."

Aislinn smiled to herself. 'Earl wisdom'—he should have
been a labour negotiator. She was inspecting the cache of
trophies from the scavenger hunt stored on a corner of Tim's
cement pad, along with tools and the stripped-down motor. The
guys were doing well so far, a pint-sized refrigerator, kitchen
cabinets painted passion pink, hell, even a small microwave
oven. Had they asked for that on one of their lists? Aislinn
noticed Corrine sitting on the back porch. "Hey," she called,
"that bus is going to be fancier than most houses in Tanis Bay."
She came up the yard. "Do you think they'll get it running?"

Corrine was gazing out across the lawn as if it were water and
she were searching for a buoy marking rocks. She roused herself.
"I don't know. Tim's pretty good with motors and Earl can give

him a hand. They've got Doug tearing out the seats on the inside."

"And the idea is for all of you to go downisland on holiday together?" Aislinn tried to imagine six adults and five children living out of a converted school bus.

"That's what they're telling us. Hard to believe, isn't it?" Corrine said. "What makes it harder to believe is they say they're going to fix that heap up on five hundred dollars. That's all they've got to spend. Have a look above the windshield." Corrine pointed to a spot just visible above the raised hood. "It's got a name already."

Aislinn had noticed earlier the black letters dribbling paint: THE SCAVENGER. "Yeah, I saw," she said. "Their little parade sure got the town stirred up."

"Don't I know it. People have been beating a path in my lawn. I finally locked the gate so they have to go around to the lane."

"It looks like you're the new attraction in town." Aislinn shifted in her chair to see who was down at the bus now.

"More like an old attraction that's making me older." Corrine lifted a chip of paint off the armrest of her chair. "Every time I put the kid down for a nap and try to get some work done, someone's at the door or Tim's in wanting rags, or beer, or food. I've given up on gardening."

Aislinn tried to sound optimistic. "Well, at least they're doing something more than drink and worry about Sewell."

"Yeah, well, I haven't stopped worrying about Sewell, especially with Tim spending money like we have some." Corrine lit up a cigarette.

"Five hundred between the three of them isn't that much." Aislinn put a thumbnail to the peeling paint on her chair.

"No, but they had to put good money out to buy that piece of junk in the first place." Corrine got up. "And Tim took it out of the savings account my parents started for the baby." She stubbed the cigarette out.

Aislinn laid her hand on Corrine's arm. "Hey, you okay?"

"I'm fed up. I'd give anything right now to take the baby and go visit my folks for awhile."

"Tell you what. I'll go down to the store and get my little yellow truck and we'll go for a drive. Get the baby dressed and I'll be back for you."

"Where are we going?" Corrine asked.

"I want to check the road into Devil's Creek. I'm going to do some fishing this weekend." Aislinn grinned. "I'm hoping to get a real big fish. The biggest."

Aislinn dreamed she lay on the deck of a boat and she slept and woke, slept and woke to test the waves that came and went, to chart the stars journeying across the night sky. The blind in her room had been up all night, the window wide open. It had been a clear night, she knew, and the dawn had been a soft invitation. As she awoke for the last time, already the day was warm and still. She could hear the mosquitoes breeding, the waterwalkers skating on the surface tension of the pool on Devil's Creek. There the trout were lazy ghosts among grey rocks and fallen trees. They were fat and choosy. She would have to take the best flies from her dad's tackle box. Maybe some salmon eggs for bottom-fishing if the trout were really finicky. They would need a lunch, lemonade and a couple of towels. She packed the knapsack and got the gear together and, click, into the truck before her mother awoke.

As Aislinn got her mother up and prepared breakfast, she reviewed her plan. Clara would be with Fern as usual and Sam would come over for supper. They could put Fern to bed. All her mother needed to know was that she wouldn't be home for supper.

Ivan and the others came into the store around noon. All of a sudden Aislinn felt shy, as if he knew she had been thinking about him, planning to get him alone.

While the others went for their purchases, Ivan came straight to the counter. He put his hands flat on the worn slab of oak and leaned on straight arms toward her. His look was expectant.

"Well," he said, "what have you decided?"

She had said "yes" last weekend. Did he think she would change her mind? "About what?" she hedged.

"What you're going to call me," he said matter-of-factly, as if no time had passed since their last conversation.

"Oh, that," she said. "I thought I'd start with Ivan and see if the rest of it's true." She tapped a few numbers into the adding machine.

"I'm not terrible at all. I'm a real pussycat. You'll see." His smile rearranged the hardline geometry of his face. "Have you got any ideas for something to do? This time we'd probably have to fight the kids for the swings."

"The kids around here are tough . . . you might lose that fight." Her smile was mocking. Then she realized he was waiting for an answer. Wonder if he hated fishing? Maybe fishing was just an example the other night? She glanced at him. "There's a special place not far from town . . . a great trout fishing hole. I thought we'd go fishing."

His face twisted—it was amazingly plastic—and lit up with pleasurable surprise.

"Great idea, what a day for it." He paused. "I'm not much of a fisherman though . . . only been out a few times."

"That's okay. Why don't you come back at two, when I close? Everything's ready to go. You might want to bring a six-pack with you."

Hugh stepped up to the counter grinning like a gargoyle, but if he had overheard their conversation, he didn't let on. "Hi, Aislinn. Are we still on tomorrow for the photographs?"

"Yup. I'll meet you here at noon and take you over to my grandmother's," she said, continuing to smile.

He smiled back in affirmation, then suddenly the pleased

look faded. "Your grandmother from Mexico? But, those old women . . ."

Aislinn noticed Hugh's struggle, but she was more aware of Ivan listening and watching. "Those old women are Indian," she said, turning her head slightly toward Ivan. "My grandmother is a Yaqui Indian from Mexico."

"There must be a story there," Ivan said.

Hugh nodded. "Yeah, I'd say all our families have stories to tell. Anyways, that's what I want my pictures to do is tell those stories so they aren't lost forever. What's even better is pictures and words, a documentary."

Aislinn looked from Ivan to Hugh, surprised at their family feeling. She sensed they understood that differences could come together, could live in families and become family history. This wasn't the reaction she expected to her declaration about her grandmother. There had been the odd kid in school who snickered when he saw Aislinn with her grandmother or Augusta. But he did it behind her back, if he knew what was good for him. The worst of it had come from her mother. Fern had never forgiven Francis for not telling her he was half Indian. Aislinn had heard this late at night from the bedroom above hers. With a name like Cleary how was Fern to know; she thought he was black Irish and that was bad enough. Her father said it had never occurred to him to give her his pedigree papers like those chappies that lined up outside her door. She had seemed happy enough with his qualifications at the time.

Aislinn shut her eyes to clear the old wrangling from her mind. She waited on the others in the store, pushing the adding machine buttons for real.

Ivan couldn't believe that a truck older than himself could run. He looked doubtful when Aislinn told him to get in. He wanted to know how far they would have to walk if the old yellow truck broke down.

Aislinn laughed at him . . . a challenge . . . he was in her territory. "Kick the front tire on your side, it's the bad one."

They drove in as far as they could on Devil's Creek road. When they got out of the truck, Aislinn gave Ivan the knapsack and one of the rods to carry. She took the other rod and the tackle box. She threaded a path through the forest and at one point turned to tell him over her shoulder that they would have a look at the slow pool and if it didn't look good, they would move downstream to a stretch of pocket water. He just nodded, his quixotic smile disarmingly silly as he tried to be as footfast as she was on the trail.

He remained smiling while she set them up on the edge of the pool. Aislinn hummed quietly to herself as she held the two sections of a rod and guided the male ferrule into the female ferrule. She tested the male end to see if it was firmly seated. She smiled at him. "A tight fit," she said. "Now, I'll show you how to mount the reel. Or do you already know how?"

He shook his head. "You seem to know what you're doing."

"I'm an expert," she said, placing his hand on the butt cap. "You insert and screw." She slid the mounting plate into place and secured the front locking mechanism.

"What other exciting things are you going to show me?" He spoke in a husky whisper. He knew enough not to frighten the fish.

"You'd be surprised," she said. "There's lots to learn. A raw beginner like you should start by stripping about eleven feet of line off the reel. It looks like you've got more than enough," she said in a throaty voice that almost broke into bubbles of laughter. But she suppressed it, fish were great voyeurs.

"How do you know?" he asked, looking at her instead of the reel.

"Oh, I'm a pretty good judge of what's coiled up in small places. Just rest your butt . . . the rod butt on the ground here."

She pointed to a flat spot. "Now double over your ample line . . . thicker is better than longer . . . and slip it through the guides."

"Girl guides?"

She ignored his query. "Pull the leader through and then we'll look at the all-important fly."

He looked down at the front of his jeans.

"I had something more colourful in mind," she said and presented him with a dry fly. "Here's one I call the Red Zinger."

"Lots of hair," he remarked.

"That's the way flies are," she said. "The thing to do is to use this brute to seduce those overfed beauties resting on their bellies down below. When you've got your line dangling in the water, you got to go slow, don't pick up the cast too soon, float along while the trout's trying to decide whether to open her mouth and accept your fly."

"How do you know the fish is a 'her'?" he asked.

"Red Zingers always appeal to lady trout." She took the rod and showed him how to cast. "Keep your wrist stiff and don't hold your rod too tight. Be gentle. Keep the back throw fairly high, don't lay back. The forward throw is fairly low, but don't get lazy and let it hang down."

"Who me? I'm tireless."

While he practised, she got her rod ready. On her second cast, a foot-long rainbow flew above the water with her hook in its mouth just as she was explaining how trout watch people. She held the rod steady and went on explaining that fish were great peeping Toms; they had to be since the surface of the water was like an opaque mirror to them. She lowered the rod to give the fish some slack so it wouldn't have a taut leader to snap in mid-air, and continued by saying that the mirror had one flaw and each fish had a window straight above it through which it directed a fisheye at the world of air. She played the fish in, a graceful, subtle dance, it leaping even as the net scooped it up.

"Great," he said, trying to keep his voice down. "That's really something. What do we do with it now?"

"Hand me that knife. You got to get the guts out right away." In one cut she opened up the underbelly to the throat. "Digestive juice in the stomach ruins the taste."

When they had a few fish to keep the beer company in the cooler, she asked if he wanted to go swimming. He looked down at the water, sceptical. She shook her head.

They walked back to the truck, unloaded the fishing gear, put the cleaned fish on ice, collected the lunch and a few cold beer. Aislinn started up the road and then off into the bush in the opposite direction to the pool they had just fished. Ivan lagged behind her on the trail. She felt the quiet which he wisely saw no need to fill. The moist green was a special caress from a cool hand. Her eyes searched out familiar plants and she wrapped her tongue around the delicious sounds of their names. When she was a kid, she'd chant them over and over again, boring the birds out of the trees with bearberry, bitter root, camas, chicken-claws, quick-grass, glasswort, soopolallie, sheep sorrel, witch-grass. They were words she made up stories around while walking trails like this with her old folks. On the way back to the truck, she would tell Ivan some of these names and show him who owned them.

At the edge of a flagstone pool in a clearing, Aislinn stretched her arms upward in a curve as if she were a slice of white moon against the primeval rainforest dark on the mountain behind her. Instead of diving into the pool, she slipped in along the line of her reflection, joining her selves. In a second, her head surfaced, looking for him. He stood sundazed at the edge of the forest. She waved him over.

He could see that the pool had been made by many different hands with gathered rock, mostly stream-rounded boulders. The stonework was rough, but moss grew along the edges, chinking the cracks. Standing above the pool he could feel the warmth of the water rising to his face. He bent down to test the temperature with his hand and she splashed him with her foot.

Taking off his shirt, he said, as if to himself, "It's a hotpool in the middle of nowhere."

He kicked off his sneakers and drew his belt through the loops of his cutoff blue jeans. She watched him as she floated just under the surface of the water. She had come prepared, a bikini under her T-shirt and shorts. He took his wallet and loose change out of his pocket, put them inside a shoe, then plunged in beside her, splashing her full in the face. Before she recovered, his hand found the top of her head and pushed her under. But she knew this game. Rather than resist his hand and force a battle, she dived away from his downward thrust. On her way, she got her fingers inside the waistband of his blue jean shorts and pulled him under. He was surprised. She was amazingly strong, strong enough to rip the riveted button out of the re-inforced waistband that held his pants together.

Underwater, he grabbed her leg as she tried to swim out of reach. She twisted onto her back to kick him with the other leg. Now he had both of them and he was pulling her in. She arched her spine and whipped her legs out of his hands.

Their heads bobbed up to the surface at the same time and they faced each other across the clear pool.

He shook the water out of his eyes and nose. "You're very strong," he said.

"So are you." She tossed the phrase back as light as a beach ball.

"How did you get so strong?"

"Beating loggers."

"I bet you have to fight the men off?" His touch was too heavy, the statement hit the water.

But she kept it from sinking. "Only if I decide to," she said.

He reached out and pulled her toward him. The water resisted. He kissed her and her strong arms curved around his waist. He reacted as if he thought she was going to pull him under again. His arms went around behind her. She could feel the muscles of his chest move against her breasts as his fingers followed the hollow of her spine down to the curve of her buttocks. She wondered if she hadn't been mistaken about him being a football jock. His fingers were deft, massaging the dimples on either side of her spine. Fine fingers with a carver's sensitive touch.

Their feet fluttered together, keeping their heads above water. She leaned back and kicked with enough force to move both of them toward shallow water. Their feet touched the spongy bottom. His fingers marched up the steps of her spine to the barrier of her swim top. He twisted the catch open and passed through to the tie behind her neck. Like a piece of sunshine on top of the water, the yellow material floated away, caught on an outgoing wave. Monkeys screeched in the tropical forest beyond the shore. Her nipples were hard points against his chest. He drew her in and the hard points flattened into round softness. She sensed that he had tightened his embrace because he expected her to push him away. Her fingers softly stroked his neck, touching his hair, soothing his head. He had come to her new, wild, from the jungle at the edge of the clearing. A young animal, his face nuzzling her throat. The hard rise in his jeans was against her stomach. The metal teeth of his zipper bit into her skin like milk-teeth. She slid a thigh between his legs and pushed her hip gently against him, her hand still playing in his hair. The other hand slipped from his waist, released the zipper, separated layers of cloth from skin and followed the ridge of his hipbone down to release his straining member. It floated in the warm sea between them, a bluntsnout creature rippling the water against her thigh.

Freed now from the shadow of the rainforest, from the pull of the earth on the soles of his feet, from the cloth binding him, he was less timid. He ran two fingers along the elastic edge of her bikini bottoms inside the upthrust thigh. His fingers stretched the elastic and the back of his hand pushed aside the fabric. She anticipated him as if they danced, guiding the water creature toward the curtain he had opened. The fingers of the hand caressing his head tightened around his soft curls, holding him from escape. She put the other hand on his shoulder and wrapped her legs around his waist. She looked at him for an instant. The first time she had really looked at his face since he kissed her. His eyelids were closed against the sun, against her chancing to see too deep. She knew his eyes were turned inward on the sensation racing his heart. Her eyes closed and she saw them together coupled under the surface, the sun striking sparks off the water around them.

Under her fingers the muscles in his shoulders seemed to expand, the skin taut. He lifted her up by the waist and pulled her into him. He planted his feet wide apart as firmly as he could on the slippery rocks. Trapped, she let go of his hair and with both hands on his shoulders, she tightened around him, moving back and forth. His fingers dug into her hips, pressing her against him so hard it took all the strength in her legs to stay in motion. She struggled to rub along him and manipulate his thrusts to meet again and again the exposed tip of swollen flesh controlling her. Moved by his own desire, his passion was the only force under the sun. But her blood raced ahead of his, the tension in her veins burning. She held onto him, a powerful wave rising to break over them. He tightened, every muscle rigid. The wave broke.

They floated together toward the edge of the pool. The water clouded as they parted. He helped her up onto the bank, then lay flat on his back against the hot stones. She lay with her head on his stomach and her feet dangling in the pool. He brought his arm up across her breasts as if to shield them from the black stare of an intruding raven.

They were quiet, shifting their attention from each others'

breathing to the birds among the trees. It was as if the birds were talking under a gigantic umbrella. The rainforest canopy echoed their calls, making them sound far away. It seemed as though the birds had purposely gone deeper into the woods. They were not voyeurs.

His forefinger drew lazy circles around one of her nipples. He was thinking how soft her skin felt. "How did you get so strong?"

She had to think about what he was saying. What strength?

He took his hand away from her breast and squeezed her bicep.

"Oh, I chop firewood."

"Is that all? You've got strong legs too. You just about crushed my ribs," he laughed.

She laughed too, slightly embarrassed. It was the same kind of feeling she had when she witnessed old Rita's idiot son playing with himself. The sensual world was so far outside the social world that viewing it with social eyes made it seem sadly absurd.

"Well," she started reluctantly, "my dad and I used to compete in loggers' sports days."

"Doing what?" He was curious.

"Sawing logs, axe throwing. I did some burling too, you know, rolling logs out in a boom on the water."

"Your dad's a logger, then?" He waited for an answer. He raised his head to look at her.

"He was a logger," she finally said. "He died when I was sixteen. We were a team, at the competitions. I was his right arm . . . literally, he lost it in a logging accident." It had been a long time since she had had to tell anyone about her dad. She had forgotton the words she used to use.

"I bet you did well too. You sure would be the prettiest contestant."

She liked him for that. Not the dubious compliment so much, but because he didn't say he was sorry.

Aislinn noticed the sun was starting to play hide-and-seek with the treetops. She pulled the knapsack over to them and got out the peanut butter sandwiches and beer.

They ate in silence, listening to sounds around them change as evening came on. The birds became quiet in voice and wing. There was a stillness that anticipated night.

Ivan fell asleep. Aislinn remained awake, her head on his stomach, rising and falling with the rhythm of his breathing. She watched the sky turn deep, electric blue, shot with light from behind. She felt released into that wide sky as if the tension of her body were concentrated in the evening star. It glowed while she rode the rising and falling skywaves free of that taut energy. And she would leave it there for the star to suck on like rock candy, while she led the man beside her across the green earth and down the yellow dust road.

Hugh was sitting on the front porch of the store when she arrived at noon. The town was still Sunday-morning quiet and his greeting seemed overloud. He was excited, she could see, and she added an excitement of her own to his. She wondered if he had talked to Ivan. She could imagine Ivan, Hugh and the others waking in the small bunkhouse, smelling of sleep and spilt beer. She wanted to ask Hugh how Ivan had slept, had he moaned or talked in his sleep? Instead, she said, "Are you ready to go?"

Hugh picked up his camera bags. "I've been here since nine," he said.

"Doing what?" she asked. It was like him to tell the truth, to give away his excitement in the guise of a straightforward answer.

"Just sitting, watching," he said. "Anyways, there's lots to see."

She looked around. "Like what?"

"Well, you've got wasps building one of those fantastic paper nests under your porch. I keep promising myself I'm going to find out how they make them. The answer probably wouldn't be nearly as interesting as how I imagine they do it."

"You know that all the wasps in the north are under contract?" she said, steering him toward the street and taking his tape recorder while he adjusted his bags.

"What?" he asked, preoccupied.

"Yeah, how do you think the big companies put out so much paper? Good quality toilet paper is hard to make. Think about it, millions of bugs digesting wood every minute of the day, no lunch breaks, no unions, it boggles the mind."

"Is that how they do it?" He seemed to be contemplating the information.

She smiled. "Would I lie to you?" As they walked toward the bay, she wondered specifically what her old women had planned for Hugh. She had asked several times during the week, but they told her not to worry, they were thinking about it.

Aislinn knocked on her grandparents' door, then opened it, not sure what she and Hugh would see. She stepped through ahead of Hugh so she could turn and see his face. The curtains were still drawn and the kitchen was grey in the light from the open door. Before she could call hello, her grandfather's rocker creaked and Shea said, "Come in, you're expected."

Aislinn approached him and signalled Hugh to join her. "Hugh, this is my grandfather."

"The women are out back," Shea said.

Augusta and Teodora sat facing each other under the tall spruce at the end of the yard. Wil softly beat a skin drum held between his knees and the women made throat music. Aislinn was surprised to see them dressed in the yellow robes of the Woman's Clan. The only time she had seen the robes was during the Clan ceremonies on First Woman's Island. And they wore their spirit masks, pushed up over their foreheads, the fringe of loon feathers almost concealed by the hoods on their robes.

Teodora spoke to Aislinn in a mix of Spanish and Yaqui words, directing her to stand between them. Hugh's camera clicked and sighed behind her. The old women stood and placed their hands on Aislinn's shoulders. They began to sing. She was alarmed. Surely they weren't going to perform the spirit dance here and in front of an outsider. She listened to the women, they were calling on the Mother, on First Woman and her children. The drum became louder and by the way they tightened their grip and swayed, she knew they were ready to begin with shuffling steps to the side. As they moved up the yard, Wil picked up the beat. The bark fringe on their robes lightly brushed her arms. Teodora dug her fingers into Aislinn's shoulders and she realized she wasn't singing. The rhythm was beating through her, echoing inside as if she were a drum on which the old women pounded. A sharp, high sound broke from her throat. It was almost a wail. Teodora and Augusta snapped their heads forward and wooden masks came down over their faces. Aislinn looked into the eyes of First Woman's spirit-helper.

The unbearable tickle in her arms spread throughout her body like fire in dry grass. She danced harder, as if she could stamp out the burning inside her. The drum was a storm in her head and she shut her eyes against the swirling sound. Blue lightning burst behind her eyelids. The wind forced hundreds of birds out of the sky, their wings beat against her as they fled the light and noise. When she looked down, she found their feathers had flayed the skin from her body. A woman wrapped her in a cape made of red and yellow feathers and her arms became wings. Joyful, she lifted them, beating hard against the air, but she could not raise herself off the ground. A necklace of black stones weighed her down and her blue feet were caught in a tangle of maidenhair ferns. Her feathers fell away, exposing a naked human being. A spirit-helper touched her in the centre of her forehead and something broke inside. It sounded like a shell cracking. The necklace of rocks slid down over her breasts and fell where she stood on black earth sprinkled with spruce needles. Teodora and Augusta stood beside her, staring at the ground as the necklace disappeared below the surface.

The drum had stopped. Aislinn looked up to see the old women pushing back their masks, revealing faces shining with sweat. For some strange reason, someone was clapping. The sound fluttered in her ears and made her left arm twitch.

Hugh came toward her. "Aislinn, tell them for me, 'that was incredible.' "

"Yes, the human spirit is incredible," Teodora said.

"But I thought . . ."

"My granddaughter is sometimes mischievous. My husband taught me good English. Will you stay for a cup of tea?"

"Well, I guess so. Sure," Hugh said. "If it's no trouble." He hurried to gather up his equipment.

"No trouble, Aislinn will make it." Teodora shook Aislinn's arm. "There's a jar of tea on the counter, a special mix of Augusta's."

Augusta looked up into Aislinn's face. "My tea be good for you, yes. I add my own dry plants to some stuff Teo got at that fair. I give it some power."

Hugh followed the women inside. "My grandmother has her own tea recipes. They've been handed down in my family. She guards them religiously. Some of them she brews up when we're sick. Anyways, she knows a lot of herb remedies. I suppose you ladies do too?"

Teodora removed her robe. "That's what happens when the wrinkles come into your face . . . beauty turns into wisdom. So grandmothers have to know a few things, otherwise who would want them?"

"Grandchildren," Hugh said, lightly touching the robe Teodora had laid carefully across a wooden chest. "What is this made of? It's very soft."

"That's Augusta's secret," Teodora said.

Augusta took Teodora's mask and her own, and placed them face down on the sofa. "No secret round here. Not for old people, anyhow. Bark of cedar tree make good clothes and blankets. Weave it with mountain goat wool, dog hair and bird feathers, yes, colour it with wolf moss. All things from the great mother."

Wil pushed Shea in his rocker up to the table. "Red and yellow cedar is used for just about anything you can think of." He turned to Hugh. "You're not planting cedar, are you?"

Shea didn't let Hugh answer. "Young man, Wil here is of the mind that we whites don't know how to leave things be. Figures our way of doing does more harm than good. What do you think?"

Hugh glanced at Aislinn pouring tea. "Well, I guess there's something to be said on both sides." He pushed his glasses up on the bridge of his nose. "I'm sure glad cameras were invented. And there are more ways now for me to get in touch with people all over the world. But I can see where we've lost some good things along the way."

Shea leaned into the table. "Aislinn says you go to university. What are you studying?"

Hugh set down his cup of tea. "Law," he said, in a quiet voice.

"So it would seem," Shea said.

"Hugh," Aislinn said, "this parting of ways is older than both of us put together and my grandad and Wil haven't settled it yet."

Hugh studied the hands of the two old men, side by side, like two kinds of fish, underwater and distorted. "Maybe there's no way to settle it," he ventured, still watching and wondering if his voice would stir the twisted fish.

The brown hand flattened on the table, fingers spread by time and a kind of surrender. "Yes, the time is passed here, for Atlakim Valley. Those scrubby spruce you're planting up there shame me, shame the valley. It can no more be called Atlakim, there is no more treasures to bring from the forest."

The pause turned to silence and Hugh felt responsible. "But the spruce will grow up in time."

"There are no blankets in them spruce," Augusta answered.

"No." Hugh looked to read the hands again.

Teodora poured hot water into the teapot. "Aislinn's friend is not concerned with blankets, Augusta."

Hugh raised his head to the brown eyes, the brown voice. Those eyes would be laughing at him, the voice said so.

"Blankets," he said, producing the querulous note of a small child.

Their laughter broke up the words forming in him and the fragments fell like crystals of salt on the open wound that was his mouth.

They laughed harder at his gaping. He pushed away from the table to rise.

Wil put his hand on Hugh's shoulder. "Old ones like us forget how it is to be young."

With the pressure on his shoulder, Hugh sat again.

"Maybe blanket not as good as camera, yes." Augusta smiled at Hugh.

Aislinn offered Hugh more tea, a curative, something for his mouth. "Now that you've captured our souls with your magic box, what are you going to do with us?"

The tea had opened his throat, he put down his cup. "Expose you." His laughter was air released from a balloon. "I'm sorry, a bad joke but sort of true. I'm making a documentary that follows a Buddhist monk from the Aleutians down the west coast to Mexico." This was Hugh's territory, he could speak with authority, reveal only what he chose.

Shea was shaking his head. "We've had all sorts here in Tanis Bay, but I don't recollect a Buddhist monk on this coast."

"No." Hugh examined the signs of Shea's age. "This monk was even before your time, Mr. Cleary." Hugh wondered at his own lack of respect, his familiarity with this ancient.

"This husband of mine is a lot older than he looks." Teodora patted Shea on the hand.

"Well, then, maybe you did know my monk. His name was Huei Shan and he was around here about fourteen hundred years ago."

"Whoa, young man, you're taking liberties with my person. If the womenfolk weren't about the place, I'd . . ."

"We know, we know, Shea, let the boy talk." Teodora kept her hand resting on his.

Augusta peered at Hugh. "How can you know this, yes. So long ago?"

"The monk went back to China and wrote down the story of his travels. His papers turned up a hundred years ago."

"They don't have no rats in China?" Wil made it sound like a serious question.

"They'd have their rats like everywhere else. Just that the Chinese take good care of those things left by their ancestors."

"So what was this guy doing over here?" Aislinn asked.

"He was a missionary."

"We've had our fill of that kind in this place," Wil said.

Augusta straightened her shoulders. "We go away, yes, take our Quan'i to Klaskish Island, away from missionary school. She dance like you saw today. She talk Kwak'wala."

"I'd like to meet her," Hugh said. "Does she live here in Tanis Bay?"

"Quan'i die." Augusta examined Aislinn's face.

Hugh looked from one to the other. "I'm sorry."

"But she still here, yes, close by."

The quiet room absorbed the sound of teacups and time, small-town Sunday silence mindful that we breathe twelve times a minute. Aislinn noticed Hugh's glance slide away to locate where he had left his equipment. "Come on, it's time I got home," she said to him. "Why don't I walk you as far as the store?"

"That's okay, I remember the way."

"Then you walk me back. I have to pick up some groceries."

Hugh slung his camera case over one shoulder and reached for his tape recorder. "I hope you'll let me come again sometime?" he said, by way of thanking the Clearys.

"We expect you'll be back," Teodora said.

As Aislinn and Hugh walked toward town, his talk kept her from searching out the itch in her brain. Distracted, she rubbed her left arm again and again.

"You know, it's strange, but I feel as if I know you better now," he said. "Your grandmother made me feel like I'd known your family all my life."

Aislinn watched Hugh out of the corner of her eye. "Yeah, the old folks went all out for you," she said.

"Do you think maybe your grandmother would tell me about Mexico?"

"Why Mexico?"

He paused, as if he didn't know where to begin. "It's this provincial competition for amateur filmmakers. Something to do with the big fair they're planning. You submit a proposal for a three-month shoot. They'll send you to six different countries to film."

"You're kidding?"

"If you're chosen, that is. But I figure I've got as good a chance as anybody. Anyway, one of the countries I proposed was Mexico."

"So that's what the province is wasting our tax money on," Aislinn said. She laughed at the indignant look on his face. "Don't take it seriously, I was only joking."

"Like you were when you told me your grandmother and Mrs. Charlie only spoke Indian," Hugh said, his voice quiet, but thin and high.

"Yeah, that was meant as a joke too," she said, embarrassed. She was surprised that the old frustrated anger had not risen in her when he spoke of the competition which could throw him into the world like a released bird.

"And I'm a joke to you? You find it hard to take me seriously, don't you?"

"I don't know what to make of you. I mean, you're so different from the people I know. You're so sure . . . so sure you can go out and do what you want. You're not trapped like everybody else."

"I got dreams, sure, but I got responsibilities too. It's a dream to do this documentary and prove myself. My parents think nobody's going to pay me good money to take pictures. They want me to be a lawyer. Chinese Canadians need Chinese-Canadian lawyers. That's their thinking. 'Take pictures later for fun,' they say. They don't take me seriously, why should you?"

"I saw how you were with my old folks today. You have a way of making people feel themselves. That's good for your pictures, it's not so good for me. . . . You know, you make me feel useless. I gave up dreaming when I was seventeen." She wondered just what dreams she had given up. She realized she had never owned any, she had always been afraid to dream.

"How could you? You got to have something to keep you going. It's this idea I have for the film that's kept me from quitting school. It's big, really special, and I knew from the start it would take more money than I could ever save working for wages and supporting myself. It's so powerful, it has to be done right. So, until the competition came along, I figured the only way to make the kind of money I needed was to get an education. I guess I'll know pretty soon whether I'm going to be a filmmaker who knows some law, or a lawyer who knows something about cameras."

"What's this big idea of yours?" Aislinn was more than curious, she was excited by the way Hugh was talking.

"Oh, no. I'm not going to give you something else to make fun of."

"Geez, don't think like that, I really want to know. I thought you said you knew me better now. Then you should know I'm serious."

Hugh hesitated and turned to look at her. "I haven't told many people about this because I got the idea in kind of a strange way. I was in the library doing homework and got bored so I picked up a magazine lying on the table and started leafing through it. There were pictures and I stopped at these to have a look. On one of the pages this name caught my eye because it was like my own, except it was spelled HUEI SHAN."

"The Chinese guy you were talking about before?"

"Yeah. Anyways, this article talked about Shan coming to North America around 499 A.D. When he got back to China, he sent five beggar priests over to what he called Wan Shan with orders to travel down the west coast to Mexico or Fusang teaching Dharma."

"And the only reason you know this is your namesake wrote it down? What if he was just making it up? Maybe he was writing the Chinese version of *Gulliver's Travels*."

"Give me a break, there's more to it than that. When you really look, there are obvious connections between ancient Asia and Mexico right down to the pre-Columbian myth of the Revered Visitor, Quetzalcoatl. He set up monasteries in what's now Mexico, where the priests were called Thamacazque or Tlama. Does that sound familiar?"

Aislinn wondered if Hugh wasn't getting on his high horse, holding up his education to her. "Hell, just get to the point, will you."

"The Tibetan word for Buddhist monk is Lama." Hugh quit talking as they reached the stairs of the store. He wasn't going to continue if she was preoccupied with getting her groceries and going home. His idea deserved a receptive audience.

Aislinn sat on the top stair of the front porch. She looked puzzled. "That doesn't prove anything, two words sounding the same."

"Right, it's coincidence. So explain how ancient Buddhist artifacts, things like coins, statues, swords, charms, ceremonial dishes"—he paused to push his glasses up on his nose—"have been found buried along this coast." Hugh stood in front of Aislinn, studying her face.

"Pirates, maybe."

He laughed. She was quick with answers, he conceded. "I like my theory better."

"Okay," she said, trying to pull together all he had given her, "but what's so strange about getting an idea from a magazine? What did you mean by that?"

"Well, that weekend I went with my sister to a used book store. While she was trying to find a textbook, I was looking over the shelves and my eye caught a bizarre title that made me curious. The book was called *Gods of the Cataclysm* and just even browsing through it there in the store it knocked me out." He looked up to see if she was listening. "In the introduction the author tells how over his own life of travelling around the world, he was storing away these images of statues and ruins, masks and weavings, all sorts of stuff from museums. And he figures that all this time his subconscious was making connections between these different artifacts from different countries, right?"

Aislinn nodded. "Yeah, so?"

Satisfied, he went on. "In my mind I see figures from pieces of pottery, breastplates, sides of altars, the walls of buildings, all coming together in the author's imagination. I see it like a strip of film with images rising to the surface. Anyways, when he was working on a book about Indians he started to wake up and began to put things together. There was this link between the New World and the Old World, you know, the Mediterranean, the Indo-Chinese coast, the Pacific and the Atlantic. He thinks that North and South America were definitely part of the Old World in prehistoric times until there was a great natural disaster." Hugh took a breath to slow himself down.

"Now, this is where the flood comes in, right? So you can throw the Bible in too." Aislinn was back to rounding off the corners of his serious side.

"Ask your grandmother about the great flood," he said, sharply. "She won't tell you the Bible story, but she'll have a story, so will Mrs. Charlie."

"Yeah, I know, I've heard them." Did he think he could tell her about her old women? Who they were, who she was? "So what's the big deal about all this stuff?"

Looking at her face, Hugh speculated on how much there was of her grandmother in the dark brown eyes. "You really want to know?"

"Yeah, I'm asking."

"The big deal is that you and I aren't that different." He ignored the derisive snort of laughter. "The stuff we read in history books is always telling us how different everyone is from everyone else. And then people take difference as a good enough reason to hate each other. I'm a chink, you're a breed. Do you hate me?"

"Keep asking questions like that and I will."

"I want to show that people are people. We're the same from country to country. And you know what? At one time we may even have talked to each other in a common language about things we all shared."

They were silent, staring at each other with the intensity of a first meeting.

Hugh looked away and continued, "It may seem funny, but I don't think it's coincidence I stumbled onto that article and then days later onto that book. You want to know something else? When I read those words, the ones about people talking the same, having the same ways and beliefs, I could see all the places in the world linked by golden chains. Like a shiny spider web on a map. I knew the words were true. And that feeling, it's been growing. Every so often something more happens that shows me I have to tell this. The competition was one of those right things. And look at Tanis Bay. I mean, it's like Huei Shan. I found the people of Wan Shan and Fusang, but I found them living together in the same house." He caught and held her gaze. "The Chinese believe in omens."

"What are you talking about?" But Aislinn knew. And what's more, she knew that there was a connection between her and Hugh. Although she denied it to her old women, she had recognized something in Hugh, a part of herself she had lost, the way you lose a childhood friend. That's what had provoked her. "You mean Augusta and my grandmother?"

"Yes," Hugh said. He was still staring at her. "You're not laughing anymore."

- 7 -

THE SKY WAS GLASSTHIN, days of rain had washed the good-weather blue out of it. The orange tarp, stretched out above the school bus, bulged with a fat puddle of water. Now that the rain had stopped, Tim shoved a broom handle into the paunch, pushing up the tarp from inside so the water spewed over the edge. He managed to shift some down the necks of people standing at the corner of the cement pad. They yelped and looked accusingly at the tarp as if it had belched wetly of its own accord. Their indignation shouted down the set of measurements Linda called from inside the bus. Aislinn, sitting on a sawhorse just below the window Linda was measuring, called back into the bus, "Gimme those last numbers again."

Linda stuck her head out the window. "Shit, I'll have to measure again, I've forgotten what they were."

While she waited, Aislinn doodled on the opposite page of the scribbler Linda had given her to calculate how much fabric they would need for curtains and cushions. She was thinking about the other night last week when they all sat out here drinking beer and watching the rain slant past the tarp. They were trying to decide what colour to paint the bus. The colour

sheet and order form lay among the empties. Tracey's Dusty
Lilac turned into Linda's Lizard Green which metamorphosed
into Corrine's Fire Engine Red to fire, to engine, to flames
coming out of the engine and licking along the fenders in Sunrise
Orange and Sunset Yellow. And Earl's sarcastic remark to Tim
that painted flames might be the only spark they got out of that
motor. Tim gave him the finger, telling him to figure out the
problem with the fucking electrical system, if he was so smart.

Linda stuck her head out the window. "Did you get that?"

"What?" Aislinn stopped doodling.

"You're about as much good as tits on a bull."

"Why don't you let me measure, then?"

"Because I'm no good at figuring and you are."

"Okay, then get off my back."

Linda muttered and pulled her head in the window.

Aislinn glanced at her doodling. It looked like something, but
what? She picked up a line with her pencil and led it away from
the scribbles as if it were a tail. A tail that curved up and rejoined
lines which appeared to be a bird's head. It seemed to have
feathers, but it also had a fanged jaw. Maybe a couple of curved
lines like a hooked beak would make it into something recognizable. The beak made a difference, so perhaps she should
spread the feathers out from the head over the long curved tail.

Linda was shouting numbers again that blended with the
hopscotch numbers the kids in one corner were reciting like a
singsong nursery rhyme. Aislinn looked at the hopscotch
squares chalked on the smoothest corner of the cement pad and
the kids forming a protective semi-circle to keep the adults from
stepping on their game. On Sundays, just about the whole town
turned up at one time or another under the orange tarp. The
Scavenger did better on Sunday than the Inter-faith Church.
Folks didn't sing and pray, but she had noticed they smiled and
laughed a lot. Even on the last two rainy Sundays, they crowded
under the tarp and the place became like a bright island rising

from the fog and mist. And when the sun shone the island turned into a carnival—people looking, talking, doing. The area around the bus was kept immaculate; townspeople brought their own brooms. Workbenches, sawhorses, stools had appeared, a set of kitchen cabinets and drawers had arrived on the back of someone's truck. These held tools and tubes, screws and bolts, wire, and words on each drawer and door to secure the order of this haven. There were always at least four male heads under the bus hood, one body per fender and two bruising their shins on the front bumper. The women, those who came early, crowded inside the bus. Aislinn stayed outside.

Linda looked out again. "That's it, Aislinn. You can start figuring."

Aislinn bit the end of her pencil, chewed up a few numbers and spit them out like lead bullets onto the page. She found the numbers less interesting than her scribbles on the opposite page. What was it? She had never been one for drawing or any of that artsy-fartsy stuff, but she liked the feel of those lines. It was like being at the pond. The pencil was a twig and putting it on the page was like gently stroking the flat water. The streaks and ripples became images. But the pond images had blended the colours of water, leaf and sky, making it easy to see clowns and unicorns, monsters and queens in that pool.

The kids in the corner were arguing over a line call. Aislinn watched the player get the benefit of the doubt only after her opponent got a piece of red chalk and thickened the disputed line. Aislinn wandered over to look at the powdery lines on the cement. The squares were drawn with several colours of chalk from a box sitting on a workbench. She collected the box of chalk and searched for a piece of concrete that was not fire-cracked or grease-stained. She cleared away some cardboard boxes of donated jetsam stacked near the back of the bus. On her knees, she ran a hand over the cement, feeling the texture and brushing away dust. It was as cool as pond water. She looked from the slab to the scribbler in her hand and back again. How should she begin? She had been absent-mindedly playing when she started the drawing, and so her fingers on a piece of red chalk could not remember what came first. She put down the red chalk, took up a yellow piece and sketched in some lines. A curved beak in profile. Too small. She erased it with the sleeve of her shirt. Began again. Too thin, it looked like a sliver of Hallowe'en moon. She rubbed a hole in the sleeve of her shirt. Why bother? This wasn't something she could do. Putting the chalk in the box, she rocked back on her heels.

The cement faced her with a spidery tattoo of cracks rubbed with yellow dust. The tattoo was a dragon with a butterfly tail. Aislinn fingered the yellow chalk again, this time laying the chalk flat on its side and pulling down. A bold, wide line appeared. It was as steady and hard as a beak. She tried another line with the side of the chalk. Yes, that was it. The jaw with its single fang went on in red under and slightly behind the beak. The head became a mass of downward-sweeping feathers chalked in crushed orange, yellow and red. Almost by accident the feathers worked themselves away from the head in a long tail of fire. When she attempted to draw quills on the feathers in white chalk the plumes fell apart. She tried to lift off the white with the corner of her cuff, but she couldn't get a good grip on the material so she ripped the cuff off the shirt sleeve. The white erased without too much damage. She sat back on her haunches to think about those feathers. They needed to be more definite, that's what the white should have done but it turned to pink and made the whole thing look like a featherduster with a yellow handle. Picking up a blue piece of chalk, she tentatively stroked in a quill line on a red feather. The line darkened to a reddish purple. The colour was as rich as grapes and she licked her lips in anticipation. With the tip of the blue chalk, she went to work on each feather. She was on her knees, backside in the air, face close enough to the feathers that her nose tickled with chalk dust.

Aislinn's humble posture had not gone unnoticed. Those individuals who had come to exercise their tongues, not their hands, had drifted over to see what she was examining so closely on the floor in front of her. It was not until the group of onlookers had swelled that Aislinn realized she had an audience. If she turned around, they would ask her what she was doing and she didn't have an answer. She tried to ignore them. A yellow eye was taking shape around a homemade purple iris when Tim tapped her on the shoulder.

He stood behind her looking down over her shoulder. "What the hell you doing?"

"Nothing. Just having some fun."

It *was* fun too, she thought. Fun and satisfying, unlike the paint-by-numbers they did as kids over every Christmas school break. That was always as tedious and boring as the weather at that time of year. No, here *she* was in control instead of the numbers and lines stamped on canvasboard by some factory machine. What happened to that piece of concrete was in her hands, her mind's eye.

Tim hunkered down beside her. "It sort of looks like a bird on fire."

"Yeah, it does, doesn't it?"

"Is that what it is?" Tim asked.

"I guess so." Aislinn examined the chalked lines through Tim's eyes and began to put the chalk back carefully into the box.

"Why are you doing this to my floor?" His eyes showed puzzled amusement.

"Well, I was fooling around . . ."

"Here, on the floor in front of everybody? That's gross." The others laughed.

"Forget it." Aislinn ripped the rest of her sacrificed shirt sleeve off and leaned forward to erase her picture.

Tim grabbed her hand. "Hey, don't do that. What were you going to say?"

Aislinn looked down at the yellow and purple eye studying her. "I was thinking about Earl's idea of painting flames on the fenders of the bus and doodling in that scribbler there and this came out. That's all."

Tim continued to grip her hand and stood up. She was forced to stand with him. They both stared at the red and yellow creature.

"It looks like I'm not the only one who can make fire," Tim said. "You know, that burning bird would look pretty good on the sides of The Scavenger." Tim turned to call over the bus's other disciples. "Hey, look at this, Aislinn drew us a mascot."

Linda stuck her head out a back window of the bus. "Aislinn did that? I don't believe it."

Earl stood with his hands on his hips. "That's The Scavenger, alright. Can you paint him on the bus, Aislinn?" Earl asked.

"Hey, hold on. I'm no artist. I was just fooling around."

"Well, you can fool around on the bus fenders." Tim raised his voice to be heard by the crowd under the tarp. "We need some autobody paint." He looked down at the bird. "Anybody got a little red, orange, yellow and purple they can lend us?" When a few hands went up, he turned to Aislinn. "Go talk to those folks, Picasso."

The cans of paint had been lined up on the workbench for days, unopened. The chalk bird on the cement floor had lifted into the wind, leaving only an impression where it had rested. The Scavenger hadn't gone far. While Aislinn sat weaving cattail mats for the bus with her back to the paint cans and the faded colour on the floor, The Scavenger perched on her shoulder pecking away at something in her brain, some clot. And when she pushed open her bedroom door at night, the bird was there, perched on the headboard of her bed, as if it had slipped into the room between the bars of striped wallpaper.

On Friday the mats were finished. And as Aislinn backed out of the bus on her hands and knees after pounding the edges of the mats flat against the floor with a rubber mallet, she turned to find Tim holding up a piece of primed scrap metal.

"Here," he said. "Try The Scavenger out on something less frightening than Doug's new paint job."

"Oh, hell," Aislinn said as she took the dull, clayred offering. "Tim, I don't . . ."

"Ah, come on, Aislinn. Don't wimp out on us. Earl's got his heart set on that bird of yours. He's even talking about us painting the whole bus like John Lennon's Rolls."

"Yeah, well, Lennon had some Gypsy mystic to do his painting, not me."

"Just give it a try," Tim said. "You might surprise yourself."

Aislinn set the scrap metal down on the cement near her faded tormentor. She found a bottle opener to pry off the paint can lids. Instead she used it to open a beer from the cooler. She noticed the bottle was almost the same colour as the primer on the metal. Useful observation, she thought. When she finished the bottle, she put it to one eye like a telescope and viewed The Scavenger's ghost on the ground in bottle brown. Following the curve of its beak through the bottom of the bottle, she felt a snap at the base of her skull as if a vertebra in her neck had popped under pressure. Another bottle cap fell into the cooler. She needed binoculars to see this bird thing, binoculars with 5% power. A bottle at each eye split The Scavenger in half. She needed another beer to deal with two of them. The third beer must have relaxed her, because she felt something click into place in her head and there was a rushing sensation as if a dam had opened. She nursed the fourth one, tucked in close to her body as she squatted, rocking back and forth on her heels, just barely touching the chalk beak. Paint was permanent, she would be trapped in the paint until the bus ran off a cliff and exploded or was crushed at the wrecker's to the size of the piece of scrap metal beside her. She stared at the scrap metal:

what was locked in under the ugly mask of primer? Suppose that metal had been part of some guy's love machine, one of those black vans with a heart-shaped window and a scene from the future painted on the side? Think about that. Making love to Ivan in a red plush van with a blacklight and a stereo. Ivan's deerskin shirt rattled with bear claws as he unwound the strip of leather from around his waist and between his legs. The blacklight made the deerskin seem as dark and rich as fur. Her hand stroked his chest for the feel of it. When her nails dug into the soft nap protecting his back, the reek of tanning smoke rose, released from the skin, deerskin, his skin sweating out smoke, sweet smoke that lifted them up and carried them to the shining grove on the side of the van where they lay under red trees.

She put the fourth bottle down carefully, a precious drinking vessel from the past. She took a piece of yellow chalk from the box because she had noticed, lying on her back looking up into those red trees, that there were no birds. A yellow canary. She would add a little yellow canary. The scrap metal chewed on the yellow chalk, hungry enough to want orange chalk, blue chalk, even some red chalk. And on its feast of chalk the canary grew fat and fanged.

Passing by close to Aislinn, Linda didn't see the fourth beer bottle and sent it spinning across the concrete pad. She looked down in surprise. "Hey, kid," Linda said. "Hey, that's not half bad. I didn't know you had it in you."

Aislinn blinked and stood up. Now there were two intruders, two Scavengers. The new one had an incredibly long, pointed beak, the fang embedded on the side near the tip. But that was wrong. She bent down and erased the fang. Linda handed Aislinn a beer.

Aislinn's head felt odd that morning, not like a regular hangover, not sluggish, just absent as if she were preoccupied with remembering a name she was positive she knew but could not bring to tongue. With the marker pen she used to price sale stock, she was adding red vines and leaves to the border of the store's accounts ledger and glancing at the door as if she suspected it of betrayal.

There were rapid footsteps on the porch, then Hugh burst through the door and almost leaped across the counter at her. She had hoped for that kind of greeting from Ivan, but he stood in the door looking as if he had walked into a room full of strangers. Hugh slapped down two envelopes on the counter in front of her.

Aislinn asked, "What is it, Hugh? You look like you died and went to heaven."

"Better than that . . . much better." His smile was humbling in its desire to share his joy.

"Well, spit it out," Aislinn said. "Come on."

"Okay, you're looking at a filmmaker. Not a law student, a filmmaker. I got it. I'm making a documentary for the Countries Coming Together competition." He waved the white, legal-sized envelope at her. He had surrendered to the magic of it.

"That's fantastic, Hugh. Really fantastic." Aislinn looked over his shoulder. "Did you hear that, Ivan?"

Ivan came up behind Hugh. "I've heard nothing else since the contractor brought the mail up yesterday." Ivan engulfed Hugh's shoulder with an arm. "Taught the kid everything he knows, I did."

Aislinn laughed at the picture the two of them made: they both seemed surprised by the world, as startled and shy as travellers in a land of flying fish.

"Well, that's it then. The three of us will have to celebrate tonight." Aislinn realized she had spoken too soon. The only place in town was the pub.

"Anyways, before we go drinking," Hugh said, "could we stop over at your grandparents' place?" Hugh patted the manilla envelope on the counter, his baby. "I've got the shots I took the other day. I'd like them to see."

Aislinn didn't hesitate. "Sure, great idea. I'll meet both of you here after supper."

Aislinn could see mischief in the eyes of her old folks when she introduced Ivan and then Hugh again. As she brought extra chairs to the table, she kept talking, tossing words into a space the old ones were ready to fill with teasing.

Teodora spoke as she opened the oven door. "Aislinn, help me get these buns served up."

Aislinn came to her grandmother reluctantly, turning to see how innocent the old folks looked, how fragile beside Ivan's shoulders and Hugh's eyes. But she knew the picture was an illusion, the young ones had no chance against the humour that lay just beneath the wrinkled voices. These old ones wore time like a disguise. The years made them look tame, hiding their power to see people for what they were. She noticed that Ivan was holding back a bit, shy perhaps, or maybe he sensed the danger. Not Hugh, he was preoccupied with getting the string on the manilla envelope unwound so he could show how he had recreated them. With her eyes she helped him unloop the figure eight from the tabs and spread the photos out on the table. Now that Ivan was safe for the moment, she could look away to find a tea towel and save her fingers from the hot buns she was taking out of the pan.

Still, she watched him. Ivan was looking around the room and she looked too, seeing what she had stopped noticing: the Indian blanket hung over the loft railing, the old rifles and the duck decoys her dad had carved, the ink line drawings of Trinity College, Dublin and a County Limerick village, the Salish loom, her grandad's violin. What did Ivan see: a whiteman gone Indian, bushed, living behind the times? She banged the plate of buns down in front of him. He smiled up at her.

Her grandfather called, "Aislinn, come tell me how beautiful you look to this young man's camera."

She came around behind Shea's chair and leaned over his shoulders, crossing her arms over his chest, feeling the beat of his heart against her wrist. As she stared at the photos spread out on the table, the slight echo of his heart was replaced by the pounding of her own. Her arms began to tingle and the sensation spread over her body so rapidly, so intensely, that she felt numb. The new skin on the scar in the middle of her forehead throbbed. In a flash she saw what had been hidden from her for days, hidden behind the closed eyes in the photos. Then, Hugh was speaking to her, his hand mixing the pictures, sorting the images. She made an effort to listen and the ringing in her ears stopped.

"Something happened to the film," he said. "I don't know when or how, but look at this. Aislinn, your face is almost lost in a blue haze, there's a kind of smudge on the photo. And these others, I can't understand where these streaks came from." He pointed to the background behind Teodora and Augusta in a couple of photographs. "At first I was disappointed. But the streaks look like feathers and with the strange light the shots are eerie. They're more powerful this way."

Ivan was holding a picture, examining it closely. "What do you call the dance you're doing?"

Meeting Aislinn's eyes, Teodora answered quickly, "It's a dance honouring our ancestor, First Woman."

Aislinn looked from Teodora to Augusta and saw the round eyes and whispering lips of their spirit-helper masks. The wooden eyes were fixed on her left arm where it crossed over her right.

Hugh stared thoughtfully at the photographs scattered across the table. "That was an incredible performance. I can't get over it. Every time I listen to the tape I made, I get shivers up my spine. You'll have to teach me how to chant down in my throat like that." Hugh turned to Ivan. "Mr. Charlie plays a mean drum."

Aislinn glanced at Ivan. He had no idea. His eyes had been closed when they made love. He hadn't seen her. Just like he couldn't really see her in Hugh's pictures. Neither of these men could know what she was. She said to him, "This is what we upislanders do for fun on Sunday afternoons."

"I thought you went fishing," he said, putting on his public smile.

"No, we only go when we're sure there's at least one big fish to catch," she said, taking up the teasing, reeling him in easy. But part of her wanted to be alone to sort her own images.

Wil gathered up the photos so Augusta could set the teapot on the table. "You a fisherman?" he asked Ivan.

"Not to speak of. Aislinn was giving me some lessons the other day."

Shea laughed. "That still works with the girls, does it? It wasn't fishing with us, it was nature study. The girls in my neighbourhood were keen on butterfly collecting and bird watching."

"What makes you so sure the girls were after butterflies, grandad? You men always think you're putting one over on women," Aislinn said.

Augusta slopped tea into Wil's mug. "That's for sure," she said. "But Wil here, he so easy to fool, yes, four little girls just about kill him."

"What are you saying?" Despite the question, there was a touch of pride in Wil's voice.

"You know I'm talking about a greedy young fellow who bit off more than he could chew up, yes, and I have to save him from choking."

"Nobody wants to hear this . . ."

"There were four of us girls, lived in different villages, so Wil figures we never find out about each other. He didn't count on us all working together at a potlatch. And when you're busy all the time making food, you talk and if you're young girls, you talk about boyfriends, yes. Aislinn knows." Augusta's eyes rested on Hugh and Ivan.

"Boyfriends," Wil chuckled, "you girls didn't have any. That's why I feel sorry for all of you, back then."

"Big talk, that's it. We girls pick up on Wil's game pretty fast and decide to have a little fun of our own. He didn't know we were working together when we all make dates with him for after the potlatch when everybody gone home again. We make sure, yes, there only a day between the four meetings. We know Wil have to do some quick travelling to get around to all the villages, so we agree when he come to each girl, we don't give him a minute's rest. We have him going for long walks picking berries, or visiting friends late into the night. Or a girl would have him canoe her out to one of the little islands to gather cedar bark. We keep Wil spinning for over a month, yes, so he lose weight and grew pouches under his eyes. He too tired even for kissing. He finally ask me to marry him. I know it's to get some rest."

Wil appealed to the others at the table. "Can you believe that? She twists the world into her own fancy knot. Sure, after a time I was just a skin bag full of bones 'cause those four girls were so hungry after me. But I wore them out first. They were so tired from chasing me, those girls, each and every one, asked me to marry her so she could settle down. They couldn't keep up their work at home and court me at the same time. Their mothers were all the time giving them hell for being slow or falling asleep at their chores. Augusta, she was the most worn out, so I finally took pity on her and said okay I would marry her. And look what I get for doing a good deed."

Teodora gave Augusta the freshly filled teapot and sat down beside Ivan. "Don't listen to those old crows cawing like shiny young birds," she said to Ivan and Hugh. "I know your mothers brought you up better than that."

Hugh seemed preoccupied with the photos as he lined the edges up, preparing to slide them into the envelope. "My grandmother has been trying to teach my sister what she calls 'The Quiet Way.' From her chair in the garden, it's my grandmother who runs our family, although I've never heard her utter an opinion. Anyways, my sister's too busy rebelling to catch on, but while my grandmother's clucking disapproval, I've noticed she's smiling at her cat."

Shea knew Teodora was across the table from him so he raised his head as if to look at her. "Yes," he said, "they always get their own way in the end, women do."

Teodora knew the banter but she sensed a seriousness in the young men that she wanted to prod. "If that was true, no mother would have to fear for her son. Women don't make soldiers. But women don't have their way in this world."

Shea held up his hands. "Wait a minute here," he said. "I've seen mothers send their sons to fight with pride. And you know full well that women fought in Pancho Villa's army."

Long ago Teodora recognized the fight in Shea, the desire to see justice done. But what he had never understood was that his justice was too costly. "I don't know how it is for every woman, but a mother cannot hold her baby and hope he is a soldier. And the soldier women in Villa's army carried guns because those with guns got fed."

"I wonder," Hugh said. "I wonder if the world would be very different today if the ancient female societies had continued to run things."

Augusta's eyes narrowed. "What's this you say?" she asked Hugh.

"There was a time when women were the leaders in most of the communities in what they call 'the cradle of civilization.' Anyways, from what they've been able to dig up, tablets . . .

inscriptions, these communities lived well and didn't war on their neighbours."

Augusta questioned Hugh closely as if she suspected him of eavesdropping on things she thought were secret. "How long ago, yes, and in what place were these ancients?"

Hugh squinted behind his glasses. "Back in the Stone Age, thousands of years ago in the Near and Middle East." He nodded at Augusta. "You know, the places we call Turkey, Arabia, Libya . . . on the other side of the world from here."

Augusta appeared thoughtful. "And stories were handed down from mother to daughter, yes. Is this how you know?"

"I don't know about that, but eventually some of the laws and history of these societies got written down and have been dug up by archaeologists." Hugh looked at Augusta as if he expected something more from her questions.

Shea filled the pause. "I thought you were studying law at university?" he asked.

"Yeah, I am. But I'm into other things too."

Aislinn abruptly stopped pouring tea into Ivan's half-filled cup. "I almost forgot with all this talk," Aislinn said, "we should congratulate Hugh. He's been chosen to make a movie about other countries."

"A celebration," Shea said. "Well, we should have more than tea. Teodora, can you find that dusty bottle of Irish whiskey you put away?"

Teodora went to an old wood and leather trunk placed against a wall. She opened the lid which groaned like a boat on rough water.

Wil was looking Hugh over. "Moviemaking must cost big money?"

"Some, but not much, really." Hugh glanced back at the trunk as Teodora lowered the lid. "I'm making a documentary film. It's not like a movie you see at the theatre. I do all the filming and sound myself and none of it's set up. I just go where the people are and let it happen. Anyways, what costs the most is getting around."

Aislinn refilled the teapot with hot water. "Hugh's going to six different countries." She noted a breathless quality to her voice. She looked up to see if anyone else had noticed. Hugh's eyes were on her.

Aislinn picked up the teapot and poured tea all around. Teodora added whiskey to Shea's tea and passed the bottle to Augusta.

Shea could smell the double hot aroma of tea and whiskey: the smell of the monsoon in northern India. They worked through the wet season living on tea and Irish. "You want to stay out of India during their summer monsoon. You might as well be a fish."

Hugh's head snapped up so fast his glasses bounced on his nose. "Fish people," he said from somewhere out of his musing.

"Yes, yes, extremely wet." Shea nodded.

"No," Hugh said, "what I meant was in prehistoric India there was a tribe called the 'Minas,' the Fish People. There's a theory that they left India and eventually settled areas around the world."

Wil was grinning into his teacup. "Must've been damn good swimmers, those Fish People."

The laughter at the table coasted on the liquor fumes.

Hugh smiled, but his head was tucked into his neck turtle-style. "You know, contrary to popular belief around here, boats weren't invented on this coast."

Aislinn patted Hugh's back as if to pop his head out from between his shoulders. "You can't tell Wil that," she said. "He figures Indians invented everything that's good."

Shea was remembering the small, dark labourers with their quick eyes in delicate faces, working in the pitiless monsoon. "They got that dam in like nobody's business. Hard workers, those Indians, specially considering their size. I was a Gulliver among them."

Hugh pushed his glasses up on the bridge of his nose. "I should fit right in then."

Aislinn lifted her teacup. "Congratulations, Hugh."

All the cups met in the middle of the table, splashing some of the brew onto the envelope with the photos. Hugh searched for a Kleenex in his pockets to wipe it off.

Ivan had been watching Shea, seemed to be waiting for more from the old man's past. "What kind of work did you do in India, Mr. Cleary?"

"I went out to India to work in the field office on a dam site. My father thought it would discourage my interest in engineering. He wanted me to be a medical man like himself."

"And did it?" Ivan asked.

"Not on your life. I've worked as a civil engineer all over the world."

"The changes you must've seen over the years," Ivan said.

Aislinn felt excluded by Ivan's intense interest in her grandfather. She noticed how his fingers restlessly turned the teacup as he listened to Shea.

"Changes, mostly on this coast. Came north after the Panama Canal work was done in '14. Would have gone back down in '15 when a landslide in the Gaillard Cut closed the canal, but a friend of Teodora's needed some help in Mexico with a revolution he had got himself into."

Teodora studied Shea for a moment. After all these years he was still trying to convince her that she judged Villa too harshly. "Pancho Villa was your friend," she said. Her voice hit "your" as if she were keying a piano up to concert pitch.

"He was a friend of the people. He fought to get them land of their own." Shea folded his arms over his chest.

"Maybe, and maybe he fought because he wanted the land-owners' wealth and power for himself." Teodora noted the holes in Shea's old sweater for the hundredth time. "Only a small drop of Indian blood ran in Villa's veins. The land meant money to him. Emiliano Zapata fought for the land of his people. He couldn't do anything else, his soul was made of pomegranate flowers that need Yucatan soil to open."

"I know what you are saying about Zapata, but you don't need to be Indian to want what's right." Shea's fingers, knitting-needle thin, pulled at the loose yarn at his elbows.

"No, but if Zapata had not been murdered, if an Indian had become president instead of that corn seller Obregon, my people would have their land and my relatives would not be scattered to the four winds like husks." Teodora got up from the table to put the kettle on the stove. She took down the tea canister and reached for a Royal Family cookie tin that held tag ends of yarn.

Teodora's last words seemed to settle in Ivan. He stopped looking embarrassed by his hosts' argument and took advantage of the silence. Turning to Teodora, he said, "Were you deported from your home?"

"No, I was hunted out of it." Teodora slipped a tangle of yarn into her skirt pocket.

Shea's fingers ceased exploring the holes and his hands cradled his elbows. "We were with Villa's army when he crossed the Sierra Madre from Chihuahua to Sonora. It was a desperate journey." Shea sat quite still, his head bent as if he were listening to some voice. "There were the mountains, sure, but Villa was going to fight men who had been his allies. The wind had changed and he had spit on his finger too late. You see, there had been a split in the Revolutionary Army with Carranza making himself president of Mexico and Obregon scheming to take it away from him. Villa got caught in the middle."

Teodora sat at the table with her hands in her lap, untangling the wool from her pocket. "Yes, and you were with the army. I was trying to get home to the village in the Bacatete mountains where my people were hiding."

Shea clutched his arms closer to his body. "That march was the beginning of the end for Villa's army. We crossed those mountains in October, trying to beat the snow into the high country. Villa started out with 6,500 men, mule teams and heavy artillery. We were battered by blizzards and the steep trails were no place for big guns. Eventually, most of the artillery was abandoned, the mule teams eaten, but Villa still lost two-thirds of the men before the army descended into the Sonoran Desert. Two-thirds . . ." He shook his head.

Teodora concentrated on the snarled strands in her lap. "Sierra Madre, mother mountain, land of souls. You know, Mexico celebrates the Day of the Dead, but one day is not enough."

Shea unfolded his arms and laid his hands palm-flat on the table. The others waited. Only Ivan stirred. "Teodora was injured in a fall from a horse and I nearly froze to death in those mountains. Some Tarahumara Indians took us in. When we were well, we travelled on together. By this time Villa's army was on the run in Sonora. He had to fight guerrilla-style from the mountains. No trains, no artillery, and no need for me."

A line of black yarn ran through Teodora's hand as she twisted it into a tight ball. "My village had been raided by federal soldiers. Only ghosts lived in it. The Yaqui band that had joined Villa found us there and helped us get across the border into Arizona." Teodora turned to Ivan, the ball of yarn like a shiny, dark nut in her hand. "Young man, you asked about deportation. All the time I was hiding in that boxcar going north, I was thinking about my aunts, uncles, cousins, and their babies locked in cattle cars. You know, the sand beside the train tracks from San Blas to Mexico City was blistered with small graves. They were shipped south . . . slaves for the henequen plantations. Few Yaquis returned from Quintana Roo."

"Boxcar, Teo?" Shea broke in. "It was a stinking cattle car with a roof. Filthy straw on the floor and dried cow shit on the walls.

Watching for the station signs, we had our noses right up against those encrusted boards. With every track crossing, the jolt sent shit dust up into our faces. And then the border crossing at Nogales, we had to hide under straw soaked in piss while trainmen stuck blades into it. We could hardly breathe, it stunk so badly it burned. Luckily the stench was enough to keep them from poking into the corners. For the rest of the trip, we watched for a small Yaqui settlement outside Tucson. We didn't know what we were looking for. Didn't expect there would be a sign. But if we didn't jump from the train at Barrio Libre, we would find ourselves in the Tucson railyard, where the American railroad police were."

Sitting beside Ivan, Teodora could sense his agitation. His breathing was shallow, coming in short jags, and when Shea said 'jump from the train,' Ivan held his breath. She could smell fear on people the way animals do. She poured whiskey into his teacup. "All the time," she said, "we're peering through the boards looking for the barrio, Shea's telling me what to do, how to jump, how to land so I don't get hurt. Telling me over and over until I know he's scared to death. We both see the place at the same time and slide the door open. The wind grabbing at us smells black with coal smoke. Shea's counting and it sounds like praying to me. So I think of the rural police who hunted us in the mountains and I think of these other police in Tucson and I'm so afraid I jump. I don't hear anything except the wind. But I can smell creosote bushes and it smells like home. Then, I hear this wailing not far off."

Shea slapped the table with a flat hand, just missing his teacup. He startled them all, bringing their attention back to the kitchen. "Let's get a few things straight here, old woman. I wasn't praying and I wasn't wailing. I may have groaned a bit when I hit that rock."

Teodora reached over and patted his hand. "He broke his leg. When I stand up all I can see is miles of fields spreading out on both sides of the track. We have to find some place to hide before the next train comes along. The corn's not waist-high yet, but I help Shea into the field and he lies down between the rows."

Shea snatched back his hand, placing it over his heart, the fingers spread in mock self-righteous indignation. "To make a long story short . . ."

Teodora smiled at Shea's genius for angelic poses. The devil himself would be halted by that nimbus of white hair and the bonewhite hand. "To make a long story short, I doctored him the best I could, then started out for Barrio Libre to get help."

Hugh had both elbows on the table, leaning into the story. "But were you safe?" he asked.

"Safe?" Shea questioned the word. "Safe from Mexican soldiers, yes, but not from the Americans. Some Mexicans had crossed the border and raided Columbus, New Mexico. Civilians were killed. The Americans swore it was Pancho Villa. There was bad blood between the white towns and the barrios."

"My people at Barrio Libre," Teodora said, "fixed it so we could stay at a Papago village in the desert while Shea's leg mended."

Shea drummed his long, white fingers on the table. "Those were dog days . . . hot, endless. Too much space and light so you felt small. The air, heavy with heat, seemed to wrap you up . . . a small worm in a cotton bandage."

Teodora's gaze was fixed on Shea's fingers. "In the desert you learn to run fast. A lizard on hot sand. Here, the forest swallows you. You're a mouse down the throat of a green snake."

Ivan was looking past Shea to the window and the early darkness brought on by the tall trees. Aislinn had not seen him so absorbed in thought. "My mother," he spoke, his eyes still examining the night, "will walk in the forest but not in the fields of my sister's hop farm. When we go up the coast to hike in the mountains, my mother spends most of her time pointing out places a person could hide. When she looks into the dark hollows between the roots of those giant cedar, she says it's a warm darkness and it makes her skin remember the air trapped under a woollen blanket in winter." Without lowering his eyes from the window, Ivan raised his cup to his lips. "She jumped from a moving train into a frozen stubble field so she wouldn't be caught carrying underground documents. She was an officer in the Polish Home Army during the Nazi occupation." He brought his gaze back to the group and he seemed to falter.

His confusion, as if he had returned from another land, frightened Aislinn. Ivan was solid and there had to be Ivans. She couldn't believe there might be black wings flapping somewhere inside him.

Teodora recognized the mother's fear in the son. "Were you born in Poland?" she prompted.

Ivan blinked. "No, my mother calls me the child of a new land. I was born the year they left Poland. 'The gift,' she says, 'of a long absence.' She had been in prison for eight years."

"So they caught her," Aislinn asked, "when she jumped?"

"No, she got away . . . her and my sister, she was just a baby. She had taken my sister so she would look less suspicious to the Germans."

Hugh's eyes widened behind the perpetual surprise of his lenses. "She jumped with a baby in her arms?"

"The word came down the train that they were searching everyone. She says they both should have died when she jumped out into the sky with no wax and feather wings, just a man's oversized overcoat flapping out behind. Instead she sprained her ankle. They spent the night in an open field, the only trees on the horizon." Ivan hit a pocket of silence, tripped for a second on it. "My sister's hands were frostbitten even though she was tucked inside the overcoat. They were smuggled back to Warsaw under a pile of straw in a peasant's cart." His face flushed as the hot tongue of tea and whiskey flicked along his veins.

Aislinn watched Ivan's eyes slowly close on his last words as if he must stop for a moment and embrace his mother with straw in her hair. He had been matter-of-fact in his telling, a family story repeated many times. He seemed pleasantly surprised to have such a mother, to find her in his story.

Teodora poured tea for Ivan but left the liquor bottle in the middle of the table. "Your mother was in jail a long time?" she said.

Ivan studied his cup. "The Soviets aren't in a hurry once they put you away. After all, they have to make the facts fit their story."

"Who?" Aislinn asked.

"Hitler's Germans never got her, it was the Russians . . . 'a political game,' she says. An attempt by the Soviets to discredit the Home Army because it had not been a Communist movement. They accused Home Army people of fighting the anti-fascist movement and somehow this helped the German Reich. So, just like that, my mother became a Nazi-Fascist criminal. Her reward for feeding and hiding resistance fighters and Jews. She was arrested in 1949 by the Security Service. They tried her secretly in 1951 and sentenced her to ten years."

Aislinn rubbed a corner of the table. "What did your dad do?"

"My dad and grandmother went from agency to agency talking to anyone they could, putting in applications for a review of my mother's case. Nothing worked. They moved my mother to the prison at Fordon a long way from Warsaw."

Wil nodded at Augusta. "That's the way we went with the Indian Agency, trying to get some answers about our oldest boy's death."

Ivan nodded too and wondered at the kinds of dying. "My

father got real down and spent weeks staring at a crucifix on the bedroom wall of their apartment. My grandmother looked after him and my sister and visited my mother by train. My sister tells how when they had finished a visit, mother kissed her and pressed a cross into her hand. It was made from bone and it was wrapped in a scrap of paper. The message on the paper was for grandmother to try and find the children of a woman who was in jail with mother. The woman's husband had been shot. My father found the children."

Shea was rocking and listening, his hand caressing the curved arm of his son's handiwork. "Aislinn's father saw action in Italy. He didn't talk about it much. It would have been bloody awful for civilians. Your mother must be a courageous woman, young man."

"It must have been hard for your mother," Aislinn said, looking across at Teodora, "when she left everything she knew and came to a new place. That takes real courage."

"Why do you say so, granddaughter?" Teodora asked.

Aislinn could not immediately put words to the panic she felt when she tried to imagine herself alone in a country she didn't know. The feeling was exaggerated by the attraction she had for the unfamiliar, the unexplored. She probably yearned to be somewhere else more than any of the others at the table, yet she feared it too.

"Well?" Teodora nudged her.

"It must be horrible not to be understood when you speak and not to understand others. Like being a baby."

Shea inched his hand along the edge of the table until it found Aislinn's elbow planted among the crumbs. "People get along. We're all pretty much the same when it comes right down to it. Others know what you want."

Aislinn would not be reassured by his hand next to her arm. "But what if you're robbed? You don't even know how to call for help."

Shea brought his hands together and rocked back as if to hide his smile in the shadows behind the table. "A scream is a scream."

Teodora shook her head slowly, her jaw tight and angular. "Listen to your inner voice, it knows."

Ivan tipped back his chair so he could reach behind Teodora and clap Hugh on the shoulder. "How will you get along, Hugh, when you stroll down some foreign street and start aiming that camera of yours at everybody? Think those foreigners will understand you're filming them to save the world?"

Hugh pushed his glasses up on the bridge of his nose. "There will be places I have to get permission from the local authorities, but as a rule I ask before I shoot."

Aislinn found her old frustration rising on Hugh's certainty. "In what language . . . pig Latin?"

"Your folks are right," Hugh said. "People know when you don't mean them any harm. Anyways, I'll get along."

"So will I." Aislinn rose and brushed her lips across Shea's cheek. "I've got to get home. I'll walk with you two in case you meet some Indians. I speak their language."

"Not good as you should, daughter." Augusta looked up as Aislinn touched Teodora's shoulder on her way to the door. "We talk about that, yes." Augusta folded her hands into a determined ball.

Aislinn saw Augusta's hands pulling her from the ocean, sprinkling her wet hair with the breast feathers of a loon, patting her on the back . . . to congratulate, to knock the water from her lungs. In the last few years she had become soft standing behind a counter; she wouldn't have the strength to do that swim again. "I may have forgotten how to be a fish, Augusta, but I've not forgotten the old songs."

They stepped out into a freshwater mist descending in torn streamers from the mountains.

"Guess it's too late for a beer?" Ivan asked.

"I can't," Aislinn said, thinking of her mother. She'd been away from the house a lot lately, since Ivan. This thought made her realize that her mom had hardly complained, seemed almost glad to be left alone.

"Past your bedtime," Ivan joked.

She saw something flick across his eyes. A kind of possessiveness drawing her into some hidden place. A mouse down the gullet of a snake.

"You know," Hugh said, "next week we're finished up here."

Aislinn looked at Ivan. "No, I didn't know." So he was getting ready to walk out of her life. That was a laugh, he hadn't really walked in. He was passing through. What did she expect?

Hugh continued absently, "Anyways, we leave next Monday."

Aislinn hesitated. "My mother's alone."

They walked on, silent. Aislinn stopped when they reached Centre Street. "Goodbye." She turned away before the word was out, seeing only the ground in front of her.

Hugh was startled out of thought. Ivan opened his mouth to speak, but Aislinn's back appeared to stop him. Her dark sweater seemed to pull the night in around her.

As she walked away, Hugh said to Ivan, "The way she spoke, you'd think she was going home to a small child. You know, she's never mentioned her mother. I hadn't thought about who she lives with. To me she belongs in the log house with the old people. They seem to flesh her out, give her another dimension. I guess, because they know her." Hugh took his glasses off to clean the lenses on his shirt. "There's secrets among those women. Did you notice all that unspoken stuff? It's the same back home."

Ivan remained quiet for a moment. "The old women watch . . . like they know what you're thinking."

"I haven't been able to get that dance they did out of my mind, you know. Those women together, it's almost as if something happens, as if they're breathing different air under the surface where they are. That's what makes us uneasy when women get together. Sounds crazy but it's a kind of tension that makes me think of a thread that's vibrating. I mean, it's right there in those shots I took."

In the mist they could barely see Aislinn now. She had shrunk in on herself again, her shoulders hunched against the cool night wind off the bay.

- 8 -

Lightning scratched across the sky above the trees. Thunder flattened the air. Aislinn stood watching the flashy inscriptions through the window above the kitchen sink. Behind her, she could hear Fern fidgeting in her chair.

A magazine slid off Fern's lap, slapping the linoleum. "I wish that bloody storm would let up. You shouldn't stand in front of that window. Glass attracts lightning."

"No, it doesn't," Aislinn said, still facing the window. She almost wished her mother was right. She could imagine herself climbing onto the window sill, her face against the glass and her feet in the kitchen sink full of water. The sky was worth tempting.

"It does. I've heard of many people who have been struck through windows. I don't know why anyone would want to watch a lightning storm."

Aislinn was straining to hear her mother's words. She turned to look at Fern. "You're whispering again. I can't hear you half the time these days."

"I'm not whispering. I am speaking the same way I always do."

Aislinn came over to the table. "Do you want to listen to the news?" She switched on the radio beside Fern. Violin music filled the heavy storm air. "Oh, shit, that dumb program "Twilight Serenade" isn't over yet."

"Why must you swear?"

Aislinn barely heard the words; she saw them on her mother's lips. Her mother had never scolded quietly. She tried to remember, did the Parkinson's do more than slow speech? Aislinn turned the radio down. "Mom, have you noticed a difference when you speak?"

"What difference? What do you mean?" Fern rubbed the nicotine stains on the fingers of her right hand. It annoyed her that the yellow-brown patches persisted even now when she no longer had the pleasure of the vice.

Standing there, looking down on the shrunken body, the too-big head, Aislinn could feel her hand itch and the boil or whatever it was on her left arm throbbed. "Mom, how do you feel?" They hadn't talked about what they would do if she got worse. Secretly, they both had hoped the medicine would keep things the same; they had given up thinking it would make things better.

"I'm alright. Why all these questions?" Fern covered the stained hand with the other.

"No reason." Aislinn reached for the radio knob. "The news is on."

"Leave the radio. I want to know what's bothering you."

"Nothing. I just wanted to know how you were."

Tears brightened the blue of Fern's eyes. "Aislinn, things are happening to me. I don't know, the hot flashes and this thing with my mouth's worse. When Clara brushed my hair yesterday, the brush was full. And it's grey. My voice is going. I never thought it would be this way."

"Ah, mom, it may be nothing. It's probably a sign that you're overdoing it with Clara and Sam taking you out so much. We'll start getting you to bed earlier and you have to eat more. I keep telling you that. And I'll get something from gran for your hair."

"No, don't say anything to Teodora." Fern took the balled-up hanky from her lap and held it to her mouth.

"Why, mom? She always asks how you are." Aislinn got a clean handkerchief from a drawer in the table.

"You mean, how well I'm doing at playing the invalid." The wet piece of linen rolled out of Fern's lap and onto the floor.

Aislinn picked it up and put it in a cardboard box inside the bathroom door. "You know gran doesn't think like that."

"I've known your grandmother a lot longer than you have, my girl, and she has a side she doesn't show you, especially you."

"Gran's not like that." Aislinn sat at the table.

"No, you're her favourite. How could you think anything else?" Fern dabbed at her mouth, missing the foam in the corners. "When you were born, she thought I wasn't fit to bring you up right."

"Ah, come on." Aislinn wanted to take the cloth from her mother and do the job properly. Instead she pressed the swelling on her arm and the pain centred on the lump under the skin. It was the kind of pain she could deal with.

"She tried to convince your father to let her raise you. Said I had my hands full with Colin and Mary." Fern folded her hands over the hanky. "He got drunk the night she asked."

Aislinn stared at her mother's tense body and trembling head, wondering what was inside. If Fern cracked open like an egg right before her eyes, what would come out? "Why didn't you tell me before?"

"Oh . . . it was just another one of the things Teodora did to make me look bad."

Aislinn piled the fruit bowls inside each other and threw the spoons in the top bowl, splashing milk across the table and onto the arm of Fern's chair. She got up and went to the sink, dropping the bowls in, the Melmac sounding brittle against the stainless steel. She ignored the spilt milk and ran water and a dishrag over the bowls in the sink. Outside the window a line of lightning crossed the sky, connecting the tops of the two tallest trees. Aislinn counted, waiting for the thunder, willing it over the house, in her mouth, so she could blast the walls apart.

As she came down the alley, Aislinn tried not to look directly at the bus. She wanted to be surprised by The Scavenger, to see the painted bird the way any passerby might. It was the beak that startled her: solid, real. The tail of fiery feathers was less recognizable: a red and yellow featherduster still came to mind. The eye was defiant. Now if she could just give that eye to the lady Scavenger, then the second fender just might be better than the first. She decided not to stop and look at The Scavenger because she would only notice the flaws and the thought of smudged paint and hesitant lines would make it hard to finish the lady bird.

Aislinn went through the back gate to find Corrine. The yard was busier than the bus pad. There were town folks in the vegetable garden, some trimming hedges, cutting grass. As the bus neared completion, some people lost interest but they still came by in the evenings and on weekends. And when the bus pad was tidied and swept, they looked for more to do. At first Corrine was put off by them standing in her yard offering advice on her cauliflower and cabbage. But they stayed and she let them and gradually the old folks showed up with gloves and garden tools. The garden looked peaceful compared to a corner of the yard near the front gate.

Aislinn called to Corrine on her knees weeding a flower bed, "What's going on?"

Corrine looked up and shaded her eyes with a stained hand. "They're building me a path down to the back gate. Jack

Chalmers felt bad about folks tramping a rut in the lawn, so he got a crew up."

"When are they going to fix your roof?" Aislinn sat down on the grass.

"What?"

"Well, if you don't want them to do your roof, send them over to the store. It needs lots of repairing." Aislinn picked a piece of coarse grass, stretched it between her thumbs and blew on it, creating a low, rude noise.

Corrine got off her knees and sat beside Aislinn. "You know, when the axe falls at Sewell, I'm going to be sorry to leave here. I'm just getting to know the oldtimers. There's real good people here."

Aislinn threw away the split stalk of grass. "A small place like this, you would think everybody would be too close for comfort. But folks like my grandparents have seen a lot of loggers come and go."

"The oldtimers feel the same way we do about the company. I didn't know that before."

"Sure, everybody says they hate the company, but Tanis Bay is a logging town. Now, it's a dying town."

They sat looking down the yard, watching the sun slant in under the tarp and reflect green off the bus's new paint job. The few people puttering around on the bus pad took on the appearance of fish in an aquarium. About now up on the mountain the men would be piling into the crumbies for the dusty trip home. Maybe Tim would find the trouble in the electrical system tonight and they could take the bus for a spin this weekend.

Aislinn stood up; she had better get her lady bird finished. "So, how do you feel about the old bus now?" she asked Corrine.

"I'm still not sold on the idea of living out of it with the others, but it's been a good thing."

Aislinn looked around the yard. "Yeah, you've done okay."

At a workbench under the tarp, Aislinn opened the paint cans and got out the brushes. She had cleaned them the night before, but it looked as if someone had put them in transmission fluid to soften up. She pulled a sawhorse over to the bus, sat down and went to work on the yellow beak of The Scavenger's mate. Each time she rested her hand and looked up, her eyes were drawn to the yard. The flowerbeds were lush, almost exotic, the vegetable garden tumbled green between the well-hoed rows, vines, trellised and tied, climbed the walls of the house and now, a stone walkway to save the grass. Save it for what? The bush knew its time was near. It would creep in the moment they rolled downisland on holiday. It would begin on the company side of town: the bush reclaiming the town, turning the dead wood of the loggers' houses to dust where new trees could take root. That's why the Indians had used mortuary poles for their dead; they knew no one can lie down on this land. They pointed their bear and beaver poles to the sky and the rainforest grew up around them, holding them fast, the quick and the dead. The stone path would disappear overnight.

And Ivan and Hugh were helping that take-over, although where they planted on the mountain would never be the same. But all they knew was that each tree they planted was worth a dime to them. So they had come here and planted, not caring, not knowing what they planted or how it would change things. In a few days they would go, leaving their ten-cent seedlings, and probably never wonder what had grown and what had died. She would be the only witness.

Aislinn banged the paint can lids down hard with the rubber mallet. She didn't feel like painting now. There didn't seem to be much point in making anything, nothing that mattered lasted. Might as well spend your time with a glass in your hand the way some did. They knew how useless it was. She dropped the brushes in a jar of solvent and started down the alley for town.

The pub was quiet; the crews weren't down yet. Aislinn got a beer and went out on the deck that overlooked the Bay. She sat in a worn wicker chair that tilted to the left with her weight and she put her feet up on the railing. She looked out across the Strait at the mountains robbed of their hard edges by the haze. When they were kids, Mary used to tell her that the mists that rose up around the mountains were the ghosts of people drowned in the Strait. Mary told her lots of things such as why a dog raised his muzzle into the breeze and half-closed his eyes: the wind made him remember that his ancestors were wolves and when he closed his eyes the wind was in him and he was thinking about turning wild. Or not to go swimming with the big boys because they could get you pregnant by jacking off in the water. Mary had theories about everything, theories that infuriated Colin whenever he happened to overhear them. He always told her to get real. She would like to hear him say that again . . . 'get real.'

A burst of noise from inside the pub brought her back to her empty beer mug. Aislinn listened for familiar voices and wondered, if she threw the mug off the deck into the bay, would it float or sink? She knew it would feel good to raise her arm and let go. If it floated, she'd stay, and if it sank, she'd leave. She heard Ivan order beer. The bush crew was done early, probably anxious to party, then get out of Tanis Bay, leave the bush and loggers behind. She sat quite still, cradling the empty mug. The confident thud of darts in the board punctuated talk of holidays before school started. She wondered if Ivan was going back to anyone.

Ivan stood in the doorway. "Hi, what you doing out here?"

"Just finishing a beer." She didn't look up at him.

"Here." Ivan walked over to where she sat. "Take mine and I'll get another."

"No thanks. I just dropped by for one." Aislinn could smell road dust in his jeans. He wore it but it didn't make him familiar. The dust belonged here.

Ivan leaned against the wicker chair and it was enough to overbalance the weak legs. The chair tottered. Aislinn couldn't get her legs down from the deck rail fast enough. She was spilled out onto the floor. Ivan stood looking at her. "Did I do that?" He grinned and reached out his hand, expecting her to grip it harder than she had to.

"You idiot, of course you did. You're like a bloody big ox. Coming here. . . . Oh, shit, I'm going home." Aislinn ignored his hand and pulled herself up off the floor using the slumped chair.

"Hey, I didn't mean to . . . ," Ivan said. She was standing now and he could see her face. "You know, I'm sorry the work's done. It's been good up here, especially the fishing. Maybe this weekend we could go again?"

"I've got work to do."

"Can I help?"

"No. I got to go."

"I'll see you at the store tomorrow," Ivan said as he followed her inside.

Aislinn was gone before Hugh could greet her. Ivan came over and sat beside Hugh.

Hugh lowered his beer mug. "What happened?"

"I'm not sure," Ivan answered.

Aislinn was clearing away the supper dishes when she heard someone on the back stairs, then a knock at the kitchen door. She looked at Fern and asked, "Are Clara and Sam dropping by tonight?"

"Not that I know of." Fern looked up from the newspaper spread in her lap.

Aislinn opened the door and peered through the dark mesh of the screen. On the other side of embedded insects and weed seeds stood Ivan and Hugh.

"What are you two doing here?" Aislinn kept her hand on the screen door handle.

Ivan came up to the top stair. "We came to see you."

Hugh looked around from behind Ivan. "We wanted to make sure we saw you before we had to leave."

"Well, we just finished supper. I was just cleaning up . . . ," Aislinn faltered. "My mom goes to bed early. . . ."

"Who is it, Aislinn?" Fern's voice was barely audible.

Aislinn wasn't sure that Ivan and Hugh had heard Fern. "Some friends, mom."

"Are they coming in?"

"Yes." Aislinn opened the screen door. "Come in. Do you want some tea?"

"Yeah, sure."

Ivan and Hugh stood just inside the door. They made the kitchen seem smaller than it already was with Fern's overstuffed sofa chair like a throne against the wall. The chair overcame her, a child in an adult chair. Suddenly it seemed impossible to Aislinn that this was her mother. She didn't know the wispy voice greeting two strangers. For a moment nothing in the room was familiar. She took in the family pictures on the shelves, the shabby furniture, then she realized there weren't enough chairs. She retrieved one from the livingroom and the men sat at the littered kitchen table. She threw the kettle on the stove and dove at the table with a wet dishrag. "I hadn't finished cleaning up," Aislinn said.

Hugh was watching Fern over Aislinn's shoulder as she reached across the table. "We didn't mean to interrupt your supper," he said.

"No, not at all," Fern said. "We had finished. I'm always glad to meet Aislinn's friends. You fellows are loggers, then?"

As Aislinn wiped Fern's mouth with a Kleenex, Ivan looked down at his hands. "We're treeplanters. Well, ex-treeplanters."

Fern's eyes, shiny and hard, were on Aislinn. "So you're from downisland," Fern said. She slid her gaze past Aislinn and rested softer eyes on Hugh. "And your name's Chan. When I came out from England there was another young bride riding in the same coach, a Mrs. Chan. I can't remember her first name. She came from Singapore. I do remember she had terrible nightmares. I gather the Japs were beastly when they took over Singapore."

Hugh leaned over the table toward Fern. "My mother came from Singapore in 1948. Is that when you came?"

"No, I came out just after the war. I was a war bride, you see."

Aislinn glanced at Fern and decided it would be hard to imagine her a bride. She brought a chipped teapot to the table.

Fern frowned. "You should have got the good teapot down. At least bring teacups, not those old mugs. The Limoges cups Colin sent." She nodded toward Ivan and Hugh. "Colin's my oldest. A geologist."

Aislinn opened a cupboard and reached up to a top shelf. "Hugh, was your mother caught in the fighting like Ivan's?" she asked as she took down the teacups.

"My mother was a nurse at St. Andrew's Mission Hospital in Singapore. She was evacuated with a bunch of medical staff when the Japanese invaded. She was supposed to go to India, but the ship she was on was sunk ninety miles out of Singapore." Hugh pushed up his glasses, covering the tense lines between his eyebrows.

Aislinn washed off the greasy brown coating the gas stove had deposited on the teacups and set them on the table.

Fern scrutinized the cups, her head shaking in its palsy. "It was the same at home in England. The ships trying to get people away across the Atlantic and the German submarines like sharks."

"There were probably real sharks where your mom was," Aislinn said to Hugh. "What happened to her?"

"She drifted with some others on a piece of wreckage for three days. I never thought to ask her about sharks. Anyways, Malay fishermen picked them up. She was real sick. She had been hurt when the ship was bombed. So the Malays hid her and the others under palm leaves on a junk and smuggled them to Sumatra."

Aislinn had to lean over Hugh to pour the tea and Fern took the interruption as her turn to speak. "The bombing in London . . ." Her voice trailed off. "We lost everything . . . if it wasn't destroyed the pickers got it before you returned the next morning. No better than scavenging gulls . . . they should have been shot on sight."

The nodding of Fern's head made Hugh feel as if he were expected to comment. "Mom had worked in a British hospital so she was considered British and put in their care. But the Japanese were invading all of southeast Asia and the British had to keep moving to stay ahead of them. Eventually, she was captured in Padang with a group of English refugees, mainly medical people." He paused, as if to think over what he had just said. "They were put in an internment camp. Mom says the Japanese called them 'British running dogs,' except they couldn't decide where she fit in."

Fern wiped her mouth before speaking. "Terrible, just terrible. At least we were spared the horror of Germans on English soil."

Ivan raised the teacup to his mouth, then held it away. The cup seemed like a fragile white ear he might speak into. "Was she a prisoner in a camp until the end of the war?" He had been quiet until now.

"Not in that camp, no. The Japanese commander at Padang tried to make her into a comfort girl. . . ."

Aislinn sat on the kitchen counter with her feet resting on the handles of the drawers beneath her. "Comfort girl?" As she said the words, she understood and felt foolish. How must Hugh feel? Could he imagine his mother like that? How would her dad feel if he were alive and sitting in this room with Ivan? Would he sense it? She couldn't have told him. Hugh's voice cut into her thoughts.

"She escaped from the hotel with the help of some Padang Chinese. But there was really no place to hide. There were soldiers everywhere and she couldn't survive in the jungle. Anyways, she was caught and put in prison. They said they were going to execute her as an example. A month later, they sent her to a cement factory to nurse the Malay and Chinese coolies. She was there until the end of the war."

Aislinn slipped from the countertop to help Fern with her cup of tea. Fern pushed it away to speak. "Those were hard times. You young people have no idea. You're lucky and don't know it."

Ivan's eyes flashed over Fern. "Sure, I don't know war firsthand, but my parents taught me to be thankful I don't. They gave up a lot."

Fern's face was smooth as if nothing could possibly disturb her. But her neck was tense and her face jutted forward like a thin moon. "We all did. Some more than others. Single girls especially. All the young men dying or made useless. What married life did we have to look forward to? That's why there's so many war brides in this god-forsaken country. We gave up our homes to come here, only to be sneered at by Canadian women and called thieves. If we had known what we were in for, most of us would have stayed home."

Red blotches appeared on Ivan's cheekbones. "It's hard to leave your home. That's what my parents say."

Hugh turned to Ivan. "Can your parents go back?"

"No."

"I mean to visit?"

"No, that's not possible for them."

Fern was staring at a shelf on the wall beside the table. Her voice seemed worn as an old sheet from the talk. "I should have gone back when I was going to. I'll not see that house again."

Ivan and Hugh followed Fern's gaze to a smudged black and white photograph propped against the wall. A brick townhouse was barely discernible.

Aislinn put the teacup down. "Mom, you're tired out. You should be in bed."

"Yes, I've had enough."

Ivan pushed his chair back. "Well, we'll be going."

"You don't have to," she said. "I won't be long. There's beer in the fridge."

"Okay," Hugh said.

"Help youself," she said, lifting Fern out of the chair. Out of the corner of her eye, Aislinn saw Ivan move as if to help her. She was glad he stayed in his chair; she didn't like fuss and Fern acted as though there was no one in the room.

Even with the bedroom door closed, Aislinn was aware of the fridge door opening and closing and a current of voices from the kitchen. She could imagine what they were saying. Sorting through a drawer, she found a nightdress and turned to her mother.

Fern looked up from the button she was struggling with. "Don't look at me like that. What kind of friends are those, a chink and a bohunk?"

"Friends? Don't talk to me about friends. Nobody was ever good enough for you." Aislinn threw the nightdress on the bed.

"I can see why you haven't spent much time around here lately."

"What are you getting at?" Aislinn undid the buttons Fern couldn't manage.

"I just hope it's not the Chinese. Even Billy Stone would have been better than . . ."

Aislinn backed away. "I'm not going to listen to this crap." She was out the door and about to slam it when she remembered Ivan and Hugh. She stood shaking in the hall. How loud had she been? Had they heard her? Maybe not, she could hear them talking in the kitchen. Hugh was saying something about her. . . .

"Anyways, when her mom was giving us the gears about how much they gave up because of the war. Shit, did you see Aislinn's face? I thought for a minute she was going to throw her tea at the old lady."

"Yeah, I couldn't keep my mouth shut. I mean, hell, I feel sorry for her mom, but it really got to me her saying we don't know how lucky we are."

"Sure, it was hard. There's a lot my mom doesn't talk about and it kills me. Jesus, Ivan, my imagination goes to work and, you know, it gets dark in my head."

"I know. Sometimes I see things in my mother's face . . ."

Hugh's voice seemed to change. "I never want to tell people she got captured. I should make something up for that part of her story."

Aislinn walked down the hall, stunned by how much they saw and knew. Suddenly she felt very close to them, as if they had always sat around the table in the kitchen. When she entered the room, she couldn't look at them. She opened the refrigerator and the handle vibrated in her hand. She sat down with her beer. "I thought you guys would have better things to do than come over here."

Ivan looked at her across the table. "You ever spend weeks at a time with a bunch of guys?" He laughed. "No, I don't suppose you know what that's like."

Laughter tickled in her throat and surfaced as a strange giggle which made the others laugh hard. She sat with her head down.

Ivan tried to catch his breath to speak. "Boy, the fumes from one beer are enough to get you going. You're a cheap drunk."

"No, it's just the clowns I'm sitting with. You guys are something else." The words sounded strange in her ears.

Hugh put on a macho movie voice. "What kind of 'something' we be talking about here?"

"You surprise me, that's all. I know more about you and your families than I know about some of my oldest friends."

"Why shouldn't you?" Hugh asked.

"You're kind of giving yourself away, aren't you? Letting people know about you?" she said, as if she couldn't believe they didn't know the danger.

"The more we understand about each other, the better. If you know people, you're less likely to distrust them," Hugh added.

"No, you may trust them too much." Aislinn was staring at her hands around the brown bottle. "And they can leave and take your trust with them."

Ivan put his hand on her arm. "Know what I think? Once you know someone, you never lose them, not really."

She could feel their eyes recording every scar and freckle, every twitch, lifting up her skin. . . . It was too much. They knew too much. She stood. "It's hot in here."

They almost had to run to catch her up at the end of the yard. Ivan put his arm around her shoulders. "You going to be a gentleman and walk us home?"

Her first impulse was to shrug him off. But they were both smiling at her. "You're not afraid of the dark, are you?" she asked, slipping her arm around Ivan's waist. Hugh brushed her hand.

Aislinn had been hoping all morning that the contractor had come up to Tanis Bay early and the bush crew had gone down-island. She hated goodbyes. She would want to snatch back some of what they were taking of her. She thrust the broom into a corner of the store behind the counter. Dust powdered up and she sprayed it with a fine mist of water. Her first job in the store had been sweeping up and every time she picked the broom up her mother would say, 'Don't sweep hard. Nobody wants dusty merchandise.' Her mother hadn't said anything this morning, good thing. Acted like nothing happened. Probably figured the fact that she slept in her clothes on top of the bedspread with just the quilt pulled up said enough. After their argument, Aislinn had come to the realization that if Ivan and Hugh were her friends, they would be acquaintances in a few days and she was tired of people coming and going in her life. She felt like a starfish spreadeagled on a rock, stuck, while the waves washed back and forth over her. And the next wave was going out and she didn't want to see it. But it broke on her anyway.

The front door burst open, and the bush crew rolled in and around the aisles. Ivan and Hugh came in last and slowly closed the door. They both looked at Aislinn, her head down, concentrating the bristles of the broom into the cracks between the floorboards. They moved like partners in a dance; obviously, they had talked about this meeting. They approached the counter together and Ivan said, "How's your mom?"

Aislinn looked up. Perhaps they had heard. She kept the broom in front of her as if to sweep them from the store. "The same. That's the way she is all the time." She began to sweep again.

Ivan and Hugh looked at each other and Hugh nodded. Ivan spoke up. "Hey, are you going to take me fishing?"

She could feel the heat in his question, and wondered how much Hugh knew. Aislinn continued to explore between boards that wear and oil had turned to the colour and texture of dark, warm taffy. "I have work to do," she said.

"I mean after you close the store."

"I mean I have work to do . . . somewhere else."

"Oh . . . can we help?" Ivan asked, trying to ignore her tone.

Aislinn stopped sweeping and rested her hands on top of the broom handle. She contemplated Ivan, as if weighing his usefulness. "What do you know about the electrical system in a vehicle?"

"So, that old yellow truck of yours let you down? Well, I've looked at a few in my time."

"Can you do more than look?"

"Yeah, I know my way around."

"Good, wait till your buddies are finished in here and I'll close."

By the time Aislinn joined Ivan and Hugh on the front porch, she had put away the danger of a fight. The guys badly needed someone who could fix the bus and Ivan had offered to help. She started down the street and they followed.

Ivan matched her long stride. "So your old reliable truck didn't even make it back to the store?"

They turned down a street that led away from the centre of town.

Ivan slowed to let Hugh catch up. "Don't tell me you broke down outside of town?"

Aislinn turned in at the last house on a street which ended without notice in bush, the pavement crumbling where fireweed and salal encroached. They followed her alongside the house, through a gate and down a half-finished stone walk. Over Aislinn's shoulder, Ivan caught sight of a brilliant green bus flanked by an orange tarp. Hugh couldn't see around Ivan but he could hear what sounded like a party. They stepped through another gate and up to the school bus. Aislinn tapped one of the men with his head under the hood.

From the area behind the block, Tim said, "Shit, what is it?"

Aislinn put her foot on the fender and looked in at Tim. "I've found someone to fix the electrical system."

Tim's face appeared above the air filter. "What?"

"Come out of there," Aislinn said.

Tim straightened up and jumped down from the crate he was standing on. "I know you," he said to Ivan. Accusation skated on his voice.

Ivan and Hugh were both looking at Aislinn; their faces showed confusion and suspicion.

Aislinn took a step forward, close enough to put herself between Tim and Ivan. "Yeah, you two know each other alright. But we're not going to let a little misunderstanding stand in the way of a holiday." Aislinn turned to Ivan, her hand on his arm, and explained about the bus.

Ivan and Tim eyed each other. A group was gathering behind

Tim, curious about the outsiders. Someone turned the radio down to a buzz. It got so quiet that the women working in the bus stuck their heads out the windows.

Aislinn broke in, "Hey, you two don't have to be enemies. What have you got to fight about? It's nobody's fault there's no more work here." Aislinn looked from one to the other, thinking that if neither of them made a friendly gesture in the next few seconds, she would leave with Ivan and Hugh. Ivan glanced at her. She knew he was trying to decipher her motives.

Ivan extended his hand to Tim. "I'm no expert."

Tim looked at the people around him. Most of them had been helping out since he and the guys had hauled the bus up to the pad. He had already imagined piling everybody into The Scavenger and heading out on the highway for a test spin. He could see them hanging out the windows yelling and whistling as they drove through town. Tim gripped Ivan's hand. "Shit, you can't be any worse than the rest of us."

"A heavy Chevy, eh?" Ivan said. "A big C/50."

"Have a look." Tim offered Ivan his crate to stand on and got himself another.

Hugh leaned toward Aislinn and said in a low voice, "What're you up to? You could've got us killed bringing us here. I thought I knew you, but I don't get this."

"I wanted my friends to get to know you," she said quietly.

"Why didn't you tell us?"

"Would you have come?"

As men crowded around the motor, she took Hugh's hand and led him inside the bus. She explained that just about everything had come from the scavenger hunt. The cabinets had come with two fresh coats of pink paint and they didn't have the heart to change the colour, even though they got chipped when she and Linda hung them on the wall. The table was from the restaurant in the Island Highway Service Station. It was perfect because the metal feet sticking out from the centre pedestal were easily bolted to the floor. Hugh watched as she ran her fingers over initials scratched in the arborite top, a reverse braille. On the table top there was another set of letters below the A.C. she was touching. "An artifact," she said to him. She wasn't sure he heard her.

"You know, ever since I met your grandparents and the Charlies, there's been something eating away at the back of my brain. But I think I've got it figured out." As he spoke, a few people got on the bus. "Let's go outside," he said.

Hugh led the way around the back of the bus. Someone was sorting through some boxes there, so he continued around to the alley side of the bus. "Did I tell you I'm going to China first . . . you know, to start the shoot?"

Aislinn leaned against the bus and rubbed her hand on a bracket holding a propane cylinder. She didn't want to hear about China or India or downisland for that matter. She felt pinned while everyone flowed over and away from her.

Hugh continued in her silence. "One of the reasons I'm going there is to film my mother's story. She was born in a village in Kwangsi, but when her father died and her mother remarried, she was taken to Singapore and sold as a slave girl. She's the link between the past and present in China." Hugh stopped talking when someone rounded the back of the bus with an armload of garbage for the bin in the alley. He moved further along the bus toward the front.

Aislinn followed. "Get off it, Hugh. Slavery. Come on, tell me another one."

Hugh moved in close to Aislinn, forcing her to take a step back against the bus. "I don't bullshit about stuff like this. Female slavery wasn't stopped in China until 1933. My mother was taken away from her master and put in a mission school."

"Okay, okay, I believe you. Lighten up. You're going to China, good for you." She ran her fingers over the swelling on her left arm. It hadn't gone down much, maybe it was a spider bite.

"I thought you were interested." Hugh stepped back, turning to go up to the front of the bus where bodies hung from the maw of the open hood. He sat on a sawhorse watching Ivan.

Aislinn crossed the alley and stretched out on the hood of a junker, stripped for parts. The sunbaked metal burned through her T-shirt and jeans and came warm to her skin. She lowered her eyelids against the sun and filtered the bus and the men through her eyelashes. That was the way the world should come to a person: muted, distorted. The way it really was, instead of pretending to be clear. Nothing was simple and straightforward. Why should Hugh want to spill out everything inside his head to her? What did he expect? She couldn't hold his hand. And what was he doing now? She opened her eyes and sat up. Hugh was bent over trying to examine her bird through the legs of one of the men headfirst in the motor. Hugh backed away, trying for a better position. Finally the man moved aside for a moment, reaching for a screwdriver sitting on top of the battery. Scavenger flashed out strong and fearless at Aislinn.

Hugh backed away a few steps more, then a little more until he was in the middle of the alley. Then he was leaning up against the windowless door of the car Aislinn was sitting on. "What's that on the side of the bus there?" he asked.

"The Scavenger." Aislinn pointed to the stencilled letters above the windshield where School Bus used to be.

"It's very Chinese. Like a dragon."

"It can't be. I drew it and I don't know anything Chinese except you."

"Hell, it's too fierce to be me." Hugh laughed. "So it's not a Chinese dragon, what is it?"

"I don't know. A bird."

"It reminds me of something I've seen in a book. But I don't know what. . . ."

"I didn't copy it from a book."

"No, I didn't mean that. Say, why are you so touchy?"

She was wrong. There was one straightforward thing in this world and it was standing beside her. "I don't have to answer to you." To look at him, Aislinn had to lower her eyelids again to shelter her eyes from the sun glinting off the broken windshield.

"No, you don't," he said, "but I wish you would tell me what's bothering you."

"What does it matter to you? You'll be gone in a day."

"I don't know why it matters, except . . . it's weird, this feeling I have, like I know you . . . really know you, maybe better than my own sister."

The shattered glass of the windshield was radiating sparks that dazzled her. Aislinn raised a hand to shield her eyes, but Hugh was becoming a blue blur.

"I'm going to miss you," Hugh said.

She squinted even more as the blue haze deepened around him.

"I didn't see that till just now."

Neither of them noticed Ivan approach until he cast a shadow over the windshield. "Come on, they're calling it a day. We're all going down for a beer." Ivan looked from Aislinn to Hugh. "Don't look so surprised. That Tim's not such a bad guy."

"Yeah, sure." Hugh blinked. "Did you fix it?"

"No, but I think I tracked down the problem. I'm coming back tomorrow." Ivan reached up a hand to Aislinn. "Nice hood ornament."

She avoided his hand and jumped down. "I thought you wanted to go fishing tomorrow." She raised her eyebrows; it felt good to the puckered muscles around her eyes.

"I thought you had work to do." Ivan countered.

"Now we both have work to do on the bus. We'll have to find something for Hugh to do."

"I'll supervise. Better still, I'll be The Scavenger's official photographer. We'll record for posterity the resurrection of a dead school bus and those people dedicated to the glorious task."

"Not so fast," Ivan said. "The spark of life isn't in it yet."

"Yes sir, God, or is it Dr. Frankenstein?" Hugh bowed. Ivan took a swipe at his head. Hugh danced out of reach.

And Aislinn, seeing them in that moment, said quietly to Ivan, "I'll take you fishing tomorrow before we come back here."

The outside seam of Ivan's jeans smudged the paint on the feather she had just finished touching up. A flash of anger, it surprised her. Everything inside her was so close to the surface. Then his leg brushed her cheek. He was too close for comfort. She tapped him. "Move over, Ivan." Meanwhile, Hugh kept calling to her to tilt her head this way and that as his camera clicked at her lady bird. She had begun imagining The Scavenger on the highway, in the city, and it made her feel the way she had when some downisland trout fishermen caught her skinny-dipping in the creek.

Just as Aislinn dabbed the brush in the paint can, the fender in front of her shuddered, stopped, then shuddered again. She looked up at Ivan who was waving at the windshield. There was a grinding sound, a shudder which became a prolonged vibration, and the fender rattled rhythmically. The bird before Aislinn's eyes seemed to ruffle its feathers. Everyone around the bus was talking, shouting, clapping. "I guess that's it," she said to the bird and backed away.

She picked up the paint cans and brushes and retreated to the workbench. She couldn't understand why she wasn't overjoyed that the bus was running. It wasn't that she hadn't finished; she would have time again to work on the bird. But the bus in working order meant motion, going forward, going away. Aislinn carefully cleaned out the rims of the paint cans, wiped the sides, pounded down the lids. She squeezed solvent through the bristles of the brushes with her fingers. Each brush cleaned to the base. The bus warmed up. She tidied the workbench, sorting the tools and hardware into their sanctioned drawers. Everyone piled on the bus. She swept under the workbench.

Hugh was rushing about taking pictures, then he had her by the hand. "Come on." They tried to push in at the door, but there was no room. Suddenly she had to get on the bus, she had to ride through town and out onto the Island Highway. In a panic she stepped down out of the stairwell. She didn't want to be left behind. She ran to the back of the bus and swung up on the ladder to the roof. She climbed into the luggage rack, her knuckles white on the metal rail. She turned to see Hugh climbing in beside her as the bus lurched forward.

Hugh tucked his camera in the front of his shirt. "I hope they take it easy."

The bus lurched again, backfired and stopped. Inside the bus the joyriders deflated like a balloon in one long moan. Ivan and Tim were out under the hood again. Minutes of silence, then the ignition ground over and The Scavenger was shaking. They moved out and away from the cement pad, launched down the alley toward town.

The wind coming over the high forehead of The Scavenger whipped Aislinn's hair around her face. The singed patches were no longer spiky. Instead they formed a soft, fine fringe that separated in puffs like the breast feathers of a dark bird. The rushing air tingled in her veins and the motion of the bus rumbled her bones. They were on Centre Street, leaving behind the old dock, a speck of black, weathered wood in the corner of her eye, climbing the hill past the Company office, its siding of two-inch skyline logging cable rusting to the colour of dried blood, to The Lighthouse where the inmates standing on the deck raised their glasses, beyond the roughcut cedarboard store with Cleary on the front, out and away past the Island Highway Service Station and down a grey slash cut through the trees. Aislinn could smell the forest sweat as it strained to reach into the ditches and close the cut. The scent was powerful. She turned her head to look back, expecting to see the trees close over behind her.

She recognized that need to be whole, the struggle to seal the wounds and smooth away the scars. To let the wind blow against you without fear you will be blown to the ground like deadfall. Aislinn tucked her legs under her and rose up, kneeling against the stream. She let go of the luggage rack, rocking back from her knees to her feet. The wind pushed at her clothes, her hair, her skin, as if to peel her back from her bones. But the wind would get nothing from her. She opened her eyes and watched it kiss her. Her lips would not be parted, they were closed, smooth as scar tissue.

The bus rounded a curve. Off balance, Aislinn swung out over the edge, aware now of Hugh's arms around her leg. He pulled her down. She landed hard on her knees, the mesh of the luggage rack cutting zigzags in her blue jeans. A corner of the railing gashed her right hand where she grabbed at it. She rocked for a minute on all fours.

Hugh held her around the waist. "Shit, you trying to kill yourself? Hell, you've cut your hand."

Aislinn sat back, strange to herself. "Don't worry. I'll close my hand, the wind won't get in." The air rushing by had taken her words with it.

"What?" Hugh was examining her hand.

"It's alright, Hugh." She put her hand on his where he held her left arm.

Hugh looked from her hand covering his to her face. "Aislinn, you have to come with me. I only know half of things, half the story. You have to tell the other half."

The wind beat against her eardrums, but she would not be robbed of what had come loose in her. She would not give in to the wind. No longer would she be pinned like a leaf in a corner. "What are you saying, Hugh?"

"Come to China with me." Hugh had his mouth against her ear. "Do this documentary with me."

"China?" The bus had slowed to make a U-turn. China? They were going back. Back . . . down the road, down the throat of the green snake. Aislinn started to shiver. "How could you let me stand up here like that?" She unclenched her fingers to look at the cut in her palm.

Hugh pushed his glasses up on the bridge of his nose. "I asked you a question," he said.

"You saw my mother." Aislinn's hand was bleeding. She sucked at it, sucking up her own life.

Hugh untied the red cotton handkerchief he used as a head-band. He wrapped it around her hand. "What about the rest of your family? Can't they help?"

"You don't know anything about my family . . . about me."

"I know you have to come with me. I need your eyes and anyways, you need to see." Hugh's voice was calm, assured.

They were rounding the curve that led off the highway and into Tanis Bay. When Aislinn looked back at the highway, it was hidden behind trees that appeared to meet at the high point of the curve.

The door on the contractor's van rolled shut with a hard metal thud. It closed Aislinn off from Hugh and Ivan and although she had the sky overhead, she was shut in. She unfolded the scraps of paper they had given her. Phone numbers. Ivan had wrapped his around a fish hook. She crumpled the bits of paper into the pocket of her jeans, and kept her hand bunched there, feeling the barbs against her skin.

Hugh rolled down the window. He refused to say goodbye. "Remember, we leave for China in two weeks."

Ivan turned to Hugh. "What's this about?" he asked.

The van started up, Hugh raised his voice over the bad

muffler. "You might see Aislinn sooner than you think, Ivan."

Ivan spoke to Hugh. "China, with you? I don't know if I like this." His eyes were on Aislinn.

"What's to like?" Hugh said.

Before they could pull away, she had turned down the street toward the old part of town.

By the time Aislinn arrived for breakfast, Teodora and Augusta had moved out to the yard to work on their mats. Shea and Wil were still at the kitchen table so there was hot tea in the pot. Aislinn helped herself to the eggs and fried tomatoes left in the pan for her. She kissed her grandfather and took her plate and cup outside to the bench against the wall.

Teodora looked up from the cattail leaves beneath her fingers. "Well, you got back alive."

"Alive? From where?"

"Wil say, you riding on roof of big green bus, yes."

"Yeah, they finally got the thing started."

Teodora was thinking how much faster a bus could go than a coal-eating train. "Why were you up there?"

"Excess baggage."

Augusta poked her ironwood needle at Aislinn. "That picturemaking boy was with you, yes?"

"He left this morning." Aislinn put her empty plate down on the bench.

"And that big fellow you had your eye on?" Teodora asked.

"Yeah. They're finished up here."

"That's too bad. Those two were good for you."

This wasn't what Aislinn wanted to hear.

Teodora glanced at her. "How's that lump on your arm?"

"It's about the same. Have you got something I could put on it?"

"No, it will go down on its own."

Aislinn watched them for awhile before she spoke. "Hugh's asked me to go with him."

"Why the little one asks you to go to city? He don't want girlfriend."

"He wants me to go to China with him and the other places he's making his film. Crazy, huh? What do I know about making films?"

Teodora pressed down hard on a row of leaves with her mat creaser. She set it aside and with eyes dark as wet rocks, she looked up at Aislinn. "Why does he want you to go?"

"Says he needs a woman's point of view. Something about the female principle . . . you know how he talks." She thought the cup would break in her hands.

"What did you tell him?" Teodora kept her eyes on Aislinn's face.

"No, of course. What else was there to tell him?"

"Do you want to go?" Teodora's hands were still.

"I can't go." Aislinn put her cup down on the empty plate hard enough to chip a corner off the handle.

Teodora's total attention was concentrated on Aislinn. "Fern could stay with Mary in the city."

"No. I told you Mary's pregnant again. She can't handle that bunch of hers and mom." Aislinn tapped her fork against the cup and more of the handle fell away.

"She could hire some help." Teodora ignored the tapping.

"On what Jim makes? Not likely." Aislinn noticed the fractured handle and stopped drumming.

"Nothing wrong with Colin helping out. It's about time he did more than send your mother expensive nicknacks from all over the world."

"I can't. Hugh leaves soon and who knows where Colin is? Anyway, mom can't travel and there's the store to think about."

"You don't want to go, then?" Teodora leaned toward Aislinn.

"No . . . oh, I don't know. I've never been anywhere. How would I talk to people? What would I eat?"

Teodora laughed. "Don't tell me it's your stomach that's keeping you here?" She reached out her hand. "Granddaughter, you should go on this journey. Nothing in this world is co-incidence. That boy was meant to come here and find you."

"But I don't see how . . ."

"Go to the store and call Mary, right now. Get your foolish fears out of the way and look inside." Teodora pressed Aislinn's hand.

Aislinn got up from the bench and paced.

Augusta shook her head. "Once you were brave, strong girl, yes. Where did that girl go?"

"Aislinn." The tone of Teodora's voice stopped her pacing. "The three of us know there is knowledge for you in this journey. It is time you went beyond here."

- 9 -

Heavy clouds lay in the strait, their shadows reaching across the water to darken the town. Inside, the store had taken on a grey light as if the room were trapped at the centre of a storm cloud. The electric light was flimsy against the overcast day. There was a letter in the mail from Hugh, and Aislinn took it out on the back porch of the store to read. Now that he was back in the city, he had probably changed his mind. She looked out at the overgrown yard; it always gave her a perverse kind of pleasure. The bush coming right up to her back door. Maybe she secretly hoped it would consume the back stairs, the porch, and move, still hungry, into the backroom. She wouldn't fight it.

Aislinn had brought a butter knife with her to slit the envelope without destroying the address in the lefthand corner. She had misplaced the piece of paper Hugh had given her. The washing machine probably turned it to pulp in the pocket of her blue jeans. The note inside the envelope simply told her to look at the accompanying photocopy. As she unfolded it, she speculated that he had photocopied his face or his hand. Instead she found a page from a book. Why was Hugh sending her pictures of totem poles? She read the caption: 'Shang dynasty bone handles.' Aislinn looked closely at the carved figures with symmetrical features, the lines always joined. Whoever had carved these had borrowed from the Indians. But there was some other figure between the face-on version of bear and beaver. It could be raven in profile, but the beak was short and curved like Scavenger's. Following the lines away from the beak, she found the fang and eye of her bird. Hugh was playing a joke. He must have blotted out that section and drawn in The Scavenger, then made a new photocopy. She wished she had a magnifying glass, with it she would likely see the smudged lines of the original. As it was, he had done a good job, the lines of the bird looked like they belonged there. On the back of the photocopy, Hugh had written, 'Shang Dynasty: 3000 B.C. The Chinese believe in omens, you have to come with me.'

She had called her sister and Mary had promised to try to find Colin and see what they could work out. That was five days ago and, as she expected, she had heard nothing. She could see why Mary wouldn't be overjoyed at the prospect of looking after their mother. Aislinn hadn't told Fern. No one other than her old folks knew. Teodora had told her to ask Sam Stone to take over the store for her, but she didn't think there was much point.

Aislinn turned the photocopy over and studied the bone handles. The resemblance to Indian totem poles was just an accident. It was possible that people in different times and places could unknowingly draw similar designs. Hugh was grasping at straws because he wanted more of China in Canada. He would have to decide where he belonged. She laughed at herself. Good advice, coming from her. How about her? Where did she belong? In this town. Sorry, it's history. She belonged to the coast, to Tanis Bay. It said so on the front of the envelope in her hand. Did that mean she should build a house down on the beach and grow old in it? Her grandfather had built a log house above the beach and had grown old there. But he wasn't alone and eventually she would be. She tried to imagine herself sitting on the porch of her bay house looking out across the water, the silent, overgrown town at her back. All she could see was a stick woman.

Aislinn went inside the store and called the long distance operator. She got Hugh's phone number and dialled. Before he came on the line, she hung up.

From the backroom, Aislinn heard the front door open and excited talk and laughter careened into the room. It sounded like the teenie tribe alternately eager and bored with summer holidays. When she parted the curtains, she found her friends huddled over a sheet of paper placed on the counter.

Linda looked up. "We're leaving this weekend."

'Leaving' flew up and caught in Aislinn's throat.

Corrine waved the piece of paper at Aislinn. "The guys arranged it."

Tracey lit a cigarette. "Shit, they may not have jobs to come back to, but who gives a damn? We're going to have a good time."

"We got to get groceries for the bus." Corrine stopped fluttering the shopping list. "We're going to do it together so we don't duplicate stuff."

Aislinn nodded. "There's some empty boxes by the mag rack."

Linda retrieved a few of the boxes and put them on the counter. "You know, we're going to get out on that highway and not stop till we hit the ferry."

Tracey put a couple of cartons of cigarettes in one of the boxes. "We're getting off this island as fast as we can. Spend a few days in the city, then head into the interior and find one of those big lakes with sandy beaches."

Aislinn could see the bus, a huge green beetle, nose down, eating up the white line. "How long you going to be gone?"

The phone rang before an answer came from between the aisles. Aislinn stepped through the curtains to the phone on the wall of the backroom.

"Two weeks," came from Linda on her knees digging out packages of toilet paper from the back of a shelf. "Do you think we'll last together that long without a murder?"

Corrine answered for Aislinn, "Not if Earl snores every night the way he does when he's passed out."

"Beer makes him snore," Linda said. "We'll only let him drink Southern Comfort."

Tracey filled another empty box with cereal, powdered milk, coffee. "Hey, how we going to get this stuff back to the bus?"

Linda stood up, her arms full of toilet paper. "The kids can carry it."

"Yeah, right."

Aislinn came through the curtains to the counter. "I'll take it in the truck. I'm going home when you're finished here." Aislinn pulled a box of groceries toward her and started punching prices into the adding machine.

Linda stopped stuffing packages of disposable diapers into a box. "Is something wrong?" she asked Aislinn.

"No, everything's just fine."

"You could have fooled me." Linda watched Aislinn mindlessly tap in numbers. "Did Clara call about your mom?"

"No, it wasn't Clara on the phone. Drop the third degree or I'll add this stuff up wrong."

Linda put a hand on Aislinn's arm. "You should be coming with us."

Aislinn looked up at her friend. "You know I snore." Their laughter drew Corrine and Tracey to the counter.

"I almost forgot to tell you," Corrine said, "the scavenger hunt party is tomorrow night at The Lighthouse. The guys are going to name the winner."

Tracey started packing up the rest of the groceries. "Doug says it's pretty close, a few folks collected everything on their lists and were working on the bonus items."

"What else is happening at the party?" Aislinn totalled the figures in the adding machine.

"Nothing . . . the usual drinking, that's all." Linda collected the money from the others.

Aislinn straightened out the crumpled bills. "A couple of days ago Hugh Chan sent me up some slides he took of the bus and the town. Maybe we can show them after the great hunter is honoured?"

"Sure, why not? If there's not too many," Corrine said. "I'll tell Jack Chambers to bring his projector and screen."

Fern was asleep in her chair when Aislinn came in from talking to Clara in the yard. The sound of the kettle grating against the rough cast iron of a stove burner caused Fern to twitch awake. "Is it teatime, Clara?"

"Clara's in the garden, mom."

"Oh, it's you. Is it that late? I just dozed off."

"No, I came home a little early. I wanted to tell you that Mary called. She wants us to come for a visit."

"Visit Mary? It's too long a trip for me. Haven't you told her how it is now?"

Aislinn came over and sat at the table. "If the travelling wasn't a problem, would you like to go?"

"Well, it would be nice to get over to the city." Fern gestured for a clean hanky. "But I'm too ill these days."

As Aislinn collected one from the cutlery drawer in the old kitchen table, she told Fern about the guys arranging a vacation. "They're taking that bus of theirs over to the mainland. I was thinking that we could go with them. You could lie in one of the bunks."

"A bunk, I don't know." Her head shook. "What about the store?"

"I think Sam would mind it for us."

"I don't know." Fern clutched the arms of her chair. "Maybe Colin could fly out to Mary's?"

"Mary has already called Colin. He's up north looking at some mine. But he's supposed to phone his office, so she left a message." Aislinn wondered what kind of message Colin would get. Would Mary have said it was important, he should call immediately?

"That old school bus would probably break down and strand us someplace. And then what would I do?"

"If you're too sick to go, I'll call Mary back right now." The tea kettle shrilled, the steam greying the window. Aislinn got up from the table.

"Can't say I like all sorts of people seeing me like this."

"Why don't I call the doctor, see what he suggests?"

"It would be fine if Colin could come out." Fern's eyes rested on the shelf of photographs.

"Fine if Colin could come . . . maybe." Aislinn lifted the kettle off the fire.

The rain rattled in bullets against the tin roof. Aislinn couldn't get comfortable enough in bed to block out the sound. It was tearing sleep to rags. She considered getting up, instead she made a cave of her pillow, covering her ears. In the muffled darkness, sleep crept in under the wing of a huge bird that perched on the end of Aislinn's bed. Then another arrived, just as large as the first. Perched there, they looked her over carefully. Then, suddenly, their wings rushed the air. They flew at her. Her arm came up to protect her eyes. Their talons tangled in her hair. Their wings beat harder. She was lifted up. She looked down on dark trees.

They altered the motion of their wings, forcing air against her face, into her eyes and mouth. They were descending. She was set down on the edge of South Point. The birds touched ground on either side of her. She couldn't bear to look down. She turned to one bird, then the other, and found Teodora and Augusta standing beside her. She was about to ask them why, when they pushed her off the cliff. She fell toward the grey beach rocks, that feeling of airiness in her stomach. She kicked at the wind weighing her down and the blanket fell off the bed. The raincold breeze coming through the window turned her sweat to shivers. Staring at the end of the bed, she groped for the twisted blanket. Had Teodora and Augusta come to her or was the dream all hers? When the blanket was pulled over her it seemed a dead weight, pinning her down.

Aislinn drove slowly back from the service station, watching how the road disappeared and appeared around curves. It cut through trees but around rock only to end in water, a scar running down to the sea. She felt bonetired and the flick of light and shadow across the road wearied her eyes. She almost wished she hadn't invited her old folks to the party; she would have given anything to go home. A heaviness had been with her all day, dragging her toward a deep consuming sleep. She shook herself and twisted the knob on the broken radio. She whistled to break the spell of the road. Her dad used to whistle "Good Night Irene" when he carved and never at any other time. It was not a favourite of her mother's. She wasn't a favourite of her mother's. Tonight she would ask her gran if what Fern had told her was true. She had put the asking off, because she would get a straight answer from Teodora and it was bound to open old hurts.

When she pulled up to the log house, Shea and Wil were sitting on the bench by the front door. She noticed someone had cut her grandad's hair and it lay flat at the sides instead of sticking out in wings above his ears as it had after she cut it. Shea stood when he heard the truck door open.

"Everybody ready?" she asked.

"We are, the old women are still in the house," Shea answered.

"The keys are in the ignition. Why don't you two go on ahead?"

Wil and Aislinn helped Shea into the cab of the truck. He sat stiff-backed, listening for the turn of the key.

As they walked toward town, Aislinn seemed to lag behind the old women. She wasn't sure she had the energy to ask her gran, but then again, an opportunity might not come before she went downisland. "Gran . . . mom and me were talking the other night . . ."

"What is it, granddaughter?" Teodora said, slowing to look at Aislinn. "Are you alright?"

"Mom said you wanted to take and raise me when I was a baby?"

Augusta was watching both of them. Teodora continued walking, her eyes focused far down the street as if searching for the tall spruce marking The Lighthouse. Teodora finally spoke, "Yes, that's true."

Fatigue enveloped Aislinn so that she no longer had the energy to be surprised. "Why?" Her voice was calm, detached.

Augusta answered her, "Quan'i . . . you have her spirit, yes. We see it in your baby eyes. The grandmothers train my Quan'i so she be keeper of First Woman's knowledge some day. When she a small girl, First Woman show her to us, yes. Our ancestor show us you, too."

"No," Aislinn whispered, fear in her eyes. "You're wrong."

Teodora stopped. Aislinn's lethargy disappeared as her gran seemed to grow before her eyes, her black, fringed shawl spread out from her shoulders and flapped around her. "Wrong, wrong." Her voice was hard. "First Woman wrong? How dare you deny what I know."

Aislinn stepped back; she had no defences when it came to Teodora. But how could her gran of all people think of separating her from her family? "What about my dad? How could you do that to him?" Aislinn demanded and her anger diminished her grandmother.

"Francis knew. He saw Quan'i in you from the very first. Saw her grow up again in you. He thought it was his punishment. We knew it was a blessing."

"What are you saying?" Aislinn could feel panic flitter in her stomach.

Augusta held Aislinn's arm to calm her. "Francis love Quan'i since they little kids, yes. He going to marry her when he come back from fighting. They already marry in the heart, in the body before he go away."

"I don't . . ." Aislinn saw her father's face clearly for the first time. She looked into his eyes and beyond the darkness there.

"You understand," Teodora said, taking Aislinn's left arm and squeezing it hard.

Her arm went numb for a moment. Then Teodora and Augusta walked on with her silently, arm in arm.

The women arrived at The Lighthouse just as Earl whistled to get the crowd's attention.

"Okay, okay, quiet down. Hey, at the back . . ." He whistled again through two fingers. "Alright, you want to know who won?"

They roared back at him.

"Good, 'cause the best scavenger in town is your neighbour and mine, Bill Amos. Shit, Big Bill, get up here. I don't like standing in front of a dartboard by myself."

Wil had to move his chair and Shea's to let Big Bill through.

Earl opened a box on the floor beside him and took out a toilet seat, lid and all. He held it up to show everyone in the room. Painted on the lid in red letters was GREAT SCAVENGER and below was a not-so-great copy of Aislinn's bird. On the toilet seat was a handpainted circular road map with a green bus following the black line between towns. Earl handed the trophy over. "Say a few words, Bill."

Big Bill just stood there studying the thing and shaking his head.

"You could wear it, Bill. The hole's big enough to get your

head through," Earl said. The crowd agreed.

"No, thanks, Earl. I'll just take it back to my table. You know, give the wife a good look at it."

"Let's hear it for Big Bill."

The room got loud again. Earl looked around for Aislinn and when he spotted her, he shouted, "Hey, hey, listen up. I been told we've got pictures or something of the bus. So, let's have a look-see, then get down to partying." He pointed to the projector and waved Aislinn over. "Why don't you switch that machine on and I'll set the screen up here."

Aislinn did as she was told, grateful for the dark that followed when Earl finished struggling with the screen. She was clicking the slides one after another onto the screen, when someone shouted to slow down. She found the right rhythm and was finally free to think. What had her gran and Augusta been doing to her all these years? What did they want? She had always thought they were her safe place, a haven. But they had plans for her, counted on her to do something. Do what?

"Hey, back up," someone called, "to the one of Sally in her nightgown."

Click.

"It's a housecoat I got on, you dumbo."

"How did that kid get a picture of you in your nightie?"

"It's not . . . he took me by surprise."

"I bet."

"Now stop that, he was a nice young man."

Click.

"Say, Teodora, you and Augusta dressed up for church?"

"You look like a couple of giant canaries."

Click.

"Now how did he do that? I've never seen a burnt snag look like that before. Aislinn, did that kid have some kind of special camera or what?"

"I don't know."

Click.

"The bay looks fine, don't it, with the morning sun on it like that?"

"Setting sun, you mean."

"Hell no, look at the angle."

Click.

"I'll be damned, the bird on the side of that bus is a dead ringer for Big Bill."

"No wonder he did so good in the scavenger hunt."

Click.

"The arteest at work."

"Hey, Aislinn, who's your model for that overdressed dickey-bird?"

Click.

"Boo, get it off the screen."

Click.

"That's better. Shit, Devil's Falls looks ten times as high in that picture."

"Come on, that picture's not from around here."

"Sure it is, idiot, can't you see?"

Click.

"Town looks a bit seedy in that one. Kind of overgrown."

"What do you expect, it's the company side of town."

Click.

Darkness.

"You got any more, Aislinn?"

Augusta touched Aislinn's arm before Earl found the light switch. "You paint those birds, yes?"

Aislinn could feel Teodora leaning close to her shoulder. The light dazzled her. "Yes," she said.

She showed the rest of Hugh's slides and listened to people surprised at themselves, at their neighbours; listened to others argue over where some of the shots were taken, why things looked different. She was surprised at how much of Tanis Bay

Hugh had seen and those folks he had talked into posing for him. He had revived parts of the place she no longer really saw and reminded her of people who kept to themselves and seemed to disappear out of mind. He also found the beauty she thought only she saw.

Aislinn shook the rain off her coat before entering the log house. The kerosene lamp was a slice of moon in the kitchen. Wil had built a small fire in the wood stove and Shea's rocker was pulled up close. Aislinn stepped up behind Shea and tilted the chair back on its rockers far enough for her to kiss him on the forehead. When he protested, she let the chair rock gently forward and went to sit at the table where Teodora was mending the elbows of Shea's old grey sweater. Augusta was sipping the last of the breakfast tea.

Teodora looked up from her darning needle and smiled at Aislinn. "We have something for you."

"Oh." Aislinn looked closely at the old women as if she expected to find black feathers in their hair.

Teodora set aside the sweater. From her skirt pocket, she took a black, braided cord with a single knot and placed it on the table. Also from a pocket, Augusta collected a circle of twisted, red cedar bark.

"What are these?" Aislinn asked.

"They are for your journey," Teodora said.

"But I'm just going to visit Mary."

"We'll see," Teodora said. "Come here and let me put the cord about your neck. I have started your map song string with the last knot from mine. It's the knot for this place." When Teodora finished tying the cord, the knot hung in the centre at Aislinn's throat.

Augusta beckoned Aislinn to her side. "This circle very old, yes. Inside is hair of First Woman. She go with you, watch you like your grandmothers." Augusta slipped the coil of bark over Aislinn's hand and onto her wrist.

"Thank you for the gifts. But I don't understand why you're acting like the city is the end of the earth."

Augusta patted Aislinn's hand. "That picturemaking boy not gone yet, yes?"

"He'll be gone next week and that's that."

"We'll see." Teodora said.

Aislinn stood looking down on her two old women. "Why are you so sure I'm going with him?"

"It is time for you to go." Teodora took Aislinn's other hand in hers.

"How do you know?" Aislinn wanted to prove them wrong. It was necessary to cling to the thought that she was going to the city to visit.

Teodora looked up at Aislinn with dark eyes, shiny and unblinking. "Stop seeing with your mother's eyes."

Augusta's fingers curled around Aislinn's hand. "You have much to do."

Aislinn stood between them and they held her hands. Below her the soft grey sweater fell over the edge of the table into Teodora's lap.

The wind that came up with the night rain had lifted off a few shingles on the store roof. Then it had marched the clouds out over the Strait and left Tanis Bay to the sun. Aislinn took advantage of the retreat to get on the roof and repair what she could. She didn't want Sam up there, Clara would have a fit. The broken shingles were nowhere to be seen. She looked over the edge of the roof, trying to spot them in the tangled back yard. Nothing, the weeds hadn't been disturbed. Sitting on the peak, she gazed down Centre Street to the bay. It was a blue flag fluttering out from the dock. It marked the spot where the street ended and began, depending upon whether you were going or coming. Or it used to before the highway. She could hear Sam below her, whistling as he swept the aisles. She shouted down to him, "That wind was so strong it must've tossed those shingles into the Strait." He called back, "Tell me another fish story, heh." The phone rang and Sam summoned her. "Long distance, Linny." Aislinn slid down the aluminum ladder, a neat trick she had learned from Sam's Billy.

Sam took up his sweeping behind the counter, raising dust that started him coughing. Aislinn stuck her head between the curtains to check on him. When she came out of the backroom, she handed him the spray bottle of water.

He nodded at her, his hand searching for his cigarettes in his shirt pocket. "Everything okay?"

"Yeah, just fine." Aislinn looked around the store as if she expected to be blindfolded and told to find the door out.

"You better get a move on. The bus will be at your place by now."

"You got the keys. The roof's okay. I'll put the ladder away." Aislinn felt rushed, confused.

"Leave it." Sam picked up the broom. "Do I have to chase you out of here?"

"No, I'm going." She hugged Sam, the cigarette on his lip dangling near her hair. "You'll check in on the old folks?"

"Yes, yes, now go."

When Aislinn shut the front door behind her, the breeze flipped over the sign in the window from OPEN to GONE FISHIN'.

Her lady bird watched her cross the street toward the bus. Its red eye was relentless, staring a hole in her forehead. The eye, the slightly open beak, she had made her bird too strong. It saw into her and laughed. Passing the bird, she ran up to the house. Aislinn carried her mother onto the bus and Earl put their suitcases aboard. The others busied themselves with shutting up the house until Fern was settled on a bench that also served as a bed, her legs covered with a blanket. It was a bit narrow, so Aislinn wedged a wooden chair between the bench and the table. Linda's five-year-old crawled up on the chair to inspect Fern through the rungs of the backrest. They were getting acquainted when the bus's engine started and Aislinn scooped up the boy and sat on the chair with him in her lap. She let him sit on the table so he could see out a side window.

As they pulled onto Centre Street, car horns greeted them and a trumpet sounded from the Company Park where it looked as if the whole town had gathered. Someone had taken down Sewell's flag and raised on the company flagpole a homemade coat of arms: a shield bearing The Scavenger birds, a chainsaw and a beer. The bus drew alongside the park and a contingent headed by Mad Dog saluted the new flag. A cheer drowned out the trumpet. Aislinn looked up the street to the store and caught Sam on the roof. He waved as they went by. The community hall and the baseball field slipped away. She could feel the ocean at her back, the tide pulling at the dock. She rubbed her arm and noticed the swelling was gone. There was just a small bump under the skin.

The boy squirmed to get down and Aislinn handed him over to Linda. "Mom, you okay?" Aislinn asked Fern.

"Yes, you've made quite sure with that blessed chair."

"Mary phoned the store just before I left. She heard from Colin." Aislinn had kept this to herself until now. "He's coming out." Since the call, she had been looping this phrase around in her mind, a tape on rewind or maybe it was more like fast forward.

"Now, that's good news." Fern said.

"Good news," Aislinn repeated. The quiet in her voice made it a question.

Aislinn fingered the knot at her throat. She turned away to look out the back window of the bus. The forest cut off her view of the town.